Missing from the Record

Missing from the Record

CLIVE EGLETON

St. Martin's Press
New York

Library of Congress Cataloging-in-Publication Data

Egleton, Clive.
      Missing from the record / Clive Egleton.
            p.   cm.
ISBN 0-312-02253-0
      I. Title.
      PR6055.G55M57   1988   88-15667
      823'.914—dc19   CIP

First published in Great Britain by Hodder and Stoughton Limited, under the title *Gone Missing*.

First U.S. Edition

10 9 8 7 6 5 4 3 2 1

this book is for those intrepid travellers
and good friends –

Viola and Bob Norman

1975

MONDAY 28 APRIL

to

FRIDAY 16 MAY

1

The cockerel began to crow shortly after first light, but it was the rising humidity and the distant sound of artillery that roused Sarah Lucas from a fitful slumber. Still not fully awake, she threw back one side of the mosquito net, then rolled off the narrow bed and walked out on to the balcony. The air base at Bien Hoa lay to the north-east of Saigon and the sky-line in that direction reflected the glow from the blazing fuel dumps. The North Vietnamese Army had been pounding the installation with their Russian-made 130mm cannon since early yesterday but Bien Hoa was a good fifteen miles away which meant the bombardment she could hear had to be much nearer.

Sarah glanced left and right to see if the Americans who lived on Tran Gian Street had moved out during the night. The pick-up used by the TV crew staying opposite was still in the yard, so too was the battered Chevrolet belonging to the Edmonds, the Quaker family next door who ran the orphanage near the Buddhist University. But there was no sign of the big ex-marine and part-owner of the Hole-in-the-Wall Club on Tu Do Street down by the river.

His absence wasn't surprising. Yesterday afternoon, a six-by-six General Motors five-ton truck had been parked outside the villa and his whole family from the Vietnamese grandparents down to the youngest child had been busy loading the contents of the house into the vehicle. But Sarah didn't care for their chances much; no ship of any size had come up the river for days and surely no one was going to find room for all his stuff on one of the Air America C130s flying out of Tan Son Nhut, even assuming the air-field was still in use.

Sarah returned to the bedroom. She wanted to strip off the check shirt and khaki drill slacks she'd slept in and stand under a cold shower but that luxury would have to wait until the signal log had been checked. The transceiver was tucked away in the cellar next to the improvised strongroom and was manned round the clock.

Le Khac Ly, affectionately known as 'Little Brother', had relieved her at 0200 hours but to her surprise, Peter Wentworth, the former SAS Warrant Officer, was on watch instead. He was the Mission's small arms expert responsible for training the local self-defence units and always projected a macho image, even in civilian clothes. Apart from the fully automatic AR-15 rifle which he'd propped against the table within easy reach, he was also sporting a Colt .45 automatic pistol in a shoulder holster.

"Be with you in a minute, Sarah," he said and keyed another four letter group into the crypto machine.

"What's happened to Le Khac Ly?"

"I told him he might as well get his head down." Wentworth pointed to the telephone. "He roused me at about 0340 hours to take a call from the embassy. It was the duty officer who'd been told to warn us we could expect to receive a UK Eyes Only signal from Hong Kong very shortly. I figured it would be a good idea if our Vietnamese friend wasn't around when it came through on the direct link."

"He isn't cipher trained, Peter."

"So what? UK Eyes Only means exactly what it says. Anyway, you don't want to underestimate 'Little Brother'; he's smart enough to know how to work this gubbins."

An outsider could be forgiven for thinking Wentworth was her superior officer instead of it being the other way round. It was a ridiculous arrangement of course; he had vastly more experience at counter insurgency operations and had served in Vietnam with the New Zealand Squadron of the SAS. Before that, he'd completed a nine year engagement with the British Army seeing active service in Cyprus, Borneo, Aden and the Oman. At thirty-six, he was eleven years her senior which was another thing she could not lightly shrug off.

"South Vietnam is about to go under, Sarah. President Tran Van Huong is on his way out and 'Big Minh' is about to take office because the Senators and Deputies of the National Assembly believe he's the one man the Viet Cong will negotiate with." Wentworth smiled lopsidedly, then added, "Pretty soon now it's going to be every man for himself, if you'll pardon the expression."

Big Minh: the nickname had been bestowed on General Duong Van Minh because at five foot eleven he was exceptionally tall for a Vietnamese. Aside from his height, he also enjoyed a reputation for being totally incorruptible which set him apart from all the other Generals and leading politicians. But Peter was right: the VC weren't about to negotiate with anyone, the whole of the North Vietnamese army had come south and between them they had Saigon by the throat.

"Seems Hong Kong agrees with me." Wentworth waited for the printer to finish chattering, then ripped off the clear text print and gave it to Sarah. "They've ordered you to get the treasure chest out of the country as a precautionary measure."

The instructions from Simon Faulkner in Hong Kong were unequivocal. The gold and foreign currency reserves they were holding were to be delivered to Bien Hoa by 1300 hours that day, for immediate transfer by Chinook helicopter to the USS *Okinawa* lying offshore outside Vietnam territorial waters.

"What's Simon playing at?" Sarah demanded. "Doesn't he know the air base is under artillery fire?"

"Search me." Wentworth shrugged. "Maybe you should advise him?"

"We don't have a secure speech link. Anyway, the telephone has only been working on and off since Friday, which is one of the reasons why Simon took off for Hong Kong when he did."

"Send a signal, then. Make it Op Immediate or even

Emergency if you feel like it, and we should get a reply in half an hour."

What Peter had suggested made good sense; grabbing a message pad, Sarah drafted a brief signal appraising Hong Kong of the latest situation and gave it to Wentworth to encode and transmit. Then she went upstairs, stripped off and took the shower she'd promised herself, except the water was nearer lukewarm than cold.

The Quaker family next door began to move out while Sarah was still dressing. If she needed proof that the war was about to end in total victory for Hanoi, their sudden departure provided it. People like the Edmonds simply didn't pack up and leave unless they'd been ordered to do so by their embassy and had been assured that their Vietnamese orphans would also be evacuated.

Just as Wentworth had predicted, the Emergency precedence had produced an electric response from Simon Faulkner, though his reply was not altogether reassuring. He had consulted his American counterpart in Hong Kong who had confirmed that the United States Marine Corps were still using Bien Hoa as a pick-up point.

"The Yanks have better communications than us," Wentworth told her. "With their satellite radio relay and secure speech facility, the CIA man in Hong Kong can talk direct with the Task Force Commander offshore, Ambassador Martin in Saigon and the forward air controller at Bien Hoa. For what it's worth, I'd be inclined to believe what I'm being told."

"I'm just wondering if the road to the air base is open. Judging by the noise, it sounds as though an artillery fire-fight is taking place somewhere on the outskirts of the city."

"There's only one way to find out, Sarah."

"I know."

She lifted the receiver and dialled the number of the Joint General Staff. The Vietnamese press liaison officer was an incurable optimist and most of the communiqués issued by his office owed a lot to a fertile imagination, but

12

there was now no other source of information she could tap.

"I wouldn't spend too long on the phone," Wentworth said. "There's a lot of money in the strongroom and we're short of labour."

"I'll give it another five minutes, okay?"

"You're in charge, Sarah." He paused, then added, "Don't take this the wrong way but I figured we could do with some help. So while I was waiting for a reply to our signal, I rang my friend Colonel Huyen and arranged to borrow four of his military policemen."

"Thanks, Peter, I can certainly use an escort."

For several days now, the Viet Cong had been reinforcing their underground cells in Saigon in anticipation of the final assault on the city. One such group of infiltrators was known to be stockpiling arms and ammunition in the Buddhist University on Truong Minh Gian Street and there was a very real danger she could be ambushed on the way to the air base.

"There is one slight problem," Wentworth said almost apologetically. "These MPs we're getting want out; they reckon they're on Hanoi's death list and they're counting on you to ease them on to a helicopter. They could turn nasty if you fail to swing it."

"I'm glad you warned me," Sarah retorted drily.

It seemed a lot of people wanted out, including most of the officers at the Joint General Staff. Then, just as she was about to hang up, a very ebullient Major in G3 Ops who could understand French finally answered the phone. The situation, he assured her, was completely under control. The army had surrounded a party of Viet Cong guerillas and the artillery was completing their annihilation.

"So what's the score?" Wentworth's question came seconds after she had put the phone down.

"It's the same old story, Peter; our side's winning."

The MPs arrived twenty minutes later in a small four-wheel-drive cargo truck which, except for the disruptive

13

camouflage pattern, was the twin of the one Wentworth had brought with him when he'd pulled out of the Central Highlands a month ago. Although the MPs' vehicle was in much better condition, there was an even more compelling reason for using it in preference to their own. In the present climate of fear, there was no telling how the soldiers manning the road blocks would react if they saw the MPs, the hated Quan Canh, in a civilian truck. The Quan Canh were universally loathed and there was a chance the foot soldiers would take the MPs for deserters and shoot them out of hand.

The treasure chest Sarah had been ordered to move consisted of US dollars, Vietnamese piasters and gold taels neatly stacked on the shelves in the strongroom in sealed canvas money bags, each one valued at the sterling equivalent of twenty thousand pounds. No one was going to bother with piasters; even at the artificial exchange rate of 850 to the US dollar it had never been popular and right now the Vietnamese currency had about as much value as yesterday's newsprint. The gold and US dollars were however a vastly different proposition and Sarah was determined that none of those sacks should go missing when the MPs moved them. Leaving Wentworth to check them out of the strongroom, she counted each one into the truck. By eight-fifteen, all two hundred and thirty sacks were neatly stowed on board, leaving just enough room for the Vietnamese escort.

"I don't like the odds," Wentworth said, anxiously eyeing the four MPs clustered round the loaded vehicle. "I think it's best if I deliver the money to Bien Hoa."

"No." Sarah smiled wanly. "Thanks all the same, Peter, but it's my responsibility. Besides, who's going to organise the evacuation of our people once Hong Kong gives the word if you're not here to do it?"

"Is that an order?" he asked quietly.

"More or less."

"Okay. Then you'd better take this with you."

She glanced at the pocket-size Beretta he had pressed into

14

her palm. "It looks like one of those gimmicky lighters you can buy on Tu Do Street," she said.

"A .22 automatic pistol is still a lethal weapon. You shoot one of those Quan Canh between the eyes and it'll give him more than just a headache. And while we're at it, there's another piece of insurance I'd like you to have." Wentworth turned away from her and went back inside the villa. A few minutes later he returned with a map and a hand-held VHF/UHF transceiver. "With this radio set you'll be in voice range all the way out to Bien Hoa. Call me every fifteen minutes with a grid reference of your location."

"And if you don't hear from me?" she asked. "What then?"

"I'll have a word with another friend of mine in 1st Airborne Brigade. The Paras still have the balls to go on fighting and they'll come looking for you."

"Simon always said you were a damned good soldier." Sarah glanced at her wristwatch, then held out her hand to shake his. "It's time I was going, Peter, there's no telling how many hold-ups we may encounter on the way."

Leaving the villa, the truck headed towards the river, then turned left into Tu Do Street and continued on up the tree-lined artery of Saigon past the Hotel Caravelle, the National Assembly Building, the Café Givral and the Continental Palace Hotel. Sarah came up on the radio twice to report their position: when they reached the basilica of Our Lady of Peace and again shortly after they had joined National Route 1 and were approaching the turn-off for Bien Hoa. On each occasion Wentworth repeated the grid reference she had given him and told her he would remain on listening watch. The noise of artillery fire was much louder now and must have been clearly audible every time she pressed the transmit button, but he never mentioned it.

The road to Bien Hoa was a four, and in places, a six-lane highway but nothing was moving either way on it that morning. The road block was on the Saigon side of the river about a ten minute walk from the New Port bridge. The

15

soldiers manning it were jittery and excitable enough to shoot anyone on the slightest pretext, especially the hated Quan Canh. The Front, one of them informed her in a mixture of broken French and Vietnamese, was just up the road and she would have to get out and walk if she wanted to go any farther. She called Wentworth on the radio again, told him what was happening and said she was going forward to take a closer look. None of the MPs wanted to go with her but the senior NCO in charge of the detail ordered the youngest Quan Canh out of the truck at gun point.

The New Port bridge was a steel frame structure which rose steeply from the four-lane highway to span the river above the new docks that the Americans had built three and a quarter miles north-east of the city centre. Using what cover she could find amongst the wooden shacks lining the road, Sarah cautiously approached the bridge, her reluctant bodyguard in tow. The Viet Cong were dug in on the far bank one hundred yards away and were blanketing the area with small arms fire from their Kalashnikovs whenever any of the paratroopers in the vicinity of the bridge tried to move forward.

The noise was deafening. Two M41 light tanks were sniping at the VC positions with their 76mm cannon, an artillery battery was pounding the river bank from somewhere in the suburbs and a Mission Fire Controller was endeavouring to direct a couple of mortars on to a particularly troublesome machine gun nest. Crouching low, Sarah inched her way towards the firing line. As she drew level with the nearest tank, the muzzle blast from the 76mm cannon was like a Force 10 gale and almost stopped her dead in her tracks. Across the river, a figure in a black pyjama suit cracked under the strain of the bombardment, climbed out of his foxhole and was promptly cut down by a hail of small arms fire.

There were very few officers in evidence at the bridge but after crawling around on her hands and knees for the best part of half an hour, Sarah eventually located a captain who seemed to know what was going on. Vietnam had become the only war in history to appear nightly on television and the captain was used to having a news reporter breathing down his neck in the middle of a battle. One glance at her bogus press card was sufficient to allay his suspicion and obtain a quick briefing. Bien Hoa was still in government hands and was operating normally. The only enemy in the area were the fifty or so VC on the far bank who had slipped through the lines during the night and were trying to block the main supply route to the Front. He was very confident his soldiers would dislodge them before the day was much older.

The attack went in at noon – and got nowhere. Three quarters of an hour later, the Airborne tried again and met with a similar lack of success, despite the air support provided by two helicopter gunships which rocketed the far bank. Every time one of the M41 tanks left its hull-down position to advance on the bridge, a guided missile sent it scuttling back to its hole in the ground; then a salvo from the artillery fell short and the mood of the troops around Sarah turned ugly.

A corporal spat at her, pointed to the hand-held VHF/ UHF set and tried to snatch it away. Although Sarah only understood one word in five, it was blindingly obvious they believed she was in radio contact with the Viet Cong and had kept them fully informed. The baby-faced MP tried to explain that they'd got it all wrong but the Airborne soldiers weren't in the mood to listen. The corporal turned his Armalite rifle on the Quan Canh, squeezed the trigger and emptied the magazine in one long burst which lifted the MP off his feet and flung him backwards into the ditch by the roadside, gutted like a fish from crotch to throat.

"Oh, you bastard." Anger overcame her fear. "You bloody miserable bastard," she screamed and hurled the radio at him.

Out of the corner of her eye, Sarah saw the diminutive paratrooper reverse his Armalite and instinctively jerked her head out of the way. She was swift, but not swift enough and the rifle butt caught her a glancing blow on the right side of

17

her face. The earth opened up to swallow her and she plunged into a dark, bottomless pit.

When she regained consciousness, the warehouses on the dockside were burning fiercely, the Viet Cong were still holding out and the Airborne forces at the bridge had been reinforced by several hundred infantrymen. Dazed and bewildered, she got to her feet and slowly made her way back to the road block. Her escort had disappeared, together with the four wheel drive cargo truck.

2

There was little to distinguish Le Khac Ly from most of his compatriots. At five foot five, he weighed one hundred and nineteen pounds, had jet black hair and a small rounded face which made him look far younger than he was. Now aged twenty-seven, he had been a lieutenant in the army's Black Panther Division until May 1974 when he had been discharged as medically unfit. During the four months between May and September 1974, when Simon Faulkner had recruited him, he had been employed as an interpreter by the United States Defence Attaché Office located at Tan Son Nhut airport. At the mission, he was employed as a jack of all trades – driver, interpreter, clerk and radio telegraphist. His wife was also on the payroll and was supposed to look after the permanent staff, but she was now heavily pregnant with their third child and latterly had had to take things easy. It was Wentworth's opinion that her husband had been doing that ever since he'd joined the mission; but then he was the one person who disliked Le Khac Ly, and made no bones about showing it.

"Thursday the twenty-fourth of April." Wentworth picked up the classified register and threw it at the Vietnamese. "You want to look it up for me, Little Brother?"

"I think you are not a very nice man, Mr Wentworth."

"I'm looking for a signal from Hong Kong – Ops 394 Date/Time Group 240800 Zulu hours – classified Top Secret."

"It is not listed here."

"Surprise, surprise," Wentworth said acidly. "Do you suppose it went astray?"

"Perhaps it did. Who knows?"

"I'm asking *you*. The signal carried an Op Immediate precedence and was transmitted direct to us and not via the embassy in Saigon. Hong Kong is eight hours ahead of Greenwich Mean Time which means it was despatched shortly after four p.m., unless the operator back there was inundated with dozens of signals carrying a higher precedence. Right?"

"I guess so," Le Khac Ly said in a pseudo-American accent.

"You guess so?" Wentworth snarled. "How many times have you known an Op Immediate signal to be delayed? Once? Twice?"

"Once."

"When was that?"

"I don't remember."

"Who was on duty last Thursday at 1600 hours?"

"Sarah – Miss Lucas."

"You've got a very convenient memory, Little Brother. You don't recall the signal but you do remember that Miss Lucas was on duty."

"She was. You ask her if you no believe me."

"I can't raise Miss Lucas on the radio. Last time I heard from her, she was held up at the New Port bridge. Since then, there's been no word." Wentworth picked up his clipboard and waved it under Le Khac Ly's nose. "Take a good look at this signal I received from Hong Kong not ten minutes ago. See what it says? Please confirm Gage withdrawn from Hieu Thien in accordance with my previous signal 240800 Zulu hours April 75."

"I no see it."

"You can bet your bottom dollar Doctor Matthew Gage never heard about it either. If he got out of Hieu Thien before the North Vietnamese cut the road to Saigon it was no thanks to you."

"Maybe Miss Lucas call him on the telephone and then forget to log the signal?"

"You're clutching at straws, Little Brother. Next thing you'll be telling me is that having spent the last twenty years

20

of his life in Vietnam, Doctor Gage didn't want to leave the country anyway."

"It's possible."

"Anything's possible. It could be your army will stand and fight but I doubt it."

Wentworth looked up at the map covering the area of the Capital Military District. A series of bold red arrows depicted the main enemy thrusts against Saigon from the north. Those in the area of Hieu Thien to the west of the capital were less definite and were meant to indicate diversionary attacks. All the same, the 25th Infantry Division defending the sector had fallen back to a point only twenty-one miles from the capital, leaving a pocket of resistance in and around Hieu Thien itself. Just who controlled the road between was open to question.

"You not record any signals today, boss." Le Khac Ly was still holding the classified register and had moved on to the entries for Monday 28 April.

"Because they're UK Eyes Only."

"Perhaps the missing signal also UK Eyes, boss?"

Wentworth knocked the register out of his hand, lifted the Vietnamese off the ground by his shirt front and shook him like a rag doll.

"I'll tell you how it was," he snarled. "You decoded a signal you'd no right to see, then you got cold feet and destroyed it. Now you're trying to put the blame on Miss Lucas because she's not here to defend herself."

"Not true, boss."

"You're a bloody liar." Still holding Le Khac Ly by his shirt, Wentworth lowered him to the ground and drew the Colt .45 automatic from his shoulder holster. One round was already in the breech; thumbing the hammer back, he pressed the barrel against Le Khac Ly's forehead. "I'm going up the road to Hieu Thien to see if I can bring Doctor Gage out and you'd better not run off the moment my back is turned."

"I stay here, boss," Little Brother assured him.

"If your name isn't already on Hanoi's death list, it soon

21

will be once they get their hands on our card index."
Wentworth turned the Vietnamese round to face the adjoining strongroom. "We've got a big fat file on you and your family in there, Little Brother," he added for good measure.

"I no run away."

"I'm glad to hear it. But any time you do feel like taking off, just remind yourself that I'm the only man who can get you and your family out of the country."

"I remember," Le Khac Ly said grimly.

"Good. Make sure you tell Miss Lucas where I've gone when she returns."

Wentworth eased the hammer forward, returned the Colt .45 to the shoulder holster, then picked up his Armalite rifle and left the cellar. The four-by-four light cargo truck parked in the yard behind the villa started first time; shifting into gear, he moved out into the road and turned right. The Edmonds next door had long since departed, as had the TV crew across the street. With everyone else up and running, he did not expect Le Khac Ly to stay put for much longer.

The road to Hieu Thien was on the north-west side of town. Heading in the opposite direction through Cholon, the Chinese Quarter of Saigon, Wentworth picked up Inter Province Route 5A on the outskirts of the city and drove on towards the small river port of Can Duoc.

Although the voice sounded a long way off, the Australian accent was unmistakable, which Sarah thought was a little strange because the tenor suggested it belonged to a much younger man than Macready. Someone raised her right eyelid but all she could see was a dazzling light. The whole of the side of her face was tender and swollen and even the lightest touch was enough to make her wince.

"Don?" Sarah moistened her lips and tried again. "Is that you, Don?" she croaked.

"No, I'm Mike Kent – *Sydney Herald*."

A blurred face appeared on the extreme periphery of her vision.

"This gentleman is Doctor Truang Chin. I asked him to take a look at you."

"Where am I?"

"The Caravelle Hotel. I found you wandering around in a daze near the road block on the turn-off to Bien Hoa."

Doctor Chin leaned across the bed, obscuring her vision while he raised her other lid and shone his torch directly into her left eye. Apparently satisfied, he switched off the pencil flashlight and asked her how many fingers she could see when he held up his hand. She told him four, then one, then three as he repeatedly clenched and unclenched his fist. Continuing his examination, Chin raised his index finger and moved it back and forth in front of her eyes to satisfy himself that she could focus on a moving object.

"I do not think Mrs Kent is suffering from the effects of concussion," he said, addressing the Australian journalist, "but I think your wife should be checked at the hospital and have some X-rays taken."

"Mr Kent is not my husband," Sarah protested, "and I'm not going to the hospital."

"My apologies, dear lady." Chin smiled at her, revealing a number of gold teeth. "However, even though this gentleman is not your husband, it would be wise to have a complete check-up."

"I can't afford the time."

"No job's that important," Kent said.

Hers was, but she couldn't tell him that. "You're very kind but I'm all right, really I am." Sarah propped herself up on one elbow and pulled out the billfold which she kept in the hip pocket of her khaki drill slacks. "And thank you too, Doctor Chin, for all you've done for me." She paused, hoping the Vietnamese physician would catch on, but her broad hint escaped him and she was forced to raise the matter of payment herself. "Perhaps it would be better if I settled your bill now?" she mumured diffidently.

Chin looked neither angry nor embarrassed, he merely shook his head and said there was no charge. On the other hand, if there was any truth in the rumour that President

23

Ford had said that every American returning home could sponsor up to ten Vietnamese, he would be eternally grateful if she would add his father's name to her list, assuming it wasn't already fully subscribed.

"I'm English," Sarah explained and was glad she didn't have to disillusion him.

"You've got the makings of a good story there," Kent told her when he returned from seeing the physician to the door.

"Yes, it has plenty of human interest."

"Who's Don?"

"Someone I know; an Australian like you, but much older."

"A fellow journalist?"

"What a lot of questions," Sarah said with a grimace.

"Well, I'm just naturally curious, especially as something like this drops out of your pocket." Kent opened the drawer in the bedside locker, took out the .22 Beretta automatic Wentworth had given her and tossed it on to the bed along with her bogus press card. "I'd have thought a notepad would have been more appropriate," he said.

"It's dangerous out there, and I felt in need of protection."

"Yeah?"

"You're not a woman, no one's going to molest you." Sarah swung her feet off the bed and sat up. "I think it's time I went, I've imposed on you long enough."

"Don't hurry away on my account, Miss Lucas. Anyway, you're not imposing on me. This is your room; one thing we're not short of in Saigon right now is hotel accommodation. The city is dying and everything is going to pot; chances are the management will forget to bill you."

"You're leaving?"

Kent nodded. "Got a story to cover. Big Minh is about to be sworn in as South Vietnam's third President in eight days. The Viet Cong said get rid of Thieu so they voted dear old asthmatic Tran Van Huong into power but the VC wouldn't have anything to do with him either. Now Big Minh is their last hope but deep down, the politicians know the Communists aren't about to negotiate with anyone."

24

He's right, Sarah thought, the enemy is knocking at the gates and it sounds as though his artillery is already bombarding the outer suburbs.

"They're getting closer every minute," she said.

"What you can hear is a thunderstorm, one's been threatening all afternoon."

The storm broke soon after the Australian departed, a gusting wind lashing the rain against the window of her hotel room. Sarah tried to ring the mission house to let Wentworth know she was all right but the operator told her the phone was out of order. Unsteadily, she dragged herself to the lifts and went on down to the lobby where she hoped one of the bellboys would get her a cab. Tu Do Street was usually like Paris in the rush hour but for once it was strangely quiet. Feeling sick and light-headed, her cheekbone throbbing painfully with each step she took, Sarah made it back to her room and collapsed on the bed.

When she woke up an hour later, it had stopped raining and the air smelt fresher and cleaner. Although a long way from being a hundred per cent, it was a relief that she no longer felt sick and dizzy. Returning to the lobby, she gave her room key to the desk clerk and checked out of the hotel.

There were still no taxis in sight but a cyclopousse was stationed outside the entrance waiting for someone to hire him. Tran Gian Street was a good four miles from the Caravelle; before Sarah had a chance to ask him, the cyclopousse informed her that the normal fare was a dollar fifty while the express service would cost five dollars. She never did discover just how fast the express service was.

The firing began shortly after they had moved off and seemed to be coming from the roof of the National Assembly building. Above the rattle of automatic rifles and the deeper pow-pow-pow of a .50 calibre machine gun, she could hear the noise of a jet engine. Glancing over her shoulder, Sarah counted five ground attack planes winging their way towards the Tan Son Nhut air base. Cessna A-37 Dragonfly converted jet trainers supplied to the South Vietnamese Air

Force by the United States Military Assistance Command: Sarah identified the aircraft for what they were even as the air raid sirens began their wailing.

The cyclopousse pedalled even faster, swung off Tu Do Street into a side road and jumped from his machine while it was still moving at speed. Moments later, the bicycle hit the kerb, toppled sideways and threw Sarah out of the basket chair. The sidewalk did not make for a soft landing. Her hands and knees skinned and bleeding, she crawled into the doorway of a house to find what shelter she could. Overhead, the planes made pass after pass, attacking the air base with fragmentation bombs, rockets and cannon fire.

Don Macready anxiously scanned the shoreline with his powerful binoculars. The last message he'd received from the mission house had been transmitted at 1350 hours local time and it had confirmed the pre-arranged RV. The chart he was using had been surveyed by the United States Navy which meant that it was a hundred per cent accurate, and there was nothing wrong with his navigation. He was in the right place at the right time, two miles down river from the small port of Can Duoc, but with the light beginning to fail, there was still no sign of Peter Wentworth, Sarah Lucas or Matthew Gage.

The column of black smoke rising into the sky above Can Duoc was an ominous reminder of what had happened a month ago in Military Region 1, north of Saigon, when the Vietnamese Navy had staged a minor Dunkirk off Da Nang. Simon Faulkner had sent him up there with the Vosper Thornycroft fast patrol boat to evacuate the command element of the Self Defence Force they'd worked so hard to establish. Macready had received some lunatic orders in his time but that had to be the craziest of them all. The whole purpose of the SDF was to wage guerilla warfare against the occupation forces, yet the Secret Intelligence Service had decided to withdraw the Vietnamese officers who were supposed to direct the local resistance movement before the enemy had actually over-run the area.

In the event, there had been a complete breakdown of discipline amongst the troops of the army's 3rd Division and in the ensuing chaos, Macready had been forced to leave without the SDF command cell. The scenes on the beaches of Da Nang had been a nightmare he was never likely to forget. Senior officers had deserted their men in order to save themselves, their wives and families, girlfriends and prized possessions. Some of the officers had discarded their uniforms in favour of civilian clothes, but all of them had retained their sidearms. They had used their submachine guns to threaten Macready and warn off other panic-stricken refugees who'd attempted to join them after they'd taken over the boat.

There had been a low tide that morning and everyone had had to wade out to the small armada of vessels lying offshore. Despite a thick mist, the beaches had been under continuous and accurate shellfire, which had created an air of total hysteria as well as giving credence to a rumour that the North Vietnamese had a number of artillery observers among the refugees. Macready recalled a fat colonel in a Hawaiian shirt who'd used his girlfriend as a human stepping stone and had then hauled her aboard with one hand while drawing a .357 magnum revolver with the other to execute one of his soldiers who was trying to follow her into the boat.

Now, these horrendous scenes were about to be repeated off Can Duoc. Roughly three-quarters of an hour ago, he'd heard several bursts of machine gun fire somewhere upstream beyond the bend in the river. Then, some twenty minutes later, a high speed ocean-going launch had shot past them on its way out to sea. Shortly after that, fires had been started in Can Duoc as looters put the village to the torch.

Macready spotted the flashing vehicle headlights at precisely the same moment as his Thai bosun in the dory moored alongside gave a triumphant whoop and pointed towards the shore. There was no need for him to give any orders. The bosun recognised the signal, told the seaman in the bows to cast off and started the outboard motor; seconds

27

later, the inflatable craft was streaking towards a narrow inlet. When it returned after what seemed a lifetime, the only passenger on board was Peter Wentworth.

"What's happened to the others?" Macready asked.

Wentworth pushed a hand through his tousled blond hair. "Matthew Gage is still up-country in Hieu Thien. Faulkner sent a signal ordering him to pull out but he never received it. I tried to get through to him but the Viet Cong have cut the road halfway between Saigon and Hieu Thien."

"And Sarah?"

Macready had taken a shine to Sarah Lucas the day he'd first met her back in Hong Kong. She had everything – looks, brains, breeding and dry sense of humour. Even though old enough to be Sarah's father, just thinking about her made him feel horny.

"Last time I heard from her, Sarah was caught up in a fire-fight at the New Port bridge on her way to Bien Hoa with the slush fund. She had an escort of four MPs but they must have abandoned her somewhere. At least I hope they did because I found their abandoned cargo truck north of Can Duoc." Wentworth dumped a bloodstained canvas money bag on the chart table, cut the drawstring above the lead seal and, opening the sack, took out a fistful of gold taels. "This was the only trace I could find of them. The cargo truck was riddled with bullet holes and there was a lot of blood inside the vehicle. I figure they were ambushed either by the VC or by a bunch of deserters."

Macready stared at the gold coins, a bitter taste in his mouth. "How long are we going to wait?" he asked huskily.

"Until it's dark," Wentworth told him. "If Sarah isn't here by then, we'll head for Ko Chang in the Gulf of Thailand."

Sarah eased her foot on the accelerator, felt the automatic drive shift down into second gear, and turned into the driveway beside the villa. The transport had been provided unwittingly by an American contractor who'd abandoned his '73 model Pontiac near the US Embassy on Thong Nhat

Avenue. The former owner had omitted to leave the keys, but that hadn't been a problem. One of the tricks the SIS had taught her at their training school near Petersfield was how to hotwire the ignition.

A neighbourhood power failure had left the whole street in darkness but Sarah fancied she could find her way round the villa blindfolded. All the same, the total blackout made her feel creepy and taking out the pocket-size Beretta, she drew the slide back to chamber a .22 round. Gun in hand, she then walked up the front steps, tried the door and found it was unlocked.

Le Khac Ly, his heavily pregnant wife and their two children had gone. Sarah could sense it the moment she stepped across the threshold and reached for the flashlight which was kept on top of the fusebox in the hall. Supposition became an established fact when neither appeared after she called to them in a loud voice. Subsequently, their two rooms on the ground floor at the rear of the villa provided mute evidence of a hasty flight. From the clothes left in the closet, it looked as though they had taken only what they could pack into one suitcase.

The strongroom in the cellar told its own story. With the aid of a hacksaw, Le Khac Ly had cut through the steel locking bar which secured the three-drawer filing cabinet and removed his personal file. The empty spaces suggested that while he was at it, he'd also removed a few other files which he'd subsequently fed into the secret waste destructor with his own documents. However, in his haste to get away, he hadn't bothered to burn the shredded paper in the incinerator. It was something she would do for him as soon as Hong Kong authorised the destruction of all personal documents and the Top Secret papers, presently housed in the combination safe in what used to be Simon Faulkner's office.

Little Brother had left a note for her which she discovered on top of the transceiver in the adjoining room. Scribbled on the back of a message pad in barely legible handwriting e gathered that a Top Secret signal from Hong Ko ordering Matthew Gage to leave Hieu Thien had gone astray. Another ungrammatical sentence informed her that Wentworth had driven off in the light cargo truck to see if he could bring him back.

Working by flashlight, Sarah drafted a situation report, marked it Personal for Simon Faulkner and encoded it. Then she unplugged the transceiver from the mains and reconnected it to a couple of standby 12-volt batteries. It took her just ten minutes to raise Hong Kong and transmit the encoded message; the reply authorising the destruction of all classified material arrived exactly half an hour later at 0105 hours.

Power still hadn't been returned to the neighbourhood which meant the secret waste destructor in the strongroom was just a piece of expensive junk. Every sheet of paper in every file had to be torn in half and half again, stuffed into a plastic sack and carried out to the incinerator in the yard. It was a slow business: the ash in the incinerator had to be raked after each burn and then saturated with a hosepipe to ensure total destruction. Half asleep on her feet, alternately sick and hungry, Sarah kept going on a diet of cheese biscuits and coffee laced with brandy which she brewed on a paraffin stove. Her first priority was to protect every Vietnamese who'd ever worked for the mission and by first light she had managed to destroy the card index and associated documents. She then started on the Top Secret papers in Faulkner's safe but was forced to abandon the task when she found it physically impossible to keep her eyes open. Completely exhausted, she dragged herself upstairs and fell into bed.

When Sarah woke up it was broad daylight and she was no longer alone in the house. At first, she thought Le Khac Ly had returned with his wife until it soon became apparent that there were at least two male voices. Sarah reached under her pillow for the Beretta automatic and remembered too late that she had left it in the strongroom. Determined not to show her fear, she went downstairs to meet the intruders.

30

They were three in number, two men and a young woman, Viet Cong guerillas from the Mekong Delta armed with a variety of weapons. For several moments they stood there gazing up at her on the stairs, then the girl raised the French MAT 49 submachine gun and took aim.

"*Américaine.*"

Sarah could not remember when she had heard so much hatred expressed in a single word by one human being to another and she knew she was about to die.

"English," she heard herself scream. "I am English."

They did not appear to believe her. One of the men found a length of flex in the cellar and tied her wrists and elbows behind her back. Then the girl removed the silk scarf she had knotted round her neck and used it for a blindfold.

"Please don't kill me," Sarah pleaded, then repeated it over and over again in French and English as they led her out of the house and down the steps and into the back of an open truck.

The VC took her to what had once been the National Police Headquarters where she was held in a cell with several other women. On the fourth day of her captivity, Sarah was taken before a Communist officer dressed in an olive green uniform without any badges of rank.

"You do bad things," he told her and pointed to a pile of Top Secret files which had been recovered from the villa.

It was the only interrogation she was ever subjected to. On Wednesday the 14th of May she was released from prison, taken to Tan Son Nhut airport and put on a plane to Vientiane in Laos where she was handed over to a representative of the International Red Cross.

Two days later, Sarah arrived in Bangkok still wearing the wide pyjama trousers and long white tunic which the North Vietnamese had given her. Simon Faulkner was on hand to greet her, so too was the Head of the South-East Asia Bureau. But despite their welcoming smiles and affectionate embraces, Sarah knew things would never be the same again.

31

1985

FRIDAY 14 JUNE

to

THURSDAY 20 JUNE

3

The rain began to ease off as Cartwright was driving through Amesbury. A few miles farther on, the evening sun broke through a lowering sky, something which had occurred all too infrequently in what so far had been the wettest June on record. Although tempted by the improved weather conditions to put his foot down, Cartwright resisted the impulse. His whole day had been one long chapter of minor disasters from the moment he'd walked out of his flat to discover someone had stolen his Mini during the night, and with the kind of luck he was enjoying it was likely that things could only get worse.

As a week-end commuter, Cartwright usually aimed to leave the office no later than four-thirty on a Friday, but today fate had intervened in the shape of a parliamentary question which the Minister had wished to answer the following Monday. As a staff officer in the army's Directorate Personal Services he was used to dealing with the issues aggrieved soldiers had referred to their Members of Parliament, but this case had been particularly difficult. By the time he had produced an acceptable draft, it was after six and although he'd tried to call Sarah from the office to warn her he'd be late, her phone had been out of order. A traffic snarl-up on the A30 out of London had delayed him further; then just when he was beginning to make up for lost time on the motorway, he'd had to pull over on to the hard shoulder to change a flat tyre on the Metro he'd hired from Avis.

Familiar with the route, Cartwright knew he was approaching the A36 trunk route long before he saw the hazard warning sign. Turning right at the T-junction, he headed towards Codford St Mary.

The house which Sarah had inherited from her maternal grandmother was on the far outskirts of the village, down a narrow lane that led to the River Wylye. A gravel drive fronted the house and led to the stables at the back where there were a couple of outhouses, one of which was used as a garage.

Coming to a halt opposite the front porch, Cartwright sounded the horn twice to let everyone know he was home, then slowly got out of the Metro. A tall man bordering on six four, he stretched both arms above his head uncoiling himself like a spring that had been overwound, then using his hands in lieu of a comb, he parted his short dark hair on the left side. Usually, his four-year-old daughter, Helen, came running out to meet him but of course it was long past her bedtime and Sarah was evidently annoyed with him for being so late. Producing a key from his jacket pocket, he unlocked the front door and let himself into the hall.

"Hi, darling," he said in a loud voice, "it's me. Home at last."

Sarah didn't answer and the house seemed unnaturally silent. He checked the reception rooms, study and kitchen, a vague sense of unease growing more positive because everywhere looked so neat and tidy, as though it was a showplace instead of a family home. It was the same upstairs: there was no sign of Sarah, Helen or their Swedish au-pair. Bergitta Lindstrom's room looked particularly bare and unlived in. Gone from her dressing table in the window alcove were the lipsticks, eye shadow and false lashes he'd come to associate with a young woman whose face had seemed different every time he'd seen her. The chest of drawers was empty, so too was the fitted cupboard; Bergitta hadn't simply gone away for the week-end, everything pointed to the possibility that she had walked out of the house for good.

Cartwright returned to their own bedroom and checked out the walk-in cupboard. The matching pair of Vuitton suitcases which Sarah's mother had given her one Christmas were missing and there was more space on the left-hand rail for his clothes than had previously been the case. Sarah

36

hadn't said anything about leaving him when he'd phoned her on Thursday evening and there was no goodbye note on his pillow where he could hardly fail to notice it.

He picked up her photograph on the dressing table and stared at it as though seeing his wife for the first time. A thirty-five-year-old woman with dark auburn hair and the sort of classical features that proclaimed her good breeding. It was not how he would have described Sarah himself but plenty of other people had, and there was no getting away from the fact that she was exceptionally well-connected. She was a Lucas, a member of an august family with an unbroken record of service to the Crown going back to the Restoration in 1660 and whose ranks included an inordinate number of Admirals and four-star Generals. Many of them had married into money, others had forged a link with the aristocracy; Sarah, he'd heard it said, had rather let the side down by marrying him.

Cartwright returned the photograph to its rightful place, then went downstairs to the kitchen and let himself out into the yard. As a matter of course, he looked into the first outhouse and wasn't surprised to find that Sarah's BMW had gone. What did shake him was the discovery that she had arranged for someone to collect both the chestnut mare and the pony belonging to Jamie, their nine-year-old son who was a boarder at Danesmead Preparatory School.

"Jenny Tyson," he said, voicing his immediate thought aloud.

Jenny owned a horsebox and was one of Sarah's closest friends but the Tysons lived the other side of Warminster and he didn't fancy driving over there to ask them if they knew where his wife had gone. Better to ring them from the public call box in the village.

The telephone. Cartwright turned about and walked back inside. The phone was usually kept on the hall table but he couldn't recall seeing it there when he'd let himself into the house. He supposed Sarah must have moved it and checked his study, then the sitting room where there was yet another socket. The only puzzling thing was how the telephone had escaped his notice the first time around when the instrument had been there all the time staring him in the face on top of the workbox.

The lead was coiled like a snake around the base of the phone, partially concealing the envelope Sarah had addressed to him. Like the envelope, the letter inside had also been typed, but there was nothing unusual about that; Sarah had her own unique form of shorthand that was virtually impossible to read and she invariably did all her correspondence on an old Remington portable.

The content of the letter was however a complete bombshell which left him numb with disbelief. Their marriage, it seemed, had been coming apart for the last eighteen months and she was beginning to feel that they were no longer compatible. He wasn't to worry about the children, she had made all the necessary arrangements, but she was going away because she needed time to herself to get things in perspective. To spare him any possible embarrassment, family and friends had been given a very different story.

Cartwright stared at the telephone, uncertain for the moment whether he really wanted to hear what sort of story Sarah had told the Tysons. Then, unwinding the flex, he inserted the bayonet-type plug into the socket above the skirting board, lifted the receiver and got a normal dialling tone. The line had been out of order when he'd tried to call Sarah earlier on but now it was evident that she had merely disconnected the phone. Checking the Tysons' listing in his pocket diary, he punched out the number and waited for someone to answer. When Jenny eventually lifted the phone, he felt decidedly awkward.

"Guess who?" Cartwright said lamely.

"Tom?"

"The same." He cleared his throat, stealing a few extra seconds to compose his thoughts. "Listen," he continued hesitantly, "I've got a bit of a problem."

"Where are you calling from?" Jenny asked, interrupting him.

"Manor Farm."

"Then you have got a problem. Sarah was expecting you to meet her at Orly. What happened to that conference you were supposed to be attending in Paris?"

"Don't ask," Cartwright said and was conscious of sounding ironic.

"It was supposed to last until the middle of next week and then you were going to take a few days' leave. Hadn't you booked Sarah into the Georges Cinq?"

"I was recalled to London, problems at the office. I tried to ring Sarah but she'd already left the house . . ."

He was surprised to find how easy it was to lie to Jenny and convince her it was the truth. By the time he eventually managed to get off the phone, it was also evident she'd no idea that Sarah had walked out on him. On the other hand, it was equally clear that if his wife had left him for someone else, she'd kept it a dark secret from her closest friend.

Cartwright found a bottle of Haig in the drinks cabinet and fixed himself a large whisky and soda. If anyone knew what Sarah had been up to it was her mother, but Lucas was almost bound to answer the phone and he didn't relish the prospect of unburdening himself to his father-in-law. Edwin Lucas was one of the least distinguished members of the family; his record of service in the army, though honourable, had been entirely without distinction and after several diplomatic appointments, he'd retired a full Colonel. His wealth, his influence, and the standing he enjoyed in the community had either been inherited or acquired through marriage. The only thing he'd achieved by his own efforts was the right to be addressed by his former army rank. That Edwin should refer to him as that young opportunist with an eye to the main chance was, in Cartwright's opinion, a piece of breathtaking hypocrisy.

The night had begun to draw in rapidly, the evening sky lit by the occasional jagged flash of lightning which, accompanied by a distant rumble of thunder, heralded the approach of yet another summer storm. Mechanically, as though programmed to respond like a microchip robot, he switched on the table lamp, lifted the receiver again and rang his

39

in-laws. Moments later, a crisp, military voice said, "Market Harborough 8729."

Then, "What's the matter this time?" Lucas demanded as soon as he'd said hullo. "Don't tell me Sarah's plane has been diverted?"

"Your guess is as good as mine," Cartwright said tersely.

Forked lightning cleaved the sky and the thunderclap which followed immediately afterwards was right overhead. If Edwin had a presentiment that something was wrong, the background noise of the storm apparently confirmed it.

"Where are you calling from?" he asked.

"Codford St Mary." Jennifer Tyson had asked him the same question and it was beginning to get a mite repetitious.

"You're supposed to be in Paris."

"So everyone keeps telling me."

"Sarah told her mother that you were over there on duty attending a symposium at the École de Guerre."

"A symposium?" Cartwright repeated blankly.

"Yes, something to do with the concept of land operations in the 1990s. Anyway, it was your idea that she should join you for a fortnight's holiday."

"Did Sarah tell you that?"

"What the hell's going on? Have you two had another row?"

"Of course they haven't, Edwin."

Lucas was partially deaf and always conversed in a loud voice. When he was angry, the whole household knew about it. His wife, Fay, had obviously heard him erupting and had picked up one of the extensions.

"As usual, you've got hold of the wrong end of the stick," she chided her husband.

"Nonsense. I distinctly remember you telling me that Sarah was going to join Tom in Paris."

"You never really listen to anything I say, Edwin, that's your trouble. One of the girls Sarah knew when she was stationed in Bonn is married to the Assistant Military Attaché in Paris and it's her husband who's attending the symposium."

40

The rest of the explanation was equally plausible. It was the old acquaintance from Bonn who'd invited Sarah to spend a week in Paris and he was supposed to join them next Friday for the second week.

There were those who said Fay was aptly named but they didn't know her as well as Cartwright did. Behind the placid, rather vague exterior, there was a very astute, very intelligent woman who could run rings round her husband. She was also adept at bringing Edwin to heel in the nicest possible way. In a soothing voice, Fay suggested that he might like to get on with whatever it was he was doing in the library before the phone rang while she talked to Tom. Lucas cleared his throat, mumbled something unintelligible, then hung up.

Fay said, "First things first. I presume you know that Helen is here with us?"

"Sarah did mention it in the note she left for me. Trouble is, I don't know what Sarah has told Jamie or even if she has been in touch with the school."

"We're all going over to Danesmead on Sunday to see him. As Helen is bound to say something, I think we should tell Jamie that his mother has gone to Paris at the invitation of the Barringtons so that she can be with you."

"Barrington is the Assistant Military Attaché we're supposed to be staying with?"

"Yes. I just twisted the facts around a bit for Edwin's benefit when I realised you weren't attending a symposium at the École de Guerre. I thought it would stop him asking a lot of awkward questions."

"Thanks, Fay. You were marvellous – in fact you succeeded in convincing me I'd got it wrong."

"Well, I've had a lot of practice at inventing plausible explanations in the last two days. It started when Sarah telephoned yesterday morning to say that Jennifer Tyson had offered to look after Helen while you two spent a long week-end in Paris but unfortunately she had gone down with a virus infection at the last moment and could I help? That was just the thin end of the wedge. Before Thursday was

41

over, a long week-end had stretched to a fortnight because your Colonel had agreed you could have seven days' leave after the symposium was over. I gathered you had phoned Sarah from Paris with the good news."

"Did she say anything about Bergitta, our Swedish au-pair?"

"Bergitta gave in her notice a month ago. According to Sarah, her father had had another mild heart attack and she felt she ought to go home and help her mother look after him. Sarah put her on a plane to Stockholm shortly before I arrived at Heathrow to collect Helen."

Cartwright stared at the portrait photograph of his wife in the silver frame next to the table lamp and wondered how many more lies she had told. He had lost count of the number of times he had phoned Sarah from London in the past month, never mind the week-ends they'd spent together, and yet she had never told him that Bergitta was working out her notice.

"Do you think Sarah has actually gone to Paris?" he asked.

"I watched her go through to the departure lounge."

"What time was this?"

"A few minutes before one o'clock. Sarah was booked on the British Airways Flight departing at 1345 hours." Fay paused, then said, "Would you like me to ring the Barringtons to see if she's arrived safely?"

"I think I'd better do that. Do you happen to have their phone number?"

"No, but I'm sure Edwin can get it for you."

Cartwright smiled wryly. If anyone could prise Barrington's ex-directory listing out of the Ministry of Defence, it was his father-in-law. Only Defence Intelligence and the Operations Branch were manned over a week-end but any duty staff officer who tried fobbing him off with that excuse, under the impression that he was merely dealing with a bellicose but unimportant old buffer, was in for a nasty surprise. By the time Lucas had finished having a quiet word with a few old friends and acquaintances, the wires would be humming and some unfortunate individual from the Services Attachés Support Staff would have to come into the office and dig out the required information. Much as he disliked asking his father-in-law for help, he could see no other alternative.

"I'd be very grateful if he would, Fay," Cartwright said flatly.

"Good. I know this sounds trite, but do try not to worry, Tom. Things are never as bad as they seem."

"I'll try to remember that," he said.

But it was difficult to be sanguine about what had happened. Sarah had always been a very private person and more than a little secretive. He recalled how, when he'd first met her, she had led him to believe she was merely one of the secretaries at the embassy in Bonn. It was only much later that he had discovered she was a brilliant linguist, fluent in French, German, Russian and Cantonese. In the circumstances, there was no telling how much else she had concealed from him over the years. Pushing the disturbing thought out of his mind, Cartwright picked up the phone and called the British Airways desk at Heathrow.

Bergitta Lindstrom was twenty-three years old, stood five foot five and a quarter in her stockinged feet and weighed a hundred and twelve pounds. She had an athletic, well-proportioned figure and looked as though she spent the greater part of her life outdoors in the fresh air. Contrary to the popular image of the typical Swedish girl, her hair and the colour of her eyes were a light brown.

Originally, Bergitta had become an au-pair in order to improve her English, but a taste for the good things in life which her wealthy boyfriend, Nuri Assad, had provided had led her to stay on long after she had begun to master the language. The Cartwrights were the fourth English family she had worked for and were country people, which made them different. She hadn't wanted to leave London for Codford St Mary but her previous employers had not given her a very good reference and none of the other interviews she'd been to had resulted in the offer of a job. So she had to take what was given.

There had been compensations for living in the depths of Wiltshire, however: her salary had been significantly better and her room had not been the poky little garret at the top of the house she'd been used to in London. If she hadn't seen quite as much of Nuri Assad as she would have liked, at least she still had the key to his luxury flat in Bayswater for her exclusive use on those alternate week-ends each month when the Cartwrights had allowed her time off.

Bergitta smiled at her reflection in the dressing table mirror. She had enjoyed working for the Cartwrights, but that chapter in her life was now closed and it was time to move on. As Nuri had so rightly said, she deserved a holiday for the way she had helped the police to protect her former employer.

Nuri: she heard the sound of footsteps in the hall and immediately assumed they were his. Slipping her feet into a pair of high-heeled court shoes, she went into the living room and came face to face with Peter Wentworth, the Detective Inspector of the Anti-terrorist Squad who had briefed her.

"Surprised?"

Bergitta nodded. "How did you . . . ?"

"Your boyfriend did me a favour and gave me his keys," Wentworth told her before she could finish the question.

It was more likely he had demanded them. Bergitta had noticed his arrogance the first time she'd met him at the beginning of May and nothing had happened since then to change her opinion. Wentworth had been very attentive and charming but Nuri had seemed almost pathetically anxious to please him. When they'd met again a fortnight later, the Englishman had produced a warrant card to prove he was a police officer. 'You could say that Nuri here is my eyes and ears amongst the Arab community in London,' he'd added, smiling. 'Thanks to him, I know who is going to do what the same day the orders come through from Damascus, Tripoli, Baghdad or wherever.' There had been more, a whole lot more. Wentworth had other informers besides Nuri and in other camps, which was how he'd learned the Israelis were planning to lift Mrs Cartwright.

"She won't come to any harm, will she?" Bergitta asked, voicing a niggling doubt that had been with her all day.

"Who? Sarah?" Wentworth found a bottle of brandy under the corner bar and fixed himself a brandy and ginger ale. "No, she'll be safe enough now." He placed another tall glass on the bar top, then stepped back a pace to eye the bottles on the shelf below. "Let's see," he murmured, "you're a vodka, lime and lemonade person. Right?"

"Yes." Bergitta frowned. "I can't understand why the Israelis should want to question Mrs Cartwright after all this time."

"Well, like I told you before, Jewish people have long memories. Sarah Lucas, as she was in those days, was known to be very pro-Arab when she was on the Mid-East desk at the Foreign and Commonwealth Office. One of the last things she did before leaving the Service was to give the Syrians a nuclear capability by shuffling a few papers in such a way that they were able to lay their hands on a quantity of plutonium. The whisper about Sarah's involvement only reached Tel Aviv a few weeks ago; that's why, years after the event, the Israelis would like to ask her just how much plutonium did reach Damascus." Wentworth unscrewed a bottle of lemonade and topped up the vodka and lime almost to the brim. "You got any other questions?" he asked.

"No."

"Good. Now suppose you tell me exactly what happened from the moment the postman arrived yesterday morning."

"He delivered a package which Mrs Cartwright had to sign for."

"A registered envelope?"

"Yes." Realising that Wentworth had no intention of waiting on her, Bergitta joined him at the bar and perched herself on a stool. "About an hour later, Mrs Cartwright told me that she was going to sell Manor Farm and divorce her husband because he was having an affair with another woman in London. She said the package had contained a detailed report from the private detective her solicitor had hired to spy on Major Cartwright." Bergitta wrinkled her nose. "I don't know why you want to hear all this. Had she told me a different story, I would have got in touch with you."

"Sarah then said something about needing some time to herself first?" Wentworth persisted.

"She said she was going off on her own somewhere to think things out and I wasn't to discuss her personal affairs with any of her friends or the neighbours. Mrs Cartwright also informed me I was to receive six months' salary in lieu of notice."

Bergitta told him about the trip to Paris which Sarah had invented for the benefit of her mother and Mrs Tyson and how she had been all friendly and loving towards her husband when he'd telephoned her on Thursday evening. As far as Bergitta could tell, he hadn't suspected anything was wrong and neither had Mrs Tyson when she had driven over to Manor Farm to collect the horses that afternoon.

"And how did it go this morning?" Wentworth asked, prompting her.

"We all drove up to London together, Mrs Cartwright, little Helen and me. I left them at Heathrow and came straight here on the Underground."

"This was before Mrs Lucas arrived to collect her granddaughter?"

"Yes." Bergitta nodded emphatically.

"And Sarah had no reason to suspect that you knew she'd no intention of divorcing her husband? She thought you believed her story about the private detective and his evidence?"

"I pretended to be very shocked when Mrs Cartwright told me she'd hired someone to spy on her husband. I was very good."

"I'm sure you were, Bergitta."

"But now I have no job."

"You've nothing to worry about, Nuri will see you right." Wentworth joined Bergitta on the other side of the bar, took

46

a bulky envelope from his inside pocket and placed it in front of her. "And you'll find we're not ungrateful either."

"For me, Peter?" she asked, her eyes widening as though she had never expected to be rewarded.

"It's got your name on it. A small present for services rendered."

"Did Mrs Cartwright also receive a present?"

"We gave her a new passport," Wentworth said. "Yours is much more exciting."

Bergitta ripped the envelope open and gave a little squeal of delight when she saw the wad of twenty-pound notes inside. Moving swiftly while her attention was still riveted on the money, Wentworth stepped behind her and smashed a clenched fist into the small of her back. The kidney punch was devastatingly effective; it left the Swedish girl writhing in agony, physically incapable of resistance. Removing his belt, Wentworth looped it round Bergitta's neck and slowly strangled her.

4

Cartwright removed the parking ticket from the vending machine, drove past the raised barrier and went on up the one-way circuit until he eventually found a vacant slot on the fourth floor of the multi-storey car park opposite the European Terminal Building at Heathrow. There was a Volvo Estate to the left and a maroon-coloured Honda saloon on the right; locking the doors on the Metro, he made a mental note of the bay number, then walked down to the ground floor.

Cartwright felt exhausted; too tired even to worry. He'd made dozens of phone calls and all of them had proved inconclusive. The Barringtons weren't expecting Sarah and they hadn't heard from her since receiving the letter she'd enclosed with a Christmas card. The Georges Cinq didn't have a Mrs Cartwright staying at the hotel, neither had they made a reservation for a Miss Lucas. On the other hand, British Airways had confirmed that Sarah had been on the 1345 hours flight to Paris. Only the fact that the Scandinavian airlines desk had no record of a Miss Bergitta Lindstrom flying to Stockholm on Friday morning had prompted him to phone British Airways again to query the information they'd given him.

The girl he'd spoken to had been very sympathetic and understanding but their records still showed that his wife had been on the plane. Furthermore, since his previous phone call, they'd checked with their staff at Orly airport who'd confirmed that Mrs Cartwright had claimed her baggage and passed through Customs. Then, perhaps anxious he shouldn't think she was being unhelpful, the girl had volunteered one particular item of information she'd

48

been given about that flight. Roughly five minutes before the passengers were about to board at Gate 12, a Miss Ellen Rothman had cancelled her seat on the plane on learning that her mother was dangerously ill in hospital. It was a slender, almost non-existent lead, but checking it out was better than sitting around worrying and at least the receptionist who'd dealt with Miss Rothman would be back on duty.

With every major airline scheduling extra flights to cope with the holiday traffic, Heathrow resembled a disturbed ant's nest. There was a small crowd three deep around the Inquiry Desk and it was a good ten minutes before he could catch anyone's eye. The information clerk was not the same girl he'd spoken to the previous evening but fortunately she had left a message for the supervisor in charge of the morning shift. All Cartwright had to do then was convince her he was a perfectly rational human being and wait a further ten minutes while a Mrs Katherine Pierce was called to the personnel manager's office over the public address system.

"I'm hoping you can help me," he said, after they'd been introduced.

"Oh, yes. Mary said something about a Miss Ellen Rothman, the lady who had to cancel her flight to Paris yesterday."

Cartwright didn't know who Mary was, nor did he care. Taking out his wallet, he extracted a snapshot of Sarah taken the previous August when they were staying at St Malo and handed it to Mrs Pierce. "Would this be the lady whose mother is seriously ill in hospital?" he asked

"I'm not sure." She smiled apologetically. "You'd be surprised at the number of domestic crises we have to deal with in the course of a working day, especially at this time of the year. As far as I was concerned, Miss Rothman was just another traveller with a problem and I didn't really pay too much attention to her appearance."

"How did she strike you?"

"What?"

49

"Miss Rothman had just received some bad news," Cartwright explained patiently. "Did she appear confused, upset or agitated?"

"I thought she seemed a bit tense but she certainly wasn't emotional or anything like that." Katherine Pierce held the photograph at arm's length and studied it carefully. "I presume this is Mrs Cartwright?"

"Yes."

"On second thoughts, her face does seem familiar. Same auburn hair but the style was different."

"Sarah wore it short last year. It didn't suit her."

"How tall is your wife?"

"Five foot eight, give or take a fraction of an inch."

"The woman I met was also fairly tall."

"You'll probably think this is a stupid question," he said, "but how did you know Miss Rothman was who she claimed she was?"

There was an awkward silence. Watching them as they exchanged glances, Cartwright was undecided whether he had merely succeeded in embarrassing Mrs Pierce and her supervisor or whether he had aroused their suspicion. They had started out thinking he was the distressed husband looking for his errant wife but now they weren't sure what to make of him.

"Because she produced her plane ticket, boarding pass and passport," Mrs Pierce told him eventually.

Cartwright thanked her, said she'd been a great help, then asked the supervisor if it was possible to find out what had happened to Miss Rothman's baggage. A phone call to left luggage established that it had been returned to Heathrow and was awaiting collection.

"How many pieces?" he asked.

"One suitcase."

"I don't suppose I could examine it?" He knew the answer before the supervisor told him it was out of the question.

"We wouldn't even allow the police to open the suitcase unless they had a warrant or could show just cause."

"Maybe they have."

"What do you mean?" The supervisor was now obviously on guard.

"Forget my wife for a moment," Cartwright told her. "Let's talk about Ellen Rothman instead. What do you really know about her? How did she learn that her mother was seriously ill in hospital? Was she paged to one of the phones in the departure lounge?"

"I haven't the faintest idea. Katherine was the one she approached."

"And I didn't think to ask her," Katherine Pierce said, frowning. "Nor did she tell me which hospital her mother had been admitted to."

"Well, has anyone heard from Miss Rothman since yesterday?" Cartwright asked. "Left luggage for instance?"

"No, she hasn't been in touch with them yet," the supervisor told him.

"Really? If I was Airport Security, I'd want to know why she was so disinterested. In fact, I'd have that suitcase X-rayed to make sure it didn't contain an IED."

"A what?"

"An improvised explosive device – a home-made time bomb."

"A time bomb?" the supervisor repeated and slowly reached for the phone.

Airport Security and a Detective Sergeant from the Special Branch cell at Heathrow arrived within a couple of minutes. The Bomb Squad was equally quick off the mark and rapidly cleared everyone out of the left luggage shed. The suitcase was identified from the baggage tag, X-rayed by a remote-controlled robot and pronounced harmless. When finally opened, it was found to contain three pairs of ladies shoes, and various articles of clothing. The underwear and clothes had been purchased from Marks and Spencer's and were at least one size too small for Sarah.

The Detective Sergeant from Special Branch took a statement from Cartwright and then gave him a few facts and figures about the number of people who were prosecuted each year by the police for wasting their time. His attitude

51

suggested he was convinced the whole episode had been an elaborate hoax and, in his shoes, Cartwright had to admit he would have drawn the same conclusion. As far as the police were concerned, British Airways had incontrovertible evidence that Sarah had been on their 1345 flight to Paris and had collected her luggage at Orly. To accept his version, they had to believe that Sarah and Ellen Rothman had switched identities while they were waiting in the departure lounge. Moreover, if they were to stand any chance of getting away with such a ruse, both women would need duplicate passports to support their adopted names.

"And let's face it," the Detective Sergeant said, winding up, "it's a pretty complicated way for a woman to walk out on her husband. Obtaining a second passport under an assumed name isn't exactly the easiest thing to do."

"I don't pretend to know how my wife did it or why," Cartwright said evenly, "but the fact remains that she did. If you don't believe me, talk to her mother and show her the snapshot. She'll confirm that Sarah and Ellen Rothman are one and the same person."

"With all due respect, she can't do anything of the kind. Mrs Pierce is the key witness and she's only prepared to say that the woman in the snapshot looks familiar." The Detective Sergeant consulted his notebook, then said, "As a matter of fact, she wasn't sure there was any similarity until you went to work on her."

"Suppose we look at this thing from a different angle? I told you that my wife drove up from Codford St Mary – right?"

"So?"

"So I'd like you to telephone Market Harborough 8729 and ask Mrs Lucas where her daughter said she'd left the BMW."

The Detective Sergeant mulled it over, his brow wrinkling as though he'd been asked to solve a problem that would have taxed an Einstein. Eventually, having weighed all the pros and cons, he asked Cartwright for the dialling code and rang his wife's parents. When he put the phone down a few

52

minutes later, it was obvious from the smile on his face that he hadn't been talking to Edwin.

"Your mother-in-law is a very charming woman," he said. "I wish I could say the same for mine."

"What did she say?"

"Your wife left her car at the Airways Garage on the Bath Road."

"The registration number is C419 GKZ." Cartwright smiled. "You can always check it out with the Vehicle Licensing Centre at Swansea."

"I'll take your word for it, Major."

The Detective Sergeant looked up Airways Garage in the telephone directory and rang their head office. The girl who took the call told him they had never heard of a Mrs Sarah Cartwright and that no one had left a BMW with them on Friday morning.

"Maybe your theory isn't quite so improbable after all," he said.

"That's a step in the right direction," Cartwright told him.

"I think you should report her as a missing person, sir."

"What good will that do?"

"Well, we'll make the usual inquiries to satisfy ourselves that she's alive and well." The Detective Sergeant glanced at the statement to make sure Cartwright had signed it at the foot of each page before he slipped it into a buff-coloured envelope. "Of course, it's not our job to bring husband and wife together and we shan't disclose Mrs Cartwright's address unless we have her permission."

"That sounds fair enough."

"Do I take it you want us to proceed on those lines?"

Cartwright simply nodded an affirmative.

The junkyard on the outskirts of Brentford was far enough removed from the Thames to escape the attention of the local environmental pressure group who were determined to clean up the riverside in that part of London. Occupying a half acre site in rear of the wharf belonging to the now defunct East India Tea Company, it was the burial ground for just about every worn-out vehicle within a radius of ten miles. Behind a tall corrugated iron fence capped with barbed wire, the rusting hulks of every known make that had ever been on the road were piled haphazardly on top of one another like a petrified forest sculptured in metal by an avant-garde artist. Thirty-six hours after lifting the Mini from outside the house in Pelham Street, Wentworth opened the gates, drove into the yard and parked the stolen vehicle behind the giant crusher where it could not be seen from the road. With the air of a man who had all the time in the world, he then got out of the car and walked back to the entrance to secure the gates.

Also concealed from view behind the crusher was a grey-coloured Dodge Transit from the Sketchley Dye and Dry Cleaning Company. The load in the back of the van consisted of a Persian carpet and one large wickerwork laundry basket weighing approximately one hundred and twenty-six pounds. Taking a bunch of keys from his pocket, Wentworth unlocked the rear doors and pulled the wicker basket towards him sideways on. Then he turned about and reaching back over his shoulders, got a two-handed grip on one of the handles and humped it over to the Mini. It had been comparatively easy to carry Bergitta out of the mews flat in Bayswater rolled up in the carpet and dump her into the laundry basket while she was still warm, but now, fourteen hours after death had occurred, rigor mortis had reached an advanced state. Tipping the basket over on to its side, he dragged out the unyielding corpse and eventually managed to heave it into the back of the Mini.

Wentworth took a swig from a hip flask of brandy, then walked over to the mechanical grabber and climbed up into the cab. He started the motor, rotated the jib until it was directly above the Mini and lowered the grabber. A touch on the button and the jaws opened and closed, the metal teeth shattering the windows. Caught in a vice-like grip, the car roof buckled and changed shape into an elongated pyramid as the teeth met below. Winching the vehicle clear of the ground, he traversed the crane through ninety degrees and deftly lowered the Mini into the trough of the giant crusher and retracted the jaws.

Wentworth stopped the motor, climbed down from the cab and set the crusher in motion. Two horizontally-opposed rams moved relentlessly forward to crush the Mini between them while a third hydraulic press positioned above the trough slowly descended. A split second before it bore down on the roof, Wentworth hit the stop button and brought all three rams to a standstill. The vehicle was already compressed to half its normal size and it was essential to arrest the process before the car was finally reduced to a parcel of scrap metal.

Although terribly mutilated, the corpse was still identifiable, which was the whole idea. Now all he had to do was fake things to make it seem that the crusher had broken down before the job could be completed. Throwing the master switch, he located the correct fuse and removed it from the box; then, moistening the 20-amp wire with spittle, he replaced the fuse, tripped the current and blew the circuit.

There remained one final touch. Parking the transit van outside the entrance, Wentworth chained and padlocked the gates, then cut one of the links in two with a pair of bolt cutters. Seen from a distance, the gates appeared to be secured, but on Monday morning the severed chain would be noticed by the workmen and the police would draw the obvious conclusion when they arrived on the scene.

5

It rained again on Monday. There was also a gusting wind swirling around the concave Empress State Building in Earls Court which created an upward draught that sucked in every scrap of litter from the surrounding area and bore it aloft. From time to time, Cartwright looked up from the work on his desk to see the same paper cup bobbing up and down like a yo-yo between the eighth and fourteenth floors of the building. His hopes of tracing Sarah had followed a similar pattern, up one moment, down the next.

After leaving Heathrow, he'd returned to Codford St Mary and spent the rest of Saturday and the greater part of Sunday working his way through Sarah's address book. Ninety per cent of the names were mutual friends and acquaintances; the remaining ten per cent were either distant relatives or people Sarah had known before they were married. Whatever their status, they had one thing in common: none of them had seen or heard from her in months. If there was another man in Sarah's life, he'd found no evidence of his existence. There had been no letters, no keep-sakes, no trinkets and no mysterious entries in the desk diary belonging to Sarah.

Cartwright wished he could have gone to Danesmead with Fay and Edwin on Sunday but of course that had been out of the question. For the sake of Helen and Jamie it had been necessary to maintain the pretence that he was in Paris with their mother, but the whole episode had left him with a nasty taste in his mouth. To assuage his conscience, he had telephoned Fay on Sunday evening to inquire after the children and had finished up talking to his father-in-law instead.

A part-time Justice of the Peace, Edwin had taken it upon himself to have a quiet word with the Assistant Chief Constable of Leicestershire. After reminding him that the police had never lost a case when he was on the Bench, he had then steered the conversation round to Sarah. "Ordinarily," he'd said, "the police try not to involve themselves in domestic problems. They don't consider it any business of theirs if a woman leaves her husband and runs off with another man, but I want my daughter found and he's promised to ginger up the Met."

Cartwright supposed he should be grateful but he couldn't help feeling that his father-in-law had probably made things worse. The Met wouldn't take kindly to the Assistant Chief Constable of a provincial force making waves and the people on the ground were likely to be particularly resentful. Furthermore, Sarah had disappeared in mysterious circumstances and matters weren't being helped by her father hinting to his friends that their marriage was on the rocks. It was too late to ask the Assistant Chief Constable to back off but at least Lucas could put him straight and there was only one person who could persuade Edwin to do that. Cartwright reached for the phone, intending to ring Fay; as he did so, the office intercom suddenly came to life and Nolan, the grade one staff officer in charge of the branch, asked him to drop into his office.

Lieutenant Colonel Nolan was not alone. His visitor was a lean, dark-haired man who looked very sure of himself and was clearly unimpressed by senior army officers below one star rank. Cartwright noticed he had merely unbuttoned his knee-length navy blue raincoat instead of removing it and wondered if this was intended to convey a sense of urgency.

"My name's Dalton," he said before Nolan had a chance to introduce him. "I'm a Detective Inspector with 'T' District over at Brentford and I believe you're the owner of a 1976 dark blue Mini, registration number KPH 187P?"

"Until it was stolen on Thursday night." Cartwright smiled. "Do I gather you have recovered it?"

Dalton ignored the question. "I've also been informed by

57

my colleagues at Heathrow that Mrs Cartwright has disappeared," he said. "Is that correct?"

"Yes."

Nolan looked sour. Although he had never met Sarah, he obviously felt that he should have been appraised of the situation instead of learning about it secondhand from the police.

"When did this happen?" Dalton asked.

"Some time on Friday. My wife told her mother that she was joining me in Paris." Suddenly, Cartwright was fighting panic; he had a horrible premonition that his whole world had collapsed in ruins. "Has anything happened to Sarah?" he asked hoarsely.

"I think you'd better come with me, sir," Dalton told him.

"Shall I fetch my raincoat from the office?" The absurdity of the question struck him forcibly even as he uttered it.

"You won't need it," Dalton said. "I have a car parked outside the front entrance."

Sarah was dead; the realisation sank in, overwhelming him with a feeling of immeasurable loss. A lump formed in his throat which threatened to choke him and it was as much as he could do to hold back the tears. A kind of paralysis set in, numbing his mind, so that afterwards he had no recollection of leaving Empress State or of the journey across town to the mortuary in Brentford.

The girl Dalton showed him looked as though she had been run over by a train. What was left of her face was barely recognisable but Cartwright didn't need a second glance to know who it was.

"Bergitta," he said in a low voice.

"Who?"

"This girl is Bergitta Lindstrom, our au-pair. She was supposed to have flown home to Stockholm on Friday because her father had had another heart attack."

"I think you'd better tell me what you know about the deceased," Dalton said. "Name and address of her next-of-kin, how long she had been in your employ – that kind of thing. The station's just round the corner from here."

58

"Do I need a solicitor?"

"Not as far as I'm aware. What prompted you to ask?"

"Because I don't believe that Miss Lindstrom stole my car and my instinct tells me she wasn't killed in a traffic accident."

"All I want from you is a tentative identification," Dalton told him. "Then we can get in touch with the Swedish Consular Office and they can inform the next-of-kin. Okay?"

"Sounds fair enough to me," Cartwright said.

The police station, which had been built around the turn of the century, resembled a fortress and was considerably farther away than Dalton had implied. One of the interview rooms on the ground floor near the detention cells happened to be vacant and Cartwright was allowed to dictate a statement to a uniformed constable without interruption. The questions only started after he had read and initialled the deposition at the foot of each page to signify it was a true record.

"When was the last time you saw Bergitta?" Dalton asked him innocently.

"It must have been a fortnight ago last Friday. She has every other week-end off."

"You don't seem very certain of your facts," Dalton observed. "Can't you be a little more precise?"

"This may come as a surprise to you," Cartwright said, "but I wasn't all that interested in Bergitta's social life. My wife didn't exactly work her to the bone and she was always having extra time off. I don't recall seeing Bergitta when I arrived home that Friday evening, but she must have been around the next day. We had dinner with Hugh and Jennifer Tyson on the Saturday evening and we would never have hired a baby-sitter to look after Helen."

"Did Miss Lindstrom have any boyfriends?"

"A few; she was a very attractive girl."

"Anyone in particular?"

Cartwright frowned. "There was someone called Nuri she was seeing in London."

59

"An Arab gentleman?"

"I assume so. She didn't talk about him all that much but from what little she did tell us, I gathered he had plenty of money to throw around."

"Did Bergitta go up to town on her evening off?" Dalton asked.

"I doubt it, the journey there and back by public transport takes too long."

"How about you, sir? Have you ever spent the odd weekend in town, supposedly on duty?"

Cartwright glared at the older man contemptuously. "Are you trying to imply we had something going?"

"Your Mini was found in a junkyard not far from here where someone had done their level best to reduce it to a neat bundle of scrap metal. If the machine hadn't blown a fuse, Miss Lindstrom would have been sealed up inside a tin box no larger than a suitcase." Dalton paused to let it sink in, then said, "Even so, it beats me how you recognised her."

The police were trying to build a case against him with bricks made of straw. Cartwright knew that unless they were ready to prefer charges, there was no way they could detain him against his will. In theory, he was free to leave the police station any time he chose to, but no matter what the law said, he wasn't at all sure Dalton would stick to the rules.

"Then there's Mrs Cartwright," Dalton continued. "A wealthy, attractive and intelligent young woman who has disappeared in very mysterious circumstances."

"What exactly are you getting at?"

"Nothing. I was just wondering if there was a connection."

Cartwright dug out a handful of loose change from his pocket and piled the coins on the table in front of Dalton. "All right," he said coldly, "where's the nearest pay-phone?"

"What?"

"I'm going to call my solicitors." Strictly speaking, Bream, Cotton and Roose were Edwin's legal advisers but Cartwright didn't know who else to approach and the firm had acted for Sarah and himself when they'd drawn up their respective wills just before Christmas.

"There's no need to do that," Dalton said.

Cartwright regarded the police constable who'd recorded his statement. "A2304," he said, reading off the silver-plated numbers on the dark blue shoulder boards of his uniform. "We may not have been introduced but I'll know who to call as a witness."

"Sir?" the police constable said, frowning.

"Your superior officer is attempting to deny me certain legal rights conferred on every citizen by the Judge's Rules. Don't let him pressure you into supporting his statement when I sue the police for wrongful arrest."

"Oh, for God's sake," Dalton said irritably, "somebody get the man a telephone. He can talk to the Lord Chief Justice for all I care."

Ellen Rothman left the Metro at Havre-Caumartin, walked up the Boulevard Haussmann as far as the Place St Augustin, then turned right into the Rue de la Pépinière to make her way towards the Gare St-Lazare. It had been very warm and humid ever since she had arrived in Paris on Friday afternoon, and today was no exception. She could feel the sun on her back and the nylon slip she was wearing under her silk dress clung to her like a second skin. The weather did have one advantage: it gave her a good excuse for ducking into a small bar just up the road from the French Officers' Club.

The bar was deserted except for two workmen drinking absinthe. Ignoring their curious stares, she perched herself on the stool nearest the window where she could watch the street and ordered a soft drink. Ten minutes later, Ellen Rothman left the bar and continued on her way, convinced that no one was following her.

The transformation from archivist to field agent had been swift and totally unexpected. A fortnight ago she had been on leave awaiting reassignment after a two year tour of duty in the Persian Gulf, then in response to a phone call to her home address, she had reported to Standard House in the Strand where she had been interviewed by Simon Faulkner.

Standard House was not part of the Foreign Office empire and she had never met Simon Faulkner before, but she had found his name in the Diplomatic Service List and his biographical details had been sufficiently detailed to put her mind at rest. During the interview, it had also become rapidly evident that Faulkner had had access to her security file. The loan from the British Bank of the Middle East to buy a car, the minor breach of security committed in March 1981 and the affair she'd had with the First Secretary Commerce at the embassy in Ankara; there had been nothing in her past he hadn't known about.

The training she had received had been minimal but as Faulkner had pointed out, in the time available they could only teach her the basics. The actual programme had consisted of a classroom exercise designed to evaluate her ability to absorb and retain information under pressure and a couple of dry runs across London which were intended to test her security awareness. None of it had made a great deal of sense to her until the final briefing; then everything had fallen into place and she could appreciate just how purposeful the programme had been. And when Faulkner had shown her a photograph of the woman she was to impersonate, it had been obvious from their physical similarity why he had chosen her for the job, despite his misgivings about the breach of security she'd committed in 1981.

"So okay, it was only a minor offence," he'd said, making the point forcibly. "You forgot there was a restricted circular in your pending tray when you locked up for the night and no harm was done because the duty officer found it when he checked your office five minutes after you'd left." Faulkner had wagged a finger at her. "But no one will be covering for you on this job and Sarah Cartwright's life will be on the line if you foul it up."

"I won't let you down," Ellen had told him, and she most certainly hadn't. In laying a false trail for the Israelis to follow, she had obeyed his instructions to the letter. She had confided in no one, not even her parents and she was not about to fall down on the job now that it was nearly completed.

Ellen turned into the Gare St-Lazare, walked past the ticket office and found a vacant phone booth at the far end of the concourse. Feeding two 1-franc coins into the box, she punched out the contact number Faulkner had given her and waited.

A few moments later, a male voice answered the phone with a cryptic *"Oui?"*

"My name is Sarah Cartwright," she told him, carefully enunciating every word in case he barely understood English. "I wish to speak to Mr Peter Wentworth."

"You've just got your wish," the man said and chuckled.

The throaty voice and the way he laughed – a cold, mirthless laugh – sounded rather familiar.

Bream, Cotton and Roose were based in Market Harborough; it was therefore only logical that they should brief a London firm of solicitors to represent Cartwright who in turn sent one of their assistants along to Brentford police station. Henry Edgecombe was an earnest-looking twenty-five-year-old whose youthful appearance did nothing to boost Cartwright's confidence. As soon as he spoke, it was obvious that past clients had shared his doubts.

"I want you to know I completed my articles some time ago," he said as they shook hands in the interview room.

"How long is some time?" Cartwright asked politely.

"Seven and a half months," Edgecombe told him in all seriousness, and promptly sat down at the table. "I've read your statement concerning Bergitta Lindstrom," he continued. "The police have also told me about your wife's disappearance and the theft of your car. Now I'd like to hear your side of the story."

"From the beginning?"

"If you would."

Cartwright nodded, then told Edgecombe how he'd tried to telephone Sarah on Friday evening to warn her he would be home late and had found that the line was apparently out of order. He described his increasing bewilderment as he had gradually discovered the web of conflicting lies Sarah had told the Tysons and her parents before she'd disappeared.

"And you can't account for your wife's strange behaviour?"

Cartwright reached inside his jacket and brought out the now crumpled envelope he'd been carrying around ever since Friday. "She left me this note which is supposed to explain everything," he said, and passed it to Edgecombe. "It doesn't make any sense to me. Perhaps it would have done five years ago when our marriage was going through a bad patch, but not now."

Edgecombe unfolded the letter, read it quickly, then looked up. "Does your wife type all her letters?" he asked.

"People were always complaining about her handwriting so she bought herself a portable."

"Have the police seen this note?"

"No. I thought they wouldn't believe Sarah was missing if I showed it to them."

"I see." Edgecombe rubbed his chin, frowning judiciously as he did so. "Is there anything else you want to tell me about your wife, Major Cartwright?"

"Like what?"

"Well, for instance, is it true that she has a private income?"

Either Bream, Cotton and Roose had been talking out of turn or else the police had got in touch with his father-in-law and Edwin had considered it his bounden duty to put them in the picture. Although potentially damaging, he saw no point in denying that Sarah was financially independent.

"We couldn't afford to live the way we do and send our son to an expensive Prep School on my army pay. I don't know how much Sarah has in her current account but her investment portfolio is worth more than sixty thousand." Cartwright paused, then said, "There's also Manor Farm at Codford St Mary which would fetch three or four times that amount if put on the market."

64

"Your wife is comfortably off then?"

"Put it this way, any police officer who suspected foul play wouldn't have to look very far for a motive. I'd be a rich man if anything happened to Sarah. Unfortunately for Dalton, he's up against Mrs Pierce."

"I'm told her evidence isn't conclusive. Apparently she merely said that your wife resembled Ellen Rothman."

"In other words, Sarah did not switch places with her?"

"Yes."

"Which means the police are convinced my wife was on the flight to Paris."

"They believe she was leaving you for another man, someone who isn't exactly a stranger to you."

"Someone who isn't exactly a stranger?" Cartwright repeated, then suddenly understood the inference. "You don't mean they actually think this unknown lover and I set Sarah up?" he said incredulously.

"The police appear to think it would explain a lot of things."

Amongst them, the lies Sarah had told the Tysons and her parents. According to the scenario the police had constructed, she had been very discreet. No one had known she was having an affair and she'd been determined to keep it that way right up to the very last moment in case her family got to hear about it and tried to make her break it off. Cartwright could see an eager police officer latching on to that premise.

"I act the part of the distraught husband while Sarah's lover is busy disposing of her body somewhere in France," he said, developing the theme. "Then, some years later when my wife is legally presumed dead, he and I split her estate down the middle."

"I wouldn't know what line the police are taking," Edgecombe said uncomfortably. "They didn't confide in me."

"I was just thinking aloud," Cartwright told him. "Presumably, it all started because I had the hots for Bergitta Lindstrom and she wanted a ring on her finger before she would allow me into her bed. Either Bergitta knew I was planning to kill my wife and was happy to go along with the idea before she began to get cold feet or else she was entirely innocent and just happened to discover what I had in mind. In any event, she knew too much and had to be silenced. Any idea how I'm supposed to have killed our au-pair?"

"She was strangled," Edgecombe said and hurriedly avoided his gaze.

"What about the time of death? Have they established that?"

"The post mortem hasn't even started yet, but the doctor who carried out the preliminary examination reckons death must have occurred at least forty-eight hours before the body was discovered."

"It's ironic to think her remains would never have been found if that damned crusher hadn't broken down."

"So Inspector Dalton observed."

"In other words, I was a bit unlucky?"

"Someone was."

"Why be so coy?" Cartwright said angrily. "We both know I'm the number one suspect. It was my car they found in the junkyard after it had been stolen from outside my flat on Thursday night. Dalton probably thinks I had to report the theft to cover myself in case anyone asked me what I'd done with the Mini."

"One has to admit it's a logical explanation."

"For God's sake, whose side are you on?"

"Yours, of course," Edgecombe said in a voice that lacked commitment.

"I'm very glad to hear it." Cartwright pushed his chair back and stood up. "Now let's see you get me out of here," he said.

"You're not under arrest so there's no way the police can detain you."

It sounded as though Edgecombe was expressing a fervent hope rather than a point of law but, in the event, Dalton could not have been nicer. He even thanked Cartwright for being so helpful.

"I told you there was nothing to worry about," Edgecombe said pompously as they walked out into the street. "I knew Dalton would have to back down the moment we decided to call his bluff."

"Maybe we should celebrate our victory in that pub across the road." Cartwright seized his elbow and steered him towards the pedestrian crossing. "I know you're going to say you ought to get back to the office, but another five minutes won't make any difference, will it?"

Most of the lunchtime crowd had already left when they walked into the lounge bar of The Star and Garter. Ordering a draught lager for Edgecombe who didn't fancy anything stronger, and a large whisky soda for himself, Cartwright paid for their drinks, then shepherded the lawyer to a corner table far removed from the bar, where they could be sure of some privacy.

"Tell me, Henry," he said casually, "what's your opinion of Dalton?"

"I think he's a hard but fair man. Of course, one isn't really in a position to judge his professional competence, but he strikes me as a very methodical, very experienced officer."

Edgecombe sounded as though he was damning him with faint praise, but that was probably unintentional. Although theirs was a very brief acquaintance, he had already persuaded Cartwright that he was incapable of expressing an unequivocal view on any subject, including the weather.

"I doubt if you'd be quite so even-handed if you were in my position," Cartwright told him bluntly.

"Oh, why's that?"

"Dalton looks as though he's in his mid-forties, which I reckon is a bit old for a Detective Inspector. If he's to go any farther, he needs a lucky break and the Lindstrom case could well be it. But he's got to wrap it up quickly, otherwise the Commander of 'T' District will appoint a more senior officer to head the investigation. That could be why Dalton is gunning for me. I'm the number one suspect and he doesn't have the time or the inclination to go looking for someone else."

"Do you have a lot to do with the police in your job at the Ministry of Defence?" Edgecombe asked.

"No. I'm with the Directorate of Personal Services. We handle redress of grievance, ministerial inquiries, disciplinary matters, the effects of civil legislation on the army, human rights, the application of the Geneva Convention – that sort of thing."

"But nothing highly secret?"

"I haven't seen a paper graded higher than Confidential since I left the Staff College last December. Why do you ask?"

"I was just wondering why anyone would go to such lengths to frame you." Edgecombe stared at his unwanted lager as though willing it to evaporate. "I expect Dalton asked himself the same question," he added.

The BMW was parked in a non-metered bay outside number 16 Eaton Place, off the Cromwell Road. The traffic warden had checked the car when he'd first come on duty at nine a.m., had noticed that the driver wasn't displaying a resident's permit and had immediately issued a parking ticket. Now, almost six hours later, the vehicle was still there; even more annoying was the discovery that, according to one irate resident, it had been occupying the parking space for a good seventy-two hours. Deciding there was just enough time to do something about it before he signed off, the traffic warden phoned in, asked the shift supervisor to send a light recovery vehicle to Eaton Place and had the BMW impounded.

The police compound had access to the computer records of the vehicle licensing department at Swansea. A routine check revealed that the owner of the maroon-coloured BMW was Mrs Sarah Cartwright of Manor Farm, Codford St Mary, Wiltshire.

6

The registered offices of the Sentinel Inquiry Agency were on the second floor of a terraced house in Gloucester Road. The chief investigator was a Mr Lionel Alderton whose name Cartwright had found in the Yellow Pages, a dozen or so entries above that of the firm. The accommodation, which consisted of one modest-sized office, a glorified cubbyhole for the secretary-typist and the shared use of the gentlemen's toilet with a bed-sit agency on the floor below, confirmed an initial impression that the Sentinel Inquiry Agency was a one-man band. Two things had led Cartwright to use the firm: the first letter of Alderton's surname had put him at the head of the list and the agency itself happened to be relatively near the Empress State Building.

Lionel Alderton was a tall, slim man in his mid-fifties whose thinning grey hair and scholarly appearance were in striking contrast to his somewhat lugubrious manner on the telephone. Despite looking the part of the absent-minded academic, there was nothing unworldly about the way he ran his business.

"I charge fifty pounds a day plus expenses and value added tax," he said crisply. "It's also my practice to give the client a written report after I've been on the case for three days. In it I summarise all the facts and then say whether or not I think it's worthwhile continuing with the investigation. The final decision is, of course, up to the client."

"Right."

"There's something else you should know," Alderton continued. "I'm not one of those private detectives you read about in books who go out on a limb for the sake of their client. As far as I'm concerned, there's no such thing as privileged information. If the police want to know what I'm doing on a case, I don't hold anything back."

"I just want to find my wife," Cartwright told him. "You can be as open as you like about that."

"Good." Alderton took out a large, brand-new exercise book from the top drawer of his desk and folded the cover back. "Do you have a photograph of your wife?" he asked.

Cartwright extracted a snapshot from his wallet and passed it across the desk. "This was taken last year when we were on holiday in St Malo."

Alderton glanced at the snapshot, nodded sagely, then said, "Photos are often deceptive; for one thing it's very difficult to judge the height, weight and age of the subject."

Cartwright said, "My wife is five foot eight, weighs approximately nine and a half stone and was thirty-five last January. She also has a faint scar on her forehead above the left eye, the result of a childhood accident when she got in the way of a hockey ball."

"Grey-blue eyes," Alderton intoned, gazing at the snapshot, "and auburn hair." He looked up. "Still the same colour as last year?"

"It was when I saw her last."

"Wives who leave their husbands for another man don't usually change their appearance to do so. At least, that's been my experience."

"There's always an exception to every rule," Cartwright said quietly. "In this instance, I think my wife could well be travelling under the name of Ellen Rothman."

"Her maiden name?"

"No."

"It's a free country," Alderton said philosophically. "I once had a client who was so taken with *Brideshead Revisited* that he went around calling himself Lord Marchmain. No one would give him a credit card, the Inland Revenue refused to recognise his title and I wouldn't accept a cheque from him."

"I'm pretty sure my wife has a passport in the name of Ellen Rothman."

"Oh yes?" Alderton gazed at him thoughtfully. "What else should I know?"

"Our au-pair was murdered soon after my wife disappeared. The police think I did it."

Cartwright outlined what he thought was their case against him. When he finished talking, Alderton gave a low whistle.

"I'm not too crazy about my situation either," said Cartwright, "but I'm learning to live with it and things can only get better."

"Got yourself a lawyer?"

"A young man called Henry Edgecombe."

"Better put your faith in him then," said Alderton. "Your problem's too big for me to handle. Besides, I make it a rule never to cross swords with the police."

"I'm not asking you to. They're looking for Sarah Cartwright; I want you to trace the woman who's now calling herself Ellen Rothman. I'm betting she caught a plane out of Gatwick, Stansted or Luton sometime on Friday afternoon."

He could tell from the bemused expression on Alderton's face that he'd lost him. Curbing his impatience, he went over the same ground again. Two women each possessing a second passport in the other person's name. All they had to do was exchange plane tickets and Sarah could walk out of the departure lounge as Miss Ellen Rothman while her namesake went on to Paris.

"A bit far-fetched, isn't it?" Alderton observed.

"I'm sure it's the way it happened. And I'll tell you something else: Sarah didn't go to all the trouble of fixing herself up with a second identity just to lie low in this country. My wife went abroad, but she couldn't risk leaving from Heathrow because she had just walked off the British Airways flight to Paris and there was a chance someone would make the connection."

"And that's why you want me to check the departure flights from Gatwick, Luton and Stansted?"

"Yes."

"Shouldn't be too difficult. How do I get in touch with you, Major?"

"During office hours you can reach me on 603-2198; after six o'clock you should ring 385-1659." Cartwright smiled. "I imagine you'd like a retainer?"

"A hundred pounds on account is the usual."

"I'll pay cash," Cartwright said.

"Good. I'll be in touch just as soon as I have any news." Alderton stood up, shook hands with him, then walked him to the door. "Meantime, my secretary will give you a receipt."

There was a message waiting for him on his desk when he got back to the Empress State Building shortly after five o'clock. Originally, it had read, 'Please see me as soon as you return from Brentford.' Before leaving the office, Nolan had deleted everything after 'me' and had substituted an ominous 'First thing tomorrow morning'. His signature on the bottom line was a furious squiggle resembling a demented snake chasing its own tail.

Detective Inspector Dalton turned into Fourteen Acre Close and stopped outside number 10. One of a number of identical dormer-type houses on a small estate that had been built in the late 1950s on the outskirts of Bookham, it belonged to a Mr and Mrs Ernest Rothman. The detective work which had led him to this part of Surrey had all been done by the Special Branch Sergeant who'd interviewed Cartwright at Heathrow on Saturday morning. At Dalton's request, he had got British Airways to check their flimsies for the 1345 hours flight to Paris in order to identify which travel agency had actually sold the plane ticket to Ellen Rothman. Armed with that information, it had then been comparatively easy for the sergeant to obtain the contact phone number she had given Thomas Cook Limited. Subsequently, British Telecom had run the number against their list of subscribers and had come up with the name and address of her parents.

Dalton got out of the car, walked up the front path and rang the bell. The man who answered the door to him could have been any age between forty-five and sixty. He carried himself like a Guardsman: head up, shoulders back, stomach in. There wasn't an ounce of spare flesh on his lean frame, his eyes were clear and there were only a few strands of grey in a thatch of dark brown hair. But for the puckered lips and scrawny neck, Dalton would have put him at the lower end of the age bracket.

"Mr Rothman?" he inquired politely.

"Yes."

"I'm Detective Inspector Dalton." Reaching inside his jacket, he brought out his warrant card and showed it to Rothman. "Actually, I wondered if I might have a word with your daughter?"

"Ellen?" Rothman backed off a couple of paces. "She's not in trouble, is she?" he asked apprehensively.

"Not with us, sir." Dalton put on his most reassuring smile. "As a matter of fact, we're trying to trace a friend of hers – a Mrs Sarah Cartwright."

"Ellen's not at home." A pause, then, "She's gone away for a few days on business."

From somewhere in the house, a querulous voice said, "Who is it, dear?"

"My wife . . ." Rothman said and smiled apologetically.

"I'm glad she's made such a rapid recovery, sir."

"What?"

"Your daughter," Dalton informed him, "was booked on the flight to Paris departing Heathrow on Friday at 1345 hours. At the last moment she cancelled her reservation because she had received a telephone call informing her that her mother was seriously ill in hospital. At least, that's what she told the BA staff on duty in the departure lounge."

"Perhaps you'd better come inside, Inspector."

A few minutes ago, Rothman had been apprehensive; now, despite what Dalton had told him about his daughter, he was quite confident, as though the initiative had passed to him and he was in control of the situation. Removing his raincoat, Dalton hung it up in the minuscule downstairs cloakroom, then followed him into the lounge-diner.

73

"This is Detective Dalton," Rothman said, introducing him to a plump, homely-looking woman whose eyes were glued to the colour TV set in a corner nook by the fireplace. "He's come to see me about the fraud case we've uncovered at the office, the one I told you about."

"That's nice," Mrs Rothman said vaguely and gave Dalton a brief welcoming smile as her husband steered him towards the dining table at the other end of the room.

"What'll you have to drink?" Rothman crouched in front of the sideboard and opened one of the cupboards. "I can offer you a choice of gin, whisky or a dry sherry."

"I think I'd like a whisky," Dalton said.

"We don't seem to have any soda – will you take it neat or with a splash of water?"

"Neat, please."

"Good." Rothman nodded as though he'd made a wise decision, then said, "I'll join you."

The half-empty bottle of Bell's looked as though it had been left over from Christmas. Judging by the amount he poured into their respective glasses, Dalton thought his host had every intention of making it last until the next.

"I'm with Customs and Excise," Rothman said in a low voice. "My field is Value Added Tax."

"Really?"

"That means I've been security cleared for access to sensitive information."

"So?" Dalton said, hedging. He hadn't the faintest idea what Rothman was talking about and wondered if the customs officer had suddenly taken leave of his senses.

"So I'd like to know if you've also been vetted, Inspector?"

Rothman was beginning to sound more and more like some oddball character in a play.

"We're not discussing a state secret," Dalton said quietly. "We're talking about your daughter who walked off a plane because she'd been told that her mother was seriously ill in hospital."

"I'm afraid that was my fault," Dalton said, unabashed. "You see, my wife suffers from angina and when I came

74

home at lunchtime on Friday, I found her in the kitchen on her hands and knees, unable to get up. In the event, it was a very mild attack and our doctor didn't even think it was necessary to have her admitted to hospital under observation, but I panicked and called Ellen at Heathrow."

It would have been a very plausible explanation but for one minor point of detail. "Tell me something," Dalton said. "Why didn't Ellen collect her baggage? It's still there at the airport."

Rothman smiled. His amusement was about as genuine as the canned laughter on the TV. "I'm not surprised," he said. "She didn't have time to collect it."

"Why not?"

"Because my daughter is with the Foreign and Commonwealth Office. Officially, she's on leave between postings but a little technicality like that doesn't weigh very heavily with her superiors. Believe me, if they want you for a job at the drop of a hat, you don't stop to argue, you just get up and go."

"Does Ellen know Sarah Cartwright?" Dalton asked.

"I don't think so."

"Did she ever mention anyone called Sarah?"

"No, but I seem to recall she was friendly with a Zara Hicks." Rothman frowned. "Or was it Hendricks? Anyway, they met in Cairo on Ellen's first overseas posting, but that was more than eight years ago and I doubt if they're still in touch."

"Did Ellen tell you about her new assignment?"

"Of course she didn't." Rothman leaned forward across the dining table and lowered his voice to a conspiratorial whisper. "It would have been more than her job was worth."

Dalton could recognise a reprimand when one was handed out. Furthermore, although Rothman might have gone over the top, there was no doubting his indignation and for that reason alone he was inclined to believe him. Ellen Rothman had intended spending the weekend in Paris when the Foreign Office had yanked her off the plane. For want of a better cover story, she had told the British Airways representative that her mother had been rushed to hospital. Quite by chance, Cartwright had learned about the passenger who had cancelled her seat at the last minute and had used the incident to throw a smokescreen around his wife's disappearance. Admittedly, there were a few loose ends but he liked the explanation a whole lot better than the one Cartwright had given him.

"Can I get you another whisky?" Rothman asked.

Dalton shook his head. "Thanks all the same," he added, "but I'm driving."

The situation comedy on the television had given way to a documentary on the common cold which Mrs Rothman appeared to find equally enthralling; she did not bother to answer when he said goodnight to her.

"I'm sorry to have taken up so much of your time," he told Rothman as they parted on the doorstep. "Especially when you've been so very co-operative."

"Not at all, I'm only too glad to have been of assistance."

"Just for the record, where did you say your daughter had served, apart from the Persian Gulf?"

"Ankara – before that, she was in Cairo."

The Foreign Office would never admit that Ellen Rothman belonged to the Secret Intelligence Service, but they wouldn't have to. Cairo, Ankara and Bahrain in the Persian Gulf: he would simply rattle off her record of service and ask them point blank if there was a Century House connection. They would deny it of course but he fancied he'd been a policeman long enough to know when someone was trying to flannel him.

The train from Paris arrived at the Gare du Nord in Amiens at 2025 hours. Observing Ellen Rothman as she walked towards the gate, Wentworth saw that she'd hired a porter to carry her suitcases and waited until she had paid him off before he approached her. Kissing her on the cheek the way an old friend would, he identified himself in a low intimate voice, then picked up the matching pair of Vuitton suitcases and walked her out of the station.

The battered-looking Deux Chevaux he'd hired from a local garage was parked round the corner in a public lot facing the Rue Barni. Unlocking the nearside door, Wentworth dumped the bags in the back and helped Ellen Rothman into the car. Then he walked round the front, got in beside her and started up. Turning left outside the car park, he headed out of town on Route 29 for Albert.

"You were Simon Faulkner the last time we met," she said in a voice brittle with tension.

"We like to remain anonymous when we're dealing with outsiders. That's why I had to use a name you could find in the Blue Book." Wentworth smiled. "Of course, it's different now that you've been accepted by Century House."

"I've served in three embassies; none of your colleagues in Cairo, Ankara or Bahrain found it necessary to use an alias."

"They were desk men, I'm a field agent. Need I say more?"

"No."

"Good. Now suppose you wrap things up and tell me how you made out?"

"I followed your instructions – everything went off without a hitch."

"I'd like a full report."

"What?" Her voice sounded incredulous.

"Right from the moment you called me from a phone booth in the Gare St-Lazare," he said calmly. "It may seem kind of funny to you but in this department we believe in debriefing a field agent thoroughly."

Her eyebrows rose fractionally and for a moment it looked as though he was going to hear a long sigh, but in the end she held it back and told him what he wanted to hear. After phoning him, she had returned to the Hôtel Lutèce in the Rue St-Louis-en-l'Ile where she had left a forwarding address in Amiens with the concierge and settled her bill; then she had wandered around Paris killing time until the train he'd told her to catch from the Gare St-Lazare departed.

"I went to a cinema on the Champs-Elysées," she said,

"but don't ask me what the film was about because I didn't understand a word."

After the movie show, she'd killed some more time over a light meal in the Café Artois and had then made her way to the station and collected her suitcases from the left luggage office where she'd deposited them earlier on in the afternoon.

"The rest was plain sailing." A small frown creased her brow. "Though I did have a few anxious moments when you didn't meet me as I came through the gate. What made you hold back?"

"Standard operating procedure. I wanted to see if anyone was following you."

"I would have known if anyone had been."

"I have news for you," Wentworth told her. "I'm the guy who dogged you across London when the Department was putting you through your paces."

"I never spotted you."

"You weren't supposed to."

"It's kind of you to say so, but all the same, I could hardly have inspired you with confidence."

"Listen, you did a great job," Wentworth said earnestly. "The whole idea was to lay a false trail for the Mossad to follow and you were a hundred per cent successful."

He had used pretty much the same Israeli angle on Bergitta Lindstrom and he could tell from the way the Rothman girl was nodding her head that she too believed the lie. Secretly pleased with himself, he went on up the long straight road to Albert.

'What happens now, Mr Wentworth?"

"Call me Peter," he said, flashing her a warm smile. "It's more friendly – okay?"

"Yes."

"So let's hear you say it then."

"Peter," she said obediently.

"Good, I knew you'd get the hang of it." Wentworth eyed her furtively. She was about the same height, same weight and almost the same shape as Sarah Cartwright, but she certainly didn't have her charisma. And unlike Sarah, it didn't take much to wind Ellen Rothman up. "Relax," he said cheerfully, "you're on your way home out of harm's way."

"I am?"

Wentworth nodded. "You'll stay the night in Brussels, then fly on to Heathrow first thing tomorrow. The hotel room is booked in your name, so's the plane ticket. One of the officers from the embassy is meeting us at a rendezvous outside Thiepval; he'll be taking you on to Brussels."

She digested the news in silence, her hands loosely clasped together and resting on the handbag in her lap while Wentworth drove through the outskirts of Albert. They had met very little traffic on the road and he knew they would encounter even fewer vehicles once he turned off Route 29. The Somme attracted few tourists and those who did visit the region were usually old and infirm, the dwindling band of survivors from a generation that had bled itself to death. It was a land of sluggish rivers, gentle slopes and a patchwork of open fields that had been hallowed by the graves of a million dead and which still bore the scars of war seventy years on.

In the centre of town he turned left into a narrow road which ran parallel with the River Ancre for roughly a mile and a half before it branched off to the village of Miraument. A few minutes after passing through the hamlet of Authille, he shifted into neutral, switched off the engine and gradually coasted to a halt. The Deux Chevaux was still doing approximately fifteen miles an hour when he suddenly put the wheel hard over to the right, bounced across the grass verge bordering the roadside and entered a small copse nestling between two spur lines. It was some moments before Ellen Rothman plucked up sufficient courage to ask him what they were doing in the wood. When finally she did, her voice was a low monotone that accurately reflected her innermost fears.

"This is the RV where our friend from Brussels is going to meet us," Wentworth told her cheerfully. "Over to your right beyond the trees is a replica of Helen's Tower, the war

79

memorial of the 36th Ulster Division. Thiepval is directly to our front on the ridge line above us."

The orientation was meaningless. They were parked in a copse choked with secondary growth and a low overcast hid what little there was to be seen of a moon in the first quarter. Yet even though she couldn't see a damned thing, Ellen Rothman seemed much more relaxed once he'd told her where they were and why they were there.

"Better let me have the passport for Sarah Cartwright." He smiled, then added, "You won't be needing it again, Ellen."

"Yes, of course." Opening her handbag, she took out a worn-looking passport, checked to make sure it was the right one, then handed it to him. It was only then that she noticed the small calibre automatic he was holding in his right hand. "Oh my God," she whispered.

"He can't help you now," Wentworth said quietly. "And I'm sorry it has to be this way, but you know too much."

"Please . . ." She swallowed nervously. "Please don't shoot me. I promise I won't say anything."

"Make it easy for yourself; turn your head away and look out of the window."

The tears welled in her eyes and brimmed over and her body began to shake as though she had a fever. The only house in the vicinity was the cottage belonging to the War Graves attendant and that was a good six hundred yards away. She could scream until she was blue in the face and no one would hear her; he knew it and so did Ellen Rothman.

"Please," she moaned, and then her voice broke and she crooned to herself.

"I'll be as quick as I can," Wentworth told her, "but you've got to help me."

The apparent hopelessness of her situation neutralised any thought of resistance and she slowly turned away from him and gazed out of the window. A kind of paralysis had set in and she didn't even flinch when he pressed the barrel of the .25 automatic against her neck, nor did she cry out in the final millisecond before he squeezed the trigger.

The pistol shot was fairly muted and sounded like the crack of a whiplash. The soft-nose bullet shattered inside the skull and she slumped against the door. Reacting swiftly, Wentworth pulled her upright, tilted her head back until she was staring at the roof, then got out of the car and moved round to her side. Speed was essential; the blood was already beginning to flow from her nose and open mouth and he didn't want it staining the interior. Raising her dress and ivory-coloured slip above her head, he tied them in a knot to mask her face and then dragged her out of the car.

Of all the defensive positions on the Somme during World War One, the Thiepval ridge had been the most formidable. The key strongpoint had been the Schwaben Redoubt, a vast underground fortress of some two and a half acres which had been hollowed out of the chalk. Although the land had long since reverted to its former use, the four entrance shafts positioned one in each corner of the field still remained. Unable to seal them off completely, the French had simply put up warning signs and fenced them off with barbed wire.

Wentworth had no idea just how many dead men were entombed in the redoubt, but he was quite certain that Ellen Rothman was destined to be the only woman.

7

Friends and acquaintances who met Nolan only on social occasions thought he was a charming Irishman. Most of his subordinates however knew different; in their experience, he was unpredictable, two-faced and bad-tempered. Some attributed his irrational behaviour to Mrs Nolan, who was said to be difficult, while others maintained he was merely one of nature's four-letter men. Whatever the reason, Cartwright was one of the very few officers in the Directorate who hadn't crossed swords with him; now that happy state of affairs was about to end. Yesterday, he'd taken the afternoon off and the cryptic note which he'd found on his desk had made it clear his absence had not gone unnoticed. This morning, British Rail had also contributed to Nolan's temper; a signal failure outside Surbiton had made him late into the office and he'd had to stand all the way from Byfleet to Waterloo.

"Where were you yesterday afternoon, Tom?" he asked curtly.

"I was sorting out my personal affairs. It seemed to me the police weren't exactly straining themselves to find my wife, so I decided to hire someone who would."

"You didn't think it necessary to let me know you wouldn't be returning to the office?"

"I'm sorry," Cartwright said. "I should have telephoned the office to let the clerks know I'd been delayed."

"You were questioned about the murder of a Swedish au-pair – didn't it occur to you that we've an obligation to keep the Adjutant General fully informed?"

The army called it an event of public interest, which was another way of saying there was a strong possibility the media would fasten on to the incident and give it maximum coverage. On the principle that forewarned was forearmed, Nolan would have fired off a signal giving the bare facts to all and sundry moments after he and Dalton had left the Empress State Building. Suddenly, he would have become the man of the hour with Public Relations, the Military Secretary's Branch and the Directorate of Security, all of whom would be looking at their files on him with fresh eyes.

"You would have heard from the police had they been going to bring charges."

"Why do I have to learn everything secondhand?" Nolan complained. "Your wife leaves you as a result of some domestic upheaval and I hear about it from a police inspector. Of course, normally your personal life is very much your own affair but I begin to take an interest when it affects your work or when you start behaving strangely. Then I'm reminded the army has to decide whether you are to be trusted with sensitive information. Do you follow me?"

"I'm way ahead of you, Colonel."

"Good, perhaps in future you'll keep me informed."

Cartwright said he would and returned to his office. In his own mind, he was certain that Nolan had submitted a Change of Circumstance report, which meant the army's vetting unit would soon be making inquiries to see if it was necessary to do anything about his security clearance. Ironically enough, he hadn't seen a Top Secret document since the day he'd joined the Directorate from the Staff College, but that wasn't the point. If they withdrew his clearance or restricted his access to classified information, it could have a detrimental effect on his long-term career.

He reached for the topmost file in an overflowing in-tray and tried to put his mind to the problem of a disgruntled Foreman of Signals who'd submitted a redress of grievance because his promotion to Warrant Officer Class One had suddenly been cancelled without any explanation. For once, the telephone was a welcome intrusion, especially when he found he had Alderton on the line.

"You've obviously got a lead," Cartwright said.

"How did you know?"

"You wouldn't have phoned me so soon unless you had."

"Would it surprise you to hear that Ellen Rothman left the country on Friday?"

"Where did she go?"

"Hong Kong," said Alderton. "She was on the Cathay Pacific flight departing Gatwick at 1630 hours. And here's something else which may interest you – it's the only airline that does the journey non-stop."

"That's a help; at least I don't have to go looking for her elsewhere. Did anyone recognise this Ellen Rothman from the snapshot I gave you?"

"I haven't shown it to anyone, Major."

"But you're going to," Cartwright insisted.

"Only if you want me to waste my time and your money. Sure, I could go down to Gatwick and show your wife's picture to the Cathay Pacific staff on flight reception, but I doubt they're going to remember her face unless she drew attention to herself. And, judging by what you've told me about Mrs Cartwright, I don't think she'd do that."

"How about the cabin staff? They might remember her."

"It's not that simple, Major. My source is a guy in airport security who owed me a favour; if I go down to Gatwick and ask the UK manager of Cathay Pacific if I can talk to a particular cabin crew, he'll want to know why. And when I tell him, it won't take much effort on his part to put two and two together and then I've lost a valuable contact."

"I think we'd better call it a day then, Mr Alderton. You've done a great job for me and I wouldn't want you to queer your own pitch. How much do I owe you?"

"Nothing. In fact, I'll be sending you a rebate."

"Keep it as a retainer," Cartwright told him. "I may need you again."

He put the phone down and leaned back in the chair. Hong Kong: Sarah had been posted there in 1973, a year after joining the Foreign and Commonwealth Office from Oxford. 'Too hot, too humid and altogether too claustrophobic for me' was how she had described the colony on those

84

rare occasions when someone happened to ask her how she'd liked it out there. 'Bonn was much more fun' she had invariably added and had then given him a conspiratorial wink when no one had been watching.

Hong Kong: maybe the Cathay Pacific staff at Gatwick couldn't say whether or not it was the real Ellen Rothman who'd boarded their direct flight last Friday but he could think of several good reasons why Scotland Yard should ask the Hong Kong Police Department to make a few inquiries on their behalf. Reaching for the phone, he rang Henry Edgecombe to explain why he wanted him to be there when he saw Dalton. Then he obtained another outside line and called the police station to make an appointment for one fifteen.

Pelham Street was a cul-de-sac off the New Cromwell Road which was close enough to the District Line station and the shops in Fulham Broadway for the landlord to claim that his converted Edwardian house was situated in a highly desirable neighbourhood. Of the six furnished apartments in the property, three were leased to junior executives in banking, insurance and commodities, one to a croupier whose live-in girlfriend was said to be a fashion model, and one to a freelance journalist called Frank Hillier who occupied the flat opposite number 6 on the top floor, which was rented by Cartwright.

Hillier was the one tenant the police had so far been unable to interview. When Dalton called on him at eleven thirty he was still unshaven and looked as though he'd only just crawled out of bed. His eyes were bloodshot and he appeared to have some difficulty focusing them on Dalton's warrant card.

"I'm the officer in charge of the Lindstrom murder inquiry," Dalton told him.

"Who?"

"Bergitta Lindstrom, the Swedish au-pair girl whose body was found in a junkyard at Brentford. Her murder was reported in the *Standard* yesterday evening and was repeated in the tabloids this morning."

85

"Oh, that girl." Hillier rubbed his jaw. "I didn't know she came from round here."

"She was employed by Mrs Cartwright, the wife of your neighbour across the landing."

"So why do you want to see me?"

"Can we go inside?" Dalton asked politely. "It'll be more private."

"Sure. I'm afraid the living room's a bit untidy."

A bit untidy was something of an understatement. Wherever Dalton looked there were books, periodicals, newspapers and magazines – on the floor, the coffee table, draped over the arms of the easy chairs and on top of the TV. Every ashtray was brimming over with cigarette and cigar stubs, the atmosphere was heavy with stale tobacco smoke and there were empty beer cans on the windowsill, the sideboard and dining table.

"Had a bit of a thrash at the Press Club last night," Hillier explained. "When the bar shut up shop, some of the boys came back here for a nightcap."

Dalton thought the journalist had turned forty, looked fifty and was unlikely to make sixty the rate he was going. He was a heavy smoker, his fingers were stained with nicotine, and he could hear the phlegm bubbling on his chest.

"I believe the girl was strangled?" Hillier said.

"That's right." Dalton sat down in an easy chair and tried to keep his eyes off the brunette in red undies on the cover of a girlie magazine which lay on the coffee table in front of him.

"Raped was she?"

"No, it was just a plain old-fashioned murder. None of the usual titbits that make a good story."

"Hey, don't get me wrong," Hillier protested, "murder's not my bag. I write articles for the trade papers and tech mags. Okay?"

"I'm sorry," Dalton apologised. "One of my detective constables told me you were a newspaperman and I jumped to the wrong conclusion."

"It's understandable." Hillier lit a cigarette, inhaled deeply enough to draw the smoke down on to his lungs and immediately started coughing. "First today," he wheezed.

Dalton waited for the paroxysm to die away, then said, "How well do you know Major Cartwright?"

"I'd no idea he was in the army. Matter of fact, I thought he was a civil servant – that's how well I know him."

"Don't you ever speak to one another?"

"Only to say good morning, good evening or whatever." Hillier shrugged. "He seems okay to me, quiet but pleasant enough. He's never given me any aggro, nor has he complained about the noise when I've had a few people in for drinks."

"Did he ever come to one of your shindigs?" Dalton asked.

"I don't think so . . ." Hillier snapped his fingers. "No, wait a minute, I tell a lie. I sent him an invite to a bottle party I gave back in January soon after he'd moved in. The invite said bring your wife, girlfriend or lover; he came alone."

"He isn't what you'd call a womaniser then?"

"Not in my book. I've never seen him with a bird." Hillier contemplated the glowing ember of his cigarette, his eyes narrowing thoughtfully. "Don't tell me Cartwright was having if off with this Lindstrom girl?"

"There's never been a suggestion of it and I don't want to see the possibility being mooted in print either."

"I've already told you," Hillier protested, "it's not my scene."

Cartwright was Mr Clean, all the neighbours said so. He didn't play the field, he never chatted up other women and he went home to his family every weekend. Dalton experienced a tinge of disappointment; from his point of view, it would be much tidier all round if the number one suspect wasn't such an upright character.

After telling Hillier how much he appreciated his help, Dalton left the apartment house and drove back to Brentford. When he was still roughly two miles from the station house, control came up on the radio with the news that Cartwright had asked if he could see him at 1315 hours together with his solicitor, Henry Edgecombe.

*

87

Simon Faulkner parted company with Roger Ingram, the Head of Station, Hong Kong, outside HMS *Tamar* and strolled along Murray Road towards the Peak Tramway. The meeting at the RN Headquarters had dragged on longer than he'd expected and despite the free exchange of information, no one there had come out of the conference room any the wiser. So far as the Tri Service Intelligence Unit was concerned, Vietnam was pretty low down on their list of priorities. The Army was anxious to know what was happening in China, the Air Force was committed to monitoring every communications satellite in space whether friendly or hostile, and the Navy spent their entire time eavesdropping on the Far East Fleet of the Soviet Navy. Until six weeks ago, the Tri Service Intelligence Unit had never heard of Doctor Matthew Gage, nor had they had any reason to.

Gage was Foreign Office. Ten years ago he'd stayed behind when the Mission had been withdrawn from Saigon and had gone over to the Viet Cong. Now he was coming back, his exit visa approved by Hanoi. The French Consul General with whom Gage had maintained contact ever since Saigon had changed its name to Ho Chi Minh City, was unable to offer any explanation for the sudden change of heart other than the one he'd been fed. Gage was homesick, his wife had died a year ago so there was nothing and no one special to keep him in Vietnam. Faulkner didn't believe that, neither did London. Gage had an entirely different reason for coming home: Hanoi was using him to spearhead an attack on the Secret Intelligence Service at the behest of the KGB. No one at Century House doubted the hypothesis for a moment; the difficulty lay in trying to ascertain the long-term aim of the Soviets. For all the reams of military intelligence at their fingertips, it had to be said that the Tri Service Intelligence Unit, Hong Kong, had had nothing to offer there.

Faulkner purchased a ticket from the booth in the tram station and boarded the waiting car. Moments later it began the near vertical ascent to Victoria Peak, clanking slowly past Government House and the Botanical Gardens. Leaving the tram at the halfway station, Faulkner turned into May Road where he was staying in an apartment rented by the Hong Kong Government on the eleventh floor of the Starnight Building. Sarah Cartwright was nine miles away in the dark hills above Marina Cove, far removed from the picturesque harbour and the neon lights of Kowloon which he could see from his sitting room. Her only contact with him was an answering machine in a one bedroom flat down by the waterfront in the Wanchai District, and he intended to keep it like that until the last possible moment.

The smile was beginning to infuriate Cartwright. He had just told Dalton that a woman calling herself Ellen Rothman had boarded the Cathay Pacific flight to Hong Kong on Friday, a fact which could be verified by one lousy phone call to Gatwick, yet all Dalton could do was sit there with a fatuous smirk on his face as though vastly amused by some private joke.

"Why don't you share it with us?" he snapped.

"What?" The smiled vanished from Dalton's mouth.

"Major Cartwright means we would be interested to hear your opinion," Henry Edgecombe said diplomatically. "Personally, I'd have thought there was some merit in asking the Hong Kong Police Department to make a few inquiries."

"Mrs Cartwright left Heathrow and drove straight to Gatwick." Dalton clucked his tongue thoughtfully, then looked at Cartwright. "Is that how you see it, sir?" he asked.

"I can't think how else she got there."

"And once at Gatwick, she presumably left her car in one of the parking lots near the airport?"

"Yes."

"I have news for you," Dalton said. "Her BMW was found in Eaton Place yesterday afternoon. One of the residents told the traffic warden it had been there since Friday."

"Afternoon or evening?"

"We don't know – does it matter?"

"Not really."

Nothing Sarah had done that day made any sense, but there were limits. The quickest way to Gatwick from Heathrow was by the M25; no one in their right mind would drive back to London, leave their car in Knightsbridge and then complete the journey by train. Someone else had parked the BMW in Eaton Place, but Dalton was never going to buy that one.

"There's something else you should know," Dalton continued. "The Ellen Rothman who flew to Hong Kong was not an impostor. I've talked to her father and to the Foreign Office and I'm satisfied we've got to look elsewhere for your wife, Major."

"What's this about the Foreign Office?"

"Ellen Rothman is one of their officers."

"And her trip to Hong Kong?" Cartwright asked. "Was that business or pleasure?"

"Business."

"Friday must have been one hell of a cock-up. I mean, there she was on her way to Paris . . ."

"She was on leave between postings and was going away for the weekend," Dalton said tersely, his temper beginning to fray. "Unfortunately, her Department needed a courier in a hurry and they ran her to ground."

"So why did she tell the British Airways staff that her mother was seriously ill in hospital?"

"Miss Rothman needed a cover story to get herself off the Paris flight at the last moment. That happened to be the best one she could think of there and then."

Cartwright shook his head in sheer disbelief. "The way you tell it, one would think she's a spook from Century House."

"She is."

"Who said so? The Foreign and Commonwealth Office?"

"Not in so many words."

"I bet they didn't."

Where security was concerned the Secret Intelligence Service were almost paranoiac. He recalled Sarah once

90

telling him that even within the privacy of the embassy they were apt to get very uptight if the rest of the staff failed to keep up the pretence that they were bona fide members of the Diplomatic.

"I've been a policeman long enough to read between the lines," Dalton said testily. "Sometimes a flat denial can be very illuminating, a lot depends on the tone of voice."

Dalton preferred his own interpretation of events and was not open to persuasion. It was all too evident to Cartwright that the police had him in the frame and were determined to keep him there.

"Seems to me I've been wasting your time," he said drily.

Dalton waved a dismissive hand. "You weren't to know we'd already eliminated Miss Rothman from our inquiries. I can also understand just how anxious you are to find your wife, Major, and believe me, you'll be the first to know when we do get a lead."

"What about my wife's BMW?"

"You'll get the car back as soon as Forensic have finished with it."

Cartwright had no idea what they hoped to find. His fingerprints would be on the steering wheel and elsewhere along with Sarah's; it was also likely they would find Bergitta's. But how far would that get them? Whatever the answer, he knew he'd handled things badly. Giving the police the information Alderton had obtained for him had seemed a good idea at the time but now he had a feeling he'd done himself more harm than good.

"I cocked it up," he told Henry Edgecombe when they were outside on the pavement. "I let Dalton get to me and lost my temper. He'd already made up his mind about Ellen Rothman before he contacted the Foreign Office. Consequently, when he did phone them, he heard only what he wanted to hear."

"He could say the same about you," Edgecombe pointed out.

"Except that I have a better excuse. Sarah was stationed in Hong Kong before we met."

91

"Do the police know that?"

"I shouldn't think so."

"You ought to have told Dalton, it could have made a difference."

"I doubt it. He would have wanted to know why my wife suddenly took it into her head to fly halfway round the world." And that was a question Cartwright knew he would be unable to answer. There were chapters in Sarah's life she was reluctant to talk about and Hong Kong was one of them. "I could ask Edwin," he said, thinking aloud.

"Who?"

"My father-in-law; he might remember the names of some of the people Sarah was friendly with out there."

"How about this Arab boyfriend Bergitta Lindstrom used to see in London?" Edgecombe asked. "Do you know who he was – what he did for a living – where he lived?"

"He was an Iraqi businessman, Nuri something or other."

"And?" Edgecombe glanced at his wristwatch and frowned at the time.

"That's it."

"I'd like you to think about Nuri, Major Cartwright, I have a feeling he could be very important."

"Right."

Cartwright watched him walk away. Edgecombe's comment about Nuri chilled him; it was, he reckoned, another way of saying they needed more than one angle to get him off the hook.

Wentworth paid off the cab outside the New Providence office block in Baker Street and walked inside, then took the lift up to the second floor where Eurcom Enterprises, a subsidiary of the Hong Kong-based Kimber Corporation, had a suite of offices. He had planned to arrive during the lunch hour between one and two o'clock when his secretary would be out, but there had been a hold-up near Ashford and his train had been late into Charing Cross. Consequently, when he walked through her office to get to his own, she was at her desk typing out a standard Eurcom house purchase contract.

"Don't ask," he said, before she had a chance to. "The whole trip was a waste of time, money and effort. The site was only half the size I'd been led to believe and the development costs would have been prohibitive."

As a cover story to account for his absence, he had told his secretary on Friday morning that he was off to France to look at a possible location for one of Eurcom's housing projects and expected to be away from the office until Tuesday afternoon. Adding to this basic legend, he now told her that he'd looked at an alternative site on the coast near Dieppe and had altered his plans accordingly.

"I decided to catch the Calais–Dover hovercraft instead of flying." Wentworth smiled. "Turned out to be my big mistake. We had a rough old crossing, all the trains into London were running late and the one I was on didn't have a buffet car." He patted his stomach and looked rueful. "Result is I'm starving. Do you think you could pop out and get me a sandwich?"

"Of course I will," she told him. "What would you like?"

"Beef or ham," Wentworth said. "I don't mind."

He went on through to his own office, waited until his secretary had left, then lifting the receiver, he obtained an outside line and dialled 010852, the international code for Hong Kong, followed by the area and subscriber's number. Six thousand miles away in a one-bedroom flat in the Wanchai District, a pre-recorded voice on an answering machine told him to wait for the tone signal before leaving a message.

8

The dining room faced south. Beyond the terrace with its weed-free gravel paths between the rose beds, a lawn sloped away to an ornamental pond and a weathered statue of a Grecian woman carrying an urn on one shoulder. Looking at the garden while he waited for the coffee to percolate, Cartwright thought it was a mirror image of Edwin Lucas, neat, orthodox and unimaginative. Given those qualities, the chances of persuading him that it was Sarah and not Ellen Rothman who'd boarded the Cathay Pacific flight to Hong Kong had always been minuscule. Add the fact that his father-in-law also disliked him and the task became well-nigh impossible. Had he conceded defeat a few minutes earlier, he could have caught the last train back to London. As it was, he'd had to spend the night under Edwin's roof, an uninvited and unwanted guest.

Cartwright heard the sound of light footsteps in the hall and turned about, percolator in one hand, a cup and saucer in the other. The click-clack of heels on the tiles stopped outside the dining room and in the momentary pause that followed, he found himself hoping that Fay would change her mind and go away. For a moment or so it seemed she might, but then the door slowly opened and she walked into the room.

"Hullo, Fay," he said quietly. "What are you doing up at this ungodly hour?"

"I couldn't sleep, Tom, so I thought I'd drive you into Market Harborough."

"There's no need for you to do that," he said. "I can easily phone for a minicab."

"I want to."

94

"Then I'll be only too happy to take you up on the offer."
He smiled and raised the percolator he was holding. "Care
to join me?"

"Please."

"You like it black with no sugar – right?" Cartwright
placed the cup of coffee in front of her, then returned to the
sideboard to pour one for himself.

"About last night," Fay began hesitantly. "I'd like to
apologise for what happened . . ."

"Don't," Cartwright said, cutting her short. "In Edwin's
shoes, I'd have wanted to know why the police hadn't
arrested my son-in-law."

"But they haven't and they're not fools." She smiled
lopsidedly. "If that rather obvious point had occurred to me
sooner, I would have paid more attention to what you were
trying to say."

"You didn't miss anything, Fay; it was mostly a lot of
nonsense."

"Last night, Edwin and I refused to let you tell us why you
thought something bad had happened to Sarah when she
was stationed in Hong Kong. But I at least see things
differently this morning and I'd like to hear your reasons."

"They're not very substantial."

"Nevertheless, I'd still like to hear them."

Cartwright frowned, uncertain for a moment where to
begin. Then he said, "Hong Kong was a chapter in her life
Sarah never wanted to talk about to me or anyone else in our
circle. If ever we met someone in the army who'd been
stationed out there, Sarah would cut short any reminiscing
with some tart remark about a shallow and totally false way
of life. Or else she'd say that's where she'd cut her teeth with
the Foreign and Commonwealth Office with such an enig-
matic expression that you were left with the impression she'd
love to tell you more but couldn't because she'd signed the
Official Secrets Acts. At first, I attributed her reluctance to
an unhappy love affair, then when I got to know her better, I
began to wonder if she had crossed swords with her superiors
and had been demoted after receiving an adverse report."

"I think you're wrong there," Fay said. "The Foreign Office didn't want her to leave the Service."

"Where did you hear that?"

"I saw the letter she received from the Head of the Personnel Branch."

When a serving officer retired, the Military Secretary automatically put pen to paper to say how keenly the army would feel the loss. There was a standard format for such personal letters and Cartwright doubted if they did things any differently in the Foreign and Commonwealth.

"The embassy in Bonn certainly weren't making the best use of her talents," he said gently. "Even in the Diplomatic Service there can't have been too many shorthand typists who were fluent in French, German, Russian *and* Cantonese."

"I didn't know Sarah had been relegated to the typing pool."

"It wasn't something she would have wanted to boast about, Fay."

"You're right, Sarah has always been an achiever and her pride wouldn't allow her to admit she'd been demoted."

"Especially if her security clearance had been suspended or withdrawn altogether."

"What?"

"Edwin wouldn't have it but the more I think about it, the more certain I am now that Sarah used to be a ranking Intelligence officer. With her family background, Oxbridge degree and flair for languages she would have been a natural for the SIS."

"Maybe."

He watched Fay closely, looking for a sign that would tell him what she was really thinking. 'Maybe' could mean almost anything from outright scepticism to a willingness to consider the possibility.

After what seemed a lengthy silence, Fay said, "I know Sarah was vetted because she asked some friends of ours who'd known her since childhood if they would mind if she nominated them as her referees. But the fact that Sarah was

96

also interviewed by the Security Service isn't particularly significant, is it, Tom? I mean, every applicant for the Diplomatic has to be Positively Vetted before the Foreign Office will accept them."

Much as Cartwright was loath to admit it, she had a point. Worse still, it undermined his whole hypothesis. "Well, I guess you should know, Fay," he said reluctantly. "After all, Edwin was a military attaché in his time."

"On the other hand, Sarah never told us what she actually did in Hong Kong. Her letters were very uninformative on that score."

"What did she write home about?" Cartwright asked.

"Her social life mostly – what she did in her spare time, where she'd been, who she'd met."

"Do you recall any names?"

"My God, Tom, it's light years ago and I didn't keep any of her letters for posterity."

"Any snapshots?" He was clutching at straws now, desperate for any kind of lead which might help him to identify the man or woman who had been Sarah's immediate superior officer.

"Carrie," Fay suddenly announced, "Carrie Jackman. She used to be Sarah's flatmate in Hong Kong until she left the Foreign Office and came home to England to get married. I can't remember the surname of her husband but I know Carrie's parents were living in Bury St Edmunds in those days."

"Are you sure it was Bury St Edmunds?"

"I'm positive," Fay told him. "It stuck in my mind because I was born there."

Cartwright smiled. He had a name and a possible address, a little incomplete perhaps but Lionel Alderton could check the parish registers and, with any luck, run the former Carrie Jackman to ground.

"There was someone called Simon. At one time I thought Sarah was getting very fond of him but then he suddenly vanished from the scene and she never mentioned him again in her letters. I don't believe she ever told us his surname."

It didn't matter. Even if the former Miss Carrie Jackman was unable to help him identify Simon, Cartwright was sure there would be other names she could recall. And once a Foreign Office connection had been established, Dalton would have to bring in the Hong Kong Police Department. If he still refused to widen the search for Sarah, there were ways and means of bringing pressure to bear. All he had to do was give the story to those daily newspapers who would be only too delighted to light a fire under the Home Secretary and Commissioner of Police.

"Do you think Sarah is still alive, Tom?"

He'd asked himself the same question when Dalton had shown him Bergitta Lindstrom's body in the morgue. Thereafter, he'd refused to consider the possibility, but now Fay had resurrected the private nightmare and he felt physically sick.

"Of course she is," Cartwright said fiercely. "It wasn't her ghost that boarded that damned plane to Hong Kong."

There was no logic in what he'd said but Fay was ready to accept any premise as long as it struck an optimistic note.

"You're absolutely right," she said eagerly. "Whatever else Edwin and I do, we mustn't let Helen and Jamie see that we're worried about their mother. Children can be very sensitive to atmosphere."

And Helen could be an inquisitive little monkey if she got a whiff of something out of the ordinary. Much as Cartwright wanted to see his daughter, he thought it was more important to keep up the pretence that he and Sarah were staying in Paris. It was for this reason that he'd deliberately arrived long after her bedtime the previous evening.

"What time is your train, Tom?"

Cartwright glanced at his wristwatch. "We've got less than fifteen minutes to catch it," he said and hurriedly swallowed the rest of his coffee.

Sarah Cartwright waited until the leathery hand had settled on her right knee, then casually brushed it away as she would a fly. Nothing had changed; Don Macready had been a

98

groper at the age of fifty-six when she'd first met him, he was still a groper ten years later.

"Better keep both hands on the wheel, Don," she said good-naturedly. "You're a fine seaman but a lousy driver and these hairpin bends on the road to Kowloon can be a real killer."

"Whatever you say, darling."

The Australian drawl hadn't deserted Macready even though he had never returned to his native land since leaving Adelaide in 1938. The accent was part of his image and there were those like Simon Faulkner who claimed he worked hard to preserve it.

"Mind you, I can't understand what you're worried about," Macready said, breaking a brief period of silence. "So long as you're with me, you won't come to any harm. I'm a born survivor."

He was all of that, Sarah thought. World War Two, Korea and Vietnam; he'd come through the lot without a scratch and somehow he'd always managed to end up financially better off in the process. Macready had started out as a lowly shipping clerk in Jardine Mathieson; the cost of real estate being what it was in Hong Kong, the house set in splendid isolation overlooking Marina Cove in the New Territories was an accurate yardstick of just how far he'd come since those long-dead days.

"I don't want to stay in Kowloon a minute longer than is strictly necessary in this heat." As if to emphasise the point, Macready took one hand off the wheel and wiped the sweat from his forehead with a checked handkerchief. "As a matter of fact, it won't take me more than an hour to finish my business. How about you?"

"I don't know, it all depends on what 'Little Brother' has to say." Sarah leaned back in the seat and closed her eyes. The temperature was in the high eighties and she had forgotten just how humid it could be at this time of the year. The silk blouse she was wearing clung to her back damp with sweat and there was a band of prickly heat around her waist. Even the air she breathed felt moist, as though someone was holding a wet towel over her face. "But don't hang around on my account," she muttered wearily. "I can always get a cab."

"What am I going to tell Faulkner if he phones while you're out?"

"Tell him the truth, he'll understand."

"I wonder; he told us both he didn't want you showing your face around Kowloon before the curtain went up. 'Surprise is what we're aiming for' – those were his very words."

"There's nothing wrong with my memory."

"Then why are we disobeying his orders?"

"Because I know Simon would change them if only I knew how to get in touch with him."

"That old whinge again," Macready drawled.

"Well, I don't like this one-way system of communication, it's too bloody inflexible. The fact that I've been isolated ever since you met me at the airport and drove me out to your place hasn't helped either."

"You've got a contact number for emergencies."

"And the one time I used it, I found myself talking to an answering machine."

Macready clucked his tongue. "Seems to me you've got a bad case of the jitters, girl."

"So would you in my shoes," Sarah retorted angrily. "Matthew Gage is coming back from the dead and he might just put me away for thirty years."

Thirty years: after a while, Tom would stop visiting her in prison and would consult a solicitor about a divorce. She would never see her children again, her mind would vegetate, her whole personality would change, and when finally she did emerge through the Judas Gate, it would be as a bloated and embittered old woman. A life without Tom and the children wasn't worth living and the knowledge that she might lose them made her feel physically sick.

"And you're hoping this 'Little Brother' can get you off the hook with Gage?"

"Yes."

"Take a tip from me, Sarah. Don't put your trust in this Vietnamese, he'll only let you down. When it comes to the crunch, he'll fold like the way they all did in Saigon towards the end."

"Le Khac Ly is not like that."

"Le Khac Ly?" Macready threw back his head and guffawed. "Are you sure you've got the right John Smith?"

"I think so."

Sarah wasn't at all sure she had. There were thousands of Le Khac Lys in South Vietnam and at least a score of them had arrived in Hong Kong with the boat people. Until last night when Macready had started reminiscing about Saigon, she had forgotten all about 'Little Brother'; then his name had suddenly come to her along with the biographical details they'd had on record at the Mission House. 'Le Khac Ly, age 27, height five five, weight one nineteen pounds, married, two children, former Lieutenant Black Panther Division ARVN, discharged May 1974 with suspected pulmonary tuberculosis having bribed the senior medical officer at Division Headquarters to certify that he was no longer fit for active duty. Civilian occupation, radio technician and salesman until employed by Mission as a wireless operator and interpreter.' Le Khac Ly had been with her at the end and could verify the orders she had received from Control; then Gage would know she hadn't betrayed him.

"So where does he hang out?" Macready asked.

"He has a retail shop in Harbour City."

"My business is in Jordan Road."

"I imagine it would be, Don," she said drily.

The geography was continually changing. Seemingly overnight, a hilltop would disappear and a condominium housing estate would rise to replace it. But some things didn't change: Jordan Road was still the place to go when you wanted a woman.

"I'll drop you off at the MTR station in Prince Edward Road and you can catch a train on down to Tsim Sha Tsui. Okay?"

"Don't worry about me, Don," she told him. "I can find my own way."

Cartwright had known it was going to be one of those days when he'd started to read the clutch of signals waiting for him at the office. At any other time of the year, the suicide of a young recruit at an infantry depot would have rated no more than a brief paragraph on one of the inside pages, but this was the silly season and there was a shortage of news. There were however other factors which had sparked off a nationwide interest. The deceased, who'd hung himself in the shower block after lights-out, had been a sixteen-year-old boy soldier with a penchant for collecting and wearing ladies underwear. These details plus a number of wild rumours that the junior soldier had also been sexually abused had reached the ears of a local freelance journalist who'd promptly sold the story to most of the newspapers in Fleet Street.

Although Defence Public Relations were fielding the questions, they needed guidance on matters touching on the disciplinary and sub judice aspects of the case. Consequently, the phone had started ringing before Cartwright had finished reading the overnight clutch file and it had scarcely stopped from then on. By two o'clock in the afternoon, he was so used to dealing with the army's PR man and other interested parties that Alderton was the last person he expected to hear on the line.

"Carrie Jackman," Alderton said in his usual crisp fashion. "Firstly, Carrie is short for Carole and secondly, her married name is Barrington. Her husband is a Major in the Royal Tank Regiment."

"And right now, he's the Assistant Military Attaché in Paris," Cartwright said flatly.

"Is he a friend of yours?"

"No, we've never even met, but I've heard of him." He didn't find it strange that Fay hadn't known that Carrie Jackman was now Carole Barrington. It was yet another example of the old Hong Kong syndrome: Sarah had simply kept her mother in the dark because she had this inexplicable hang-up about the place. The only puzzling thing about the whole business was why she had kept in touch with Carole Jackman, but that was a question which would have to wait until he caught up with her. "How did you run Carrie to ground?" he asked.

"It wasn't difficult, Major. Soon as you'd finished telling me what you wanted, I dug out a copy of the telephone directory for the Suffolk area and looked up the Jackmans. There were only a dozen subscribers with that surname living in Bury St Edmunds and I got the right one at the second attempt. Getting her married name and address from her father was also child's play. I led him to believe a former colleague had put his daughter down as a referee for the period May '73 to January '75 and he assumed I was with the Foreign Office vetting section."

"How would you like to do a repeat performance in Paris?"

"What?"

"I want you to talk to Carole Barrington and get the names of everyone she knew in Hong Kong who worked for the Foreign and Commonwealth Office. As soon as you've seen her, you're to phone a Mr Henry Edgecombe on 01-406 9998 and give him the information."

"Who's this Henry Edgecombe?"

"My solicitor," said Cartwright. "His offices are in Chancery Lane but at the moment he's taking his instructions from Bream, Cotton and Roose. They will prepare the ground for you with the embassy and pay your fee and expenses."

Edwin would probably blow a fuse when he heard about it, but he knew he could rely on Fay to talk him round.

"Why do I have to deal with Edgecombe then?" Alderton asked not unreasonably.

"Because you won't find it easy to get in touch with me during the next few days. All right?"

"Yes."

"Good," said Cartwright. "I'll get back to you as soon as I've had a word with the solicitors."

He put the phone down and leaned back in the chair. Sooner or later he would have to go to Hong Kong and he was damned if he was going to hang around until Alderton came up with a list of names when Sarah's life could well be in danger. His bank account was looking very sick the last time he saw a statement and certainly there weren't enough funds to cover the air fare, but first things first. Before he could think of booking a seat, it was essential to clear the decks with Nolan. He would ask for a fortnight's leave out of his annual entitlement in the confident expectation that Nolan would have to agree to seven days on compassionate grounds.

Sarah paid off the cab at the end of the private slip road where Macready had had the Chinese workmen tunnel into the hillside to make a garage for his Mercedes, and then followed the narrow footpath which led to the ranch-style house on the plateau below. A full moon picked out a junk riding at anchor in Hebe Haven, behind her the night sky reflected an orange-coloured glow from the street lights of Kowloon. Preoccupied with her own thoughts, neither view aroused the slightest interest.

Trying to contact Le Khac Ly had been a long, frustrating and ultimately unsuccessful business. She had got the address of his shop in Harbour City from the Yellow Pages and had found it without too much difficulty thanks to one of the security guards on the third level who'd been able to give her more precise directions. But there had been no sign of 'Little Brother' and according to one of the sales assistants, he hadn't been in all day. In a mixture of French and English, the same Vietnamese had also volunteered the information that Le Khac Ly had another shop in Tsun Wan on the outskirts of Kowloon. His directions had been nothing like as precise as those she'd received from the security guard and it had taken her almost an hour to find it. From there, Sarah had been guided to a high-rise apartment building where eventually she had run his wife and children to ground, only to learn that 'Little Brother' had gone to

104

Macau on business and was likely to be away for two, maybe three, days.

Sarah reached the plateau and started towards the house. The coach lamp on the wall to the right of the nail-studded oak door was burning and she could see the reflected lustre of the hall light through the window of the downstairs cloakroom. The melodic chimes started to peal, triggered by the photo-electric beam which had been interrupted as she stepped inside the porch.

The jingle ended. After a brief pause, the synthesisers began to repeat the four-bar melody, but there was still no reaction from the Chinese houseboys. Macready too managed to ignore the carillons, but he would have started drinking before the sun disappeared below the horizon and it was now gone eight. Knowing that, Sarah made her way round the side of the house expecting to find the Australian on the patio sprawled in a wicker armchair, a pitcher of brandy sour within easy reach. The broken glasses and the drinks table on its side suggested that he'd already had one too many. It was not an unreasonable assumption but it ceased to have any validity the moment she entered the sitting room through the open sliding doors and saw him lying on his back in front of the TV set, a dozen stab wounds in his chest and stomach, his throat cut from ear to ear.

9

There was blood everywhere she looked: on the carpet, on the furniture, on the walls. If a typhoon had swept through the room it could not have done more damage. The two Monets, which Macready had said were his nest eggs, had been slashed from their frames with a bloodstained knife, the porcelain in the display cabinet had been smashed underfoot and the sofas and armchairs had been cut to ribbons in an orgy of destruction. Crouching beside the dead Australian, Sarah placed a hand on his chest and found it was still warm to the touch. Just how long he'd been dead was impossible to guess. True, the arterial bleeding had stopped, but that didn't mean a lot the way the jugular had been severed.

'I'm going to throw up,' she thought and hurriedly turned her head away. Closing her eyes, she took a deep breath and held it until the nausea passed, then steeling herself, she went through his pockets looking for the key to the Mercedes. The nearest house was at least half a mile away down by Marina Cove and was the week-end retreat for some mandarin over on the island. The Chinese houseboys were either dead or had run off into the night, the telephone was in the study across the hall and she wasn't going out there.

The lights dimmed and went out. At first she thought a fuse had blown but then it dawned on her that she could no longer hear the low background hum from the generator in the outhouse. Instead, there was a rustling noise that sounded like a rat nosing around for something to eat. In one of the rooms upstairs, a man called softly in Cantonese and there was an answering grunt from his companion on the patio.

The killers were above and behind her and they knew she

was somewhere in the house. The damned chimes had alerted them and they had probably caught a glimpse of her before she disappeared from view round the back. Her hand closed on a keyring in Macready's pocket and she carefully transferred it to her shoulder bag for safe keeping, then crawled flat on her belly behind the sofa. The kind of fanciful unarmed combat the physical training instructors had taught her twelve long years ago was okay for a work-out in the gym but the Chinaman out there on the patio was a professional killer and she needed a weapon. Some blunt instrument like the heavy table lamp which was now lying on the floor. It would do very nicely if she could just unplug the damned thing without making any noise.

Where the hell was the intruder? Was he still out there on the patio or was he now standing just inside the room, waiting for his eyes to become accustomed to the dark interior? Fear drained the saliva from her mouth and every breath in and out sounded in her ears like a foghorn. Her hands were slippery with sweat and easing the three-pin plug out of the socket took what seemed a lifetime.

She gripped the heavy lamp around its narrow stem and slowly raised herself from the floor until she was in a crouching position behind the sofa. It was impractical to use the lamp as a club while the shade was still attached and she didn't have time to remove it. She would have to swing, twist and release it like a hammer-thrower but aiming to catch him broadside-on across the face.

The same voice called again, this time from the hall, and was answered by the intruder. How close was he? Five, six feet? The other side of the sofa? What the hell did it matter anyway?

She came up fast and let fly. They were only an arm's length apart and she couldn't miss. The lamp cannoned into his forehead and dropped him in his tracks. At the same time, Sarah was cut above the right eye by the trailing power plug which caught her a glancing blow.

She ran out on to the patio and turned left. The other direction led to the outhouse where the generator was kept

107

and she thought it likely that a third intruder had switched off the power supply. The footpath was the quickest way to reach the garage on the hilltop above but it was also the quickest way to get herself killed. Avoiding the easy route, she went straight at the hill and started climbing. Some twenty feet or so above the roof level of the house, she went to ground in the scrub and lay still.

Sarah could hear the intruders calling to one another, their voices high-pitched with suppressed anger. There were three of them advancing in extended line like a row of beaters, one over to the right, the other two left and slightly in rear of her position. The man she had felled with a table lamp kept telling his companions that he was bleeding like a pig and needed medical attention, but they didn't take any notice. A figure moved across her front towards the footpath, searching the ground to his left and right as he went. Speed, not silence, appeared to be paramount and he took a straight line not caring how much noise he made going through the scrub.

Sarah listened to his progress until he was out of earshot, then slowly got to her feet. Zigzagging to avoid the thicker clumps of brush, she went on up the hill, heading diagonally across the slope to meet the footpath near the summit. Only two men had moved due east; the third, who was halfway down the hillside, was squatting on the steps nursing his head between his hands. As she broke cover, he twisted round, looked up and saw her in the moonlight silhouetted against the skyline. There was an extended pause like a freeze frame in a movie, then he found his voice and yelled to his companions.

The knowledge that the killers were fitter, leaner and hardier spurred her on. Compared with a possible knife thrust between the ribs, the stitch lancing into her side was only a minor irritant. Gasping for breath, she reached the summit and ran towards the garage, the shoulder bag which she wore bandolier-fashion bumping her hip with every stride. 'Keep calm,' Sarah told herself, 'don't lose your head. Shoulder bag – key ring – unlock and raise the up-and-over door – reduce everything to a simple drill and you'll be okay. Get in the Merc – close the door – seat belt on – no, damn the seat belt – ignition – check drive in neutral – crank and fire.'

The engine caught first time. Releasing the handbrake, Sarah moved the gearshift into drive and put her foot down on the accelerator. The Mercedes swept out of the garage like a greyhound springing from the trap with the electric hare running. She put the headlights on full beam, swung the wheel hard over to the left, then realised there wasn't enough space to complete the turn and stamped on the brakes. Even so, all four wheels bounced over the kerbstone and there was an expensive grating noise under the chassis as the differential fouled the uneven ground beyond the slip road. Shifting into reverse, she gunned the engine and backed out of the rough on a right-hand lock. For a split second, the injured Chinaman appeared in the rear view mirror, his mouth open, eyes bulging; then there was a sickening thud as the rear fender smashed into his legs. She heard his body land on the trunk before sliding off sideways on to the road, could visualise the kind of damage the concrete surface would do to his skull and found she didn't care.

'Into forward drive, foot down, straighten up, watch the first bend – it's tight.' Sarah talked herself through every twist and turn between Macready's place and the outskirts of Kowloon. 'Grinding noise getting worse, differential probably cracked and leaking oil, could seize up any time, but what the hell, Kai Tak airport's coming up.' The running commentary continued in a low murmur. 'Lion Rock over on the right – flyover ahead – the inside lane passing within a few feet of a huge tenement building – no air-conditioning units, just open windows – a blur of faces – speedo reading 40 – too damned fast, slow down. Jesu, I'm lost – the geography's all wrong, I don't recognise the neighbourhood.'

She took a deep breath, then chided herself for getting uptight over such a small and insignificant problem. The solution was simple enough: all she had to do was leave the flyover, turn right at the next intersection and keep heading

west until she hit Nathan Road, the main artery of Kowloon.
There was no mistaking the main north-south boulevard
with its dazzling neon lights, shopping arcades, bars, hotels,
theatre signs, crowded pavements and traffic jams. Joining it
closer to the Peninsula Hotel than she wanted, Sarah headed
up town on the look-out for a pay-phone. They were few and
far between. The locals usually walked into a neighbourhood
bar or a shop and picked up the nearest phone without even
bothering to ask the owner's permission, but she wanted
somewhere less public. Finally spotting a kiosk at the
junction of Argyle Street, she turned left, then made another
left turn to park the Mercedes in a relatively quiet back
street.

It was then that she noticed dried blood on her hands, on
the blouse and cotton skirt, on her knees – most of it had to be
Macready's blood surely? Sarah leaned across the adjoining
seat and inspected her face in the vanity mirror. There were
a few scratch marks from the scrub but the nick above her
right eye where the plug had caught her had stopped
bleeding and no one was likely to look at her twice.
Rummaging in her shoulder bag, she found a handkerchief
and cleaned herself up as best she could, then got out of the
car and walked back to the pay-phone: 5-91214, the contact
number, was imprinted on her mind. Feeding a dollar coin
into the meter, Sarah lifted the receiver and punched it out.
A few moments later, a metallic voice told her to wait for the
tone signal before leaving a message.

"We've got a problem," Sarah announced, her voice
tense. "Don Macready's been killed, hacked to death by
three Cantonese and I'm running scared. I'll call you again
at eleven fifteen, exactly two and a half hours from now and
you'd better be there, Simon." She paused, racking her
brains for something that would make him sit up and take
notice, and then added, "If I end up talking to this
answering machine, I swear to God I'll walk into the nearest
police station and tell them what I know."

She replaced the phone, left the kiosk and walked away. At
a small emporium in Nathan Road on the fringe of the

110

Golden Mile, she purchased a complete change of clothing, then used one of the cubicles to change. After that, she killed a couple of hours in an air-conditioned cinema before retracing her steps to Argyle Street. This time when she rang 5-91214, Simon Faulkner was waiting for her call.

The *Bryanskiy Baymak* was a 9000 ton cargo tramp. Launched at Nikolayev on the Black Sea in 1956, she was the last of a long line that bore a remarkable resemblance to the wartime Liberty ships built by Kaiser in the United States. In any other merchant navy, the *Bryanskiy Baymak* would have been sent to the breakers' yard long ago, but as part of a concerted effort to transform the Soviet Merchant Marine into the world's foremost carrier of bulk cargo, she had been transferred to the Far East to end her days plying between Vladivostok, Wonsan, Haiphong, Saigon, Bangkok and Singapore. A leaky bucket held together by layers of paint, it was hardly the sort of cruise ship 'In Tourist' would advertise in their glossy travel brochures, but then the passengers who did sail in her from time to time were not the sort of holidaymakers the bureau had in mind. At least that was the opinion of Vladimir Gorshkov, Second Officer and KGB operative.

The Englishman was however a possible exception. He had come aboard at Saigon and had been seen off by the French Consul General, his exit visa had been signed by a high-ranking Vietnamese official in the Ministry of the Interior but, instead of the usual British passport, he had been issued with a temporary identity card. Vladimir Gorshkov was intrigued and although no one had ordered him to do so, he considered it his duty to discover everything he could about the mysterious Englishman. His decision had been largely prompted by the thought that his report might well impress some ranking officer in the Fifth Chief Directorate. However, apart from this important consideration, he'd also seen the task as a welcome diversion from monitoring the off-duty activities of the ship's crew and a golden opportunity to practise his English.

Unfortunately, up till now, Matthew Gage had proved to be one of the strong silent types of Englishmen Gorshkov had read about in books. All he had been able to learn about the man could be encapsulated in a few sentences. A Doctor of Medicine, Matthew Gage had spent the last twenty years of his life working in Vietnam as a senior medical officer of health. Although employed by the reactionary Fascist government led by President Nguyh Van Thieu for more than half that time, Hanoi had evidently been content to allow him to continue in office. Tonight, however, Vladimir Gorshkov was determined that he was going to penetrate the Englishman's reserve, and to this end he had been plying him with vodka all evening in the privacy of his cabin. By nine thirty he considered Gage was sufficiently drunk for him to ask a few leading questions.

"Tell me, Mr Gage," he said, choosing his words carefully, "as one friend to another, why are you leaving Vietnam after all these years?"

"Because I have cancer and will be dead in six months." Gage held his vodka up to the light as though studying its quality and texture. "I suppose you could say that was the basic cause of my sudden desire to see England again."

"I'm sorry," Gorshkov murmured sympathetically. "Have you broken the news to your family?"

"I have no family in England. My wife was Vietnamese and died in April 1983; fortunately, we had no children." Gage smiled. "Cheer up, Mr Gorshkov," he said, "it could be worse."

Gorshkov didn't see how it could be, but then he wasn't seeing anything too clearly. The funny, hollow-chested little Englishman with his sharp features and fringe of dark hair was slowly revolving in front of his eyes.

"Why are you going to Bangkok?" he asked, his voice slurred.

"It's on the way home." Gage finished his vodka and filled the glass again from the bottle.

"You could have gone by train."

"What?"

"To Bangkok. The Kampuchea State Railway from Phnom Penh connects with the Thai network at Aranya Pradet," Gorshkov told him, proudly displaying his knowledge.

"I thought it best to give the Mekong Delta a wide berth. The Khmer Rouge are still contesting the area and I didn't fancy getting shot."

Gorshkov started to giggle. The Englishman had been given six months to live and here he was worrying about getting shot by Pol Pot guerillas.

"You're right, it is a hell of a joke," Gage said and laughed uproariously.

Sarah could not recall the last time she had been quite so relieved to see Simon Faulkner. It was an accepted maxim that any woman who entered a bar in Kowloon on her own had to be on the game and the two Europeans in the booth across the aisle had been giving her the eye ever since she had walked into the place. Both men had had too much to drink; as she went forward to greet Simon, the drunker of the two patted her behind and made some obviously obscene remark in what sounded like Swedish.

"Has that oaf been annoying you?" Faulkner asked grimly.

"Not enough for you to do something about it." Sarah put a hand on his elbow. "Come on," she said, "let's get out of here before you make a scene."

"Whatever you say." Faulkner moved aside to let her pass. "My car's parked opposite the entrance – a dark blue Honda."

Sarah walked outside into the bright lights of Nathan Road, spotted the car immediately and got in. A few moments later, Faulkner left the bar and joined her.

"Are you all right?" he asked.

"You don't know how glad I am to see you, Simon. It's been a hell of a night one way and another."

"Poor love, you've really had a time of it."

"I'm okay now," Sarah told him and wondered why she

113

should feel grateful when Simon was responsible for jeopardising her safety in the first place.

"You want to elaborate on the brief telephone conversation we had a short while ago?"

"There's not a lot more I can tell you. I spent the afternoon and early evening in Kowloon; when I returned to the house a few minutes after eight, the place looked as if it had been hit by a typhoon and Don was lying on the floor of the living room with his throat cut. As the killers were still on the premises, I didn't stop to find out what had happened to the servants." Sarah frowned. "Did I tell you that I've probably killed one of the intruders?"

"No."

"Well, it's odds-on I did. He got in the way of the Mercedes when I was reversing. I eventually abandoned the car in a lane off Argyle Street; my fingerprints will be on the steering wheel."

"It doesn't matter," Faulkner told her. "The Hong Kong Police Department won't have them on record." A wan smile lit up his youthful and far too handsome face. "Good job you disobeyed orders; you'd be dead now if you hadn't."

"I suddenly remembered Le Khac Ly . . ."

"You don't have to justify yourself to me, Sarah."

"But you don't understand. Don happened to mention that he'd escaped from Vietnam with the boat people and it occurred to me that he was the one person Gage would believe."

"Yes, well, that's something we can talk about later. Right now, we've got to find you a new hideaway."

"And where might that be, Simon?"

"A safe house in Wanchai."

Faulkner tripped the indicator, filtered left into Gascoigne Road and continued on past Tsai Park, then looped down to the Kowloon-Canton Railway terminal at the Hung Hom flyover and took the cross harbour tunnel to the island. The safe house was a one-bedroom flat on the twelfth floor of a tower block on Canal Road East.

"Home sweet home," Faulkner said.

114

"I'd hardly call it that."

"No, I don't think I would in your position." He put an arm around her shoulders in a spontaneous gesture of affection that reawakened old memories. "But we don't want to take any unnecessary risks. I don't believe the intruders who killed Macready were after you as well, but for the time being I'm going to assume they were."

"Dammit, they were lying in wait for me, Simon."

"Then you were very lucky to get out of there alive. Personally, I think your arrival on the scene gave them a nasty surprise. Don made a lot of enemies out here over the years and it's likely one of the Chinese Secret Societies decided it was time to settle a few old scores."

"I always thought Don was too wily an old hand to cross the Triads."

"You're wrong there," Faulkner said.

Sarah didn't agree. Macready had always been a survivor. A lance corporal in the Hong Kong Volunteers, he'd been taken prisoner by the Japanese in December '41. Transferred to a POW camp on the outskirts of Hiroshima in the winter of '43, he had been working in the hold of a freighter one and a half miles from ground zero when the first 'A' bomb had been detonated. In the immediate post-war years, he'd gravitated to Shanghai and had made a small fortune getting some of the wealthy Chinese merchants and White Russians out of the city before the Communists marched in. Part of the small fortune had consisted of four ex-Liberty ships which had earned their keep several times over during the Korean War when the Ministry of Shipping and Transport had been chartering anything that floated in order to keep the United Nations Forces supplied. For the better part of forty years, the Australian had managed to stay just the right side of the law; a man who'd sailed that close to the wind would make sure he didn't cross swords with one of the Triads.

"Why are we excluding Gage?" Sarah demanded. "If it's revenge he wants, he could have had Macready killed."

Faulkner shook his head. "The Chinese would never do the Vietnamese a favour, the situation being what it is

115

between the two countries. Besides, there are more effective ways of damaging the SIS than killing one of their former part-time contractors. That's why Gage is coming home."

"I'm beginning to believe it's just a rumour."

"I wouldn't be here if I thought there was any chance of that. So all right, Gage is proving a little shy but the French Consul General in Saigon is looking after him and he'll show up any day now."

Sarah looked round the flat, her eyes taking in the austere accommodation with its tatty kitchen hidden away behind a curtain and the lavatory-bathroom no bigger than a walk-in cupboard. "And am I supposed to stay here until he does?" she asked dejectedly.

"No, this is purely a temporary bolthole. I need time to square things away at Macready's place." Faulkner opened the end cupboard of a cheap-looking sideboard, took out a bottle of whisky and poured two large doubles into a couple of tumblers. "Is there anything back there which would enable the police to identify you?"

"No, I kept everything in my shoulder bag – passport, credit cards and UK cheque book."

"In whose name?"

"My own, of course. I needed it to pay for the plane ticket to Paris – remember?"

"I'm sorry." Faulkner smiled ruefully. "I'm obviously getting absentminded in my old age."

He was forty-five but looked no older than he had done when Sarah had fallen in love with him twelve long years ago. Perhaps the monk's patch in the blond hair was a little bigger but he was still the same urbane, good-looking and charismatic Simon. And even though she was now older and wiser, he continued to have a very disturbing effect on her.

"I don't mind admitting I'm also a little on edge in case your cover is blown. There'd be hell to pay if the old MI5 crowd discovered we had whisked you out of the country under their noses."

"I know the risks you've taken on my behalf, Simon, and believe me, I'm very grateful."

The Security Service had kept her under some form of surveillance ever since the débâcle in Saigon. Although they had appeared to lose interest after she had resigned from the SIS, the news that Gage was coming back had apparently reawakened it.

"What about the real Ellen Rothman?" Sarah asked. "Will she be okay?"

"Miss Rothman won't talk out of turn; she's a very ambitious lady and she'll do anything to get herself transferred out of the Grade 6 administrative pool to our side of the house." He smiled again, this time like a mischievous schoolboy. "Besides Ellen Rothman has signed the Official Secrets Acts which means that not only is she forbidden to disclose our secrets to any unauthorised person, but she will find herself in equally hot water if she talks to our so-called friends in MI5."

"That isn't what I meant."

"The Security Service doesn't know about the switch."

"How can you be so sure?"

"Because I was there. I saw your bird dog leave when you went through into the departure lounge and he wasn't in the concourse when you reappeared as Ellen Rothman. It went like a dream; she flew out under your name and came back under her own." Faulkner swallowed the rest of his whisky and put the empty glass down on the sideboard. "I've got to be on my way, Sarah, there are things that need doing."

"I know."

"I'll move you out of here just as soon as I can. Meantime, there's food in the kitchen and drink in the cupboard."

"You're a good friend, Simon."

"It's nothing. Don't talk to any strange men while I'm away," he said and grinned.

Sarah kissed him goodbye, locked the door and then went into the kitchen. The food consisted of bacon, luncheon meat, butter, sausage and pineapple, all of it tinned. It was the sort of larder a man in a hurry would buy.

117

10

The alarm was set for seven a.m. Ten minutes before it was due to go off, Cartwright opened his eyes, stared blankly at the shaft of sunlight entering the room through the gap between the partially drawn curtains, then sat bolt upright suddenly wide awake. Nuri Assad and Bergitta Lindstrom: the day before yesterday he'd been unable to recall the full name of her boyfriend, this morning it had come to him without any effort. There was something else he now recalled seeing some weeks ago on the hall table back home – a letter in a blue envelope addressed to Bergitta which had been posted in the Bayswater area. It wasn't much to go on but if Assad was a businessman, he would have applied for a visa or a work permit and the Home Office might therefore be able to trace him through Immigration. He would call Henry Edgecombe before he left and give him the information in the hope that he might be able to nudge Dalton into doing something about it.

Cartwright switched off the time set before it triggered a pulsating warble guaranteed to rouse the heaviest sleeper, then went into the bathroom, stripped off his pyjamas and stood under the shower. Nolan had reluctantly agreed he could take a week off to sort out his personal affairs and he'd put a couple of addresses in the leave book in case the army wanted to contact him in an emergency. Although there was no crisis looming on the horizon, Nolan was in a sour enough mood these days to get the chief clerk to phone him up on some pretext or other. If he did, Fay had been primed to stall all inquiries for a day or so before she told anyone that he'd gone to Hong Kong.

There had been no need for Fay to point out that he was

putting his whole career at risk. He had already considered that probability and dismissed it as of secondary importance. An intensely private man, he could not even begin to explain to Fay exactly what her daughter meant to him. He only knew that Sarah was his life force and without her he was merely a husk.

Cartwright towelled himself dry, ran an electric shaver over his beard and got dressed. On his way home from the office last night, he had drawn a hundred pounds from the cash point at the Walham Green branch of Lloyds Bank which had just about drained his current account. A week might not give him enough time to run Sarah to ground but it was all he could count on before the credit people gummed things up. American Express would take care of the plane ticket and hotel bill, but incidental expenses could be a bind. Although he didn't like the idea, buying goods on credit and hocking them to a back street trader was the only means he could think of to resolve an obvious cash flow problem. Even to contemplate such a thing would have appalled him a week ago but moral principles were now a luxury he could no longer afford. If it meant the difference between abandoning the search or continuing it for just a few more hours, he was now prepared to steal pennies from a blind man.

He breakfasted on two slices of toast, the last of the orange juice in the fridge and a cup of coffee. Tucking his washbag into the suitcase he'd packed the night before, he then left the apartment a few minutes before eight and walked to the Underground station. The rush hour was just beginning and as far as he could tell, no one was following him.

Cartwright checked the price structure displayed in the entrance hall to the station, fed a 50p coin into one of the vending machines and passed through the gate. Boarding a District Line train, he changed on to the Northern at Embankment and got out at Waterloo. The clock above W. H. Smith's bookstall was showing eight thirty-six and the main concourse was already beginning to resemble a disturbed ants' nest. At the ticket office, he exchanged the railway warrant he'd been issued with for a second class

119

return to Salisbury. Then he retraced his steps to the concourse, glanced up at the departure board, noted the time of the stopping train to Exeter and made his way to Platform 13.

The platform was almost deserted, which he supposed was only to be expected. At that hour of the morning, the commuters were travelling in the opposite direction and very few people were on their way out of London. He walked on past the diesel-hauled train, went down the steps to the transverse subway below the platforms, showed his ticket to the collector at the barrier and turned right. Exiting into York Street, Cartwright flagged down a passing cab and told the driver to take him out to Heathrow.

He sat cornerways on, directly behind the driver, with his left arm casually draped along the back of the seat, which enabled him to observe the traffic behind them through the rear window without it appearing obvious. While willing to accept the possibility that the police had been following him since he'd left the house in Pelham Street, he found it hard to believe they would have had the foresight to position at least two unmarked cars at Waterloo. Yet despite the fact that nothing happened on the way to Heathrow to cause him to revise his opinion, he couldn't shake off a vague feeling of unease. What prompted it was the disturbing thought that if in fact he really had given the police the slip at Waterloo, it didn't call for much intelligence on their part to guess where he was going.

As his first priority was to get out of the country before the police relieved him of his passport, it seemed only sensible to avoid the British Airways desk. Drawing a blank with Air France and Lufthansa, KLM came up with just the solution he was looking for – a flight departing for Amsterdam in thirty-five minutes which connected with a long haul TriStar to Hong Kong via Delhi and Bangkok. Just before boarding the plane, he called Edgecombe from a pay-phone in the departure lounge and briefed him about Nuri Assad.

Dalton couldn't remember the last time he had been to

Salisbury, but whenever it was, he was quite certain that parking hadn't been quite such a problem, nor had there been such a complicated one-way circuit. The nearest car park to Lloyds Bank in Blue Boar Row appeared to be a good route march away down by the river and his driver had gone round the circuit damn near three times before he'd spotted it. As a result, Dalton had arrived fifteen minutes late for his appointment with the branch manager and had had to cool his heels in the outer office while he dealt with another customer. When finally he did get to see him, there was yet another minor hiccup: despite the court order, the manager insisted on consulting head office before he would allow Dalton to see the print-outs he'd asked for.

The bank statements were worth waiting for. The pay and allowances Cartwright received from the army went into a joint account which was invariably overdrawn towards the end of the month. With almost a fortnight to go to the next pay day, it was already teetering on the brink and Dalton noticed that two withdrawals for a hundred pounds in each case had been made from cash points in Earls Court and Walham Green in the past few days. On the other hand, Sarah Cartwright had £53,000 on deposit and a credit balance of £603.79 in her own current account.

"I can see Mrs Cartwright isn't short of a bob or two."

"She also has an investment portfolio which gives her an income of approximately one thousand pounds a month after tax, Inspector."

"I'm suitably impressed." Dalton placed the two current accounts side by side and compared the entries. "Tell me something," he said presently, "why is the sum of two hundred and eighty pounds a month transferred from the joint account to Mrs Cartwright's own personal account on the first of every month?"

"It's her housekeeping allowance; of course, it isn't anything like enough to pay for the au-pair. That particular expense is met by Mrs Cartwright."

"What else does she pay for?" Dalton asked.

"The rates, water and telephone. Major Cartwright

121

invariably settles the gas and electricity bills as well as the school fees for their son."

The print-outs appeared to reflect the various transactions the manager had described, but the penultimate entry on the current account belonging to Sarah Cartwright intrigued Dalton even more the second time he glanced at it.

"Two thousand pounds; that's a hell of a lot to draw in cash, isn't it?" he said.

"Yes. Naturally, we urged Mrs Cartwright to draw the sum in traveller's cheques but she said she was departing for Paris the following day and had a million last minute things to do, and waiting for our cashier to make up a book of traveller's cheques wasn't one of them."

"And this final entry," Dalton said, reversing the print-out to let the branch manager see it. "Could you tell me who the cheque was made payable to?"

"If you don't mind waiting while the staff go through the cancellations?"

"I'm a very patient man," Dalton told him, "and I'm used to waiting."

It took the staff slightly less than five minutes to produce the relevant cheque which had been made out to British Airways on the date of her departure from Heathrow. The amount looked about right for a return economy-class fare to Paris.

"I suppose that is her signature?" Dalton asked.

"If it isn't, it's a very good forgery."

Although the cheque appeared to clinch matters, Dalton had an uneasy feeling that Sarah Cartwright had issued it with the express intention of proving that she had been on the Paris flight. Considering she had drawn two thousand pounds the day before, he couldn't understand why she hadn't paid for the plane ticket with cash. Taking it a stage further, she had more than enough money on her to fly Cathay Pacific to Hong Kong and back under another name.

"Is there anything else we can do for you, Inspector?" the manager asked politely.

"I was wondering if there was a phone I could use?"

"My assistant manager is on holiday, you can use the one in his office."

Dalton went next door and rang the divisional station at Brentford to get an up-date from the Detective Sergeant he'd put in charge of the crime index. One of the few officers in 'T' District who understood automated data processing, the Detective Sergeant could also regurgitate information almost as quickly as his favourite ICL computer. Amongst other things, he informed Dalton that the post-mortem report on Bergitta Lindstrom had finally arrived and the pathologist was adamant that death had occurred between seven p.m. and midnight on Friday.

Cartwright was off the hook; even though it destroyed his case, Dalton knew there was no avoiding that inescapable conclusion. Much as he disliked his son-in-law, Lucas would testify that during those five vital hours he had phoned Manor Farm at Codford St Mary several times and had spoken to him on each occasion.

The DS droned on, a buzz-saw voice in Dalton's ear. Edgecombe had phoned a few minutes after eleven to say that his client had suddenly remembered the name of Bergitta's boyfriend, a certain Mr Nuri Assad who was some sort of Iraqi businessman living at an unknown address in Bayswater. There was more to come. Yesterday evening, Lieutenant Colonel Nolan had informed the police that he was giving Cartwright seven days' compassionate leave to sort out his personal affairs. Acting on the information, Dalton had arranged for the uniform branch to keep an eye on the flat in Pelham Street. This morning, two police constables in plain clothes had tailed him to Waterloo where of course he'd given them the slip.

The way the investigation was going, Dalton wondered why he should be surprised to hear that the Commander of 'T' District wanted to have a word with him. The Lindstrom case was proving to be anything but straightforward and he'd decided the time had come when the Detective Superintendent of the District should take charge. One more lost opportunity, Dalton thought, then heard the DS

123

bumbling on about a hunch he'd had that Cartwright was on the way to Heathrow and how the KLM desk had eventually confirmed he was on a connecting flight to Hong Kong.

"Well done," Dalton told him, his voice completely matter-of-fact. "Now get someone on to Nuri Assad. Check Immigration and Home Office records and the electoral roll for Bayswater."

"What do I do about Cartwright?" the Detective Sergeant asked.

"Nothing. I'll take whatever action is necessary when I get back."

Dalton put the phone down in a happier frame of mind. He didn't think the Hong Kong Police Department would find it too difficult to keep track of Cartwright. The request for their assistance would have to go through the Home Office, but that was something the Commander of 'T' District could take up with the Assistant Commissioner of Police. It also occurred to Dalton that while Commander 'T' was doing that, he might even think twice about putting someone else in charge of the case.

The bell rang a second time, emitting a long strident note that underlined Faulkner's irritation as he ineffectually rattled the key in the lock with his free hand. Completely unruffled, Sarah walked over to the door and peered through the spyhole to make sure her visitor really was Simon before she withdrew the bolts top and bottom.

"You certainly took your time," Faulkner said, smiling tightly. "For a moment there, I thought you weren't going to let me in."

"I was just being cautious."

"Seems to me you were overdoing it a bit. Who else do you suppose has a key to this flat?"

"The janitor for one. I think he'd hand it over under duress."

"And who's going to apply the duress, the people who chopped Macready?"

"If his execution was ordered by one of the Triads, it

124

wouldn't take the killers long to run me to ground with the intelligence network they've got."

"Hell, Sarah, those people wouldn't bother with a key, they'd simply use a sledgehammer to break into the flat."

"I'm not naïve enough to believe the draw bolts on the door would keep them out." Sarah reached behind her back and withdrew the switchblade she had tucked into the waistband of her skirt and showed it to Faulkner. Then for good measure, she pressed the button in the hilt to release a deadly-looking four inch stiletto.

"I'm impressed," he said. "Do you still remember how to use a knife in combat?"

"No one who's been to Petersfield is likely to forget the basic rules, Simon."

Judo, aikido, karate, close-quarter combat with a knife or a hand gun; they'd given her a thorough grounding in the martial arts at the SIS training school. But no matter how well she had performed in the gym and on the range, there had always been that doubt in her mind whether she could do it for real.

"How long have you had that little toy, Sarah?"

"Since about ten o'clock this morning."

"I thought we'd agreed you wouldn't show your face on the street?" He tried to say it teasingly but there was a slight edge to his voice which betrayed his anger.

"I don't recall giving any such undertaking," Sarah told him coldly. "And I don't see how you could expect me to stay cooped up in this rabbit hutch without a change of clothing."

"I've put my neck on the block for your sake."

"I know you have, that's why I didn't go too far afield."

"I don't care if you only poked your nose outside this building, someone could have seen you."

"Oh, come on," Sarah protested. "How many of my former colleagues are stationed in Hong Kong?"

"It's not your former colleagues I'm worried about. L. H. Kimber is still the big wheel in the bullion market out here."

Lance Havelock Kimber: the Mr Fix-it who'd laundered their money in 1975 and had purchased a small fortune in

125

gold on behalf of the Mission. She might have known Lance Kimber wouldn't leave Hong Kong while it remained an entrepreneur's paradise.

"I doubt if any of his cronies saw me. I got everything I wanted in the Excelsior shopping centre and came straight back here."

"Everything?"

Sarah followed his glance and realised he was looking at the copy of the *South China Mail* she'd left on the sideboard.

"There's a bookshop in the centre which sells newspapers and magazines. I wanted to see if there was anything about Don in the papers. Of course there wasn't, not even in the Stop Press."

"The *South China Mail* started rolling at four a.m.; the Chinese houseboys didn't report the murder until three hours later. According to the statements they made to the police, Macready is supposed to have given them the night off and they claim it was almost seven when they returned from Kowloon. One of the houseboys went into the house to wake him up at seven, the time Don liked to be roused every morning, and that's when his body was found. The CID officers reckon Macready must have pulled one trick too many for the Red Dragon Triad to stomach and they decided he had to go."

"How can you be so sure?" Sarah asked.

"I have my sources."

"The police will know Don had a woman staying with him when they find my clothes."

"They won't know anything of the kind." Faulkner smiled and looked enormously pleased with himself. "I went out to the house last night after I left you and packed your things into the luggage belonging to Ellen Rothman. I've got the suitcase and vanity hold-all downstairs in the trunk of my car."

"You took an awful chance going out to Marina Cove."

"It was a calculated risk. I was pretty sure the killers wouldn't hang around the place once they realised you'd got away; my only worry was the fear that someone might have phoned the police." Faulkner went over to the sideboard,

126

took out the bottle of whisky and poured himself a generous measure. "You want to join me?" he asked.

"Please."

"I'm sorry if I was a bit short with you earlier on."

"You had every right. When I think of what you've done for me, I'm ashamed of the way I behaved."

"Nonsense. What I did for you, I also did for myself. If the police succeeded in identifying you, Ingram, the SIS Head of Station out here, would soon get to hear about it and then the fat really would be in the fire. You're not supposed to be in Hong Kong." Faulkner poured a tot of whisky into another glass and gave it to Sarah. "Anyway, that's not why I'm so uptight."

"Then what is the reason?"

"Gage isn't coming here."

Sarah froze, the glass halfway to her lips. "Not coming?" she repeated blankly.

"We had a signal from London late this afternoon. Seems the French Consul General in Saigon informed the Foreign Office through the Quai D'Orsay that Matthew sailed for Bangkok on the *Bryanskiy Baymak*. The damned tub docked this morning, hours before the signal was even despatched." Faulkner ran a hand through his thinning blond hair. "I wish to Christ we knew what he was doing on board a Soviet vessel but unfortunately we've lost track of him for the time being."

"So what happens now?"

"Well, I'd like to slip you into Bangkok because, sooner rather than later, Gage is going to surface in Thailand and you'd be in place when he does. Alternatively, you could return home and carry on as though nothing had happened and trust to luck that Gage won't go out of his way to destroy you. Personally, I wouldn't be inclined to take that chance but of course the decision is up to you."

A few more days' separation from Tom and the children or thirty years? It wasn't difficult to reach a decision when the problem was reduced to a simple equation. "Tom is in the picture, isn't he?" she asked.

"Of course he is. Peter Wentworth was detailed to brief him." Faulkner took a long pull at his whisky and drained the glass. "You think a lot of Tom, don't you?"

Sarah nodded. "He came along at a bad time in my life and put me together again."

"And you'll have repaid him a hundredfold for that. I only hope he realises what a lucky man he is. I didn't until it was too late."

Another time, another place: Simon's flat in Repulse Bay one wet Sunday afternoon in June '74. The two of them frantically coupling on the sofa, the culmination of a growing awareness of each other which had started in the office four months previously. 1974 – the Year of the Tiger – natural air of authority, stubborn, cautious, violent, daring, lucky, intensely loving and emotional. Those attributes certainly applied to the mercurial Simon Faulkner even though he hadn't been born under the sign. He could make her do anything he wanted and even now, after all that had happened, the old charisma could still make her go weak at the knees.

"All right, Simon," she said briskly, "when do I leave for Bangkok?"

"Tomorrow, if we're lucky, more likely the day after." He saw the look on her face and made a small fluttering motion with a hand as if to pacify her. "Believe me, I'd like to get you out of here tonight, Sarah, but I need a little time to make the necessary arrangements at the far end. Okay?"

"Yes." She smiled. "I didn't mean to seem ungrateful, it's just that this place tends to have a claustrophobic effect on me. All these thousands of Chinese living on top of one another; I must be the only European in the block."

"There aren't too many of you, which is why I wanted you to keep a low profile." His voice tailed away and he frowned at the empty glass in his hand as though wondering where all the whisky had gone. "When you arrived at Kai Tak, did you put Don's name and address on the card you handed to the Immigration Officer?"

"Yes, you told me to when we were driving to Gatwick."

128

"We've got a problem."

Simon didn't have to spell it out for her. He might have removed all her clothes from the house but the Chinese servants knew that Macready had had a woman staying with him and it could only be a question of time before the police wormed that piece of information out of them. It didn't stop there either: they'd called her Missy Ellen and knew she'd just arrived from England. The police would get the surname from Immigration and would trace Ellen Rothman to Bangkok.

"Can we do anything about it?" she asked.

"If this was official, I could get a passport out of Ingram. As it is, I think I know where to get hold of an Australian one at a price."

"How much will you need?" Instinctively, Sarah touched the money belt she was wearing around her waist.

"Nothing. I'll take care of it."

Good old Simon, she thought a touch acidly. He takes care of so many things, including perhaps the telephone and answering machine which the barren socket suggested had once been located in the living room.

1985

FRIDAY 21 JUNE

to

WEDNESDAY 26 JUNE

11

The KLM Lockheed TriStar came in on the west flight approach path over Stonecutters Island, headed towards Lion Rock on the outskirts of Kowloon, then banked to make a tight right-hand turn before rapidly losing height over the city. According to the in-flight magazine provided by the airline, this was the moment when the traveller enjoyed a breathtaking view of the island and The Peak towering above Victoria, but all Cartwright could see from where he was sitting was the runway pointing out to sea.

There was a slight jolt as the pilot set the plane down; a few moments later, the co-pilot put the engines into reverse pitch and the landscape ceased to be a fast moving blur. Swinging on to the dispersal apron near the end of the runway, the Lockheed TriStar taxied over to the Terminal Building.

Cartwright glanced at the landing card he'd completed for Immigration and wondered if Sarah had entered a fictitious address in the box marked 'Intended Place of Residence' or had simply plucked the name of a hotel from the airline's brochure as he had done. His first task however was to discover exactly what she had put on the form and cracking that particular problem could be more than a little difficult. The army, though, had taught him one valuable fact of life: the successful resolution of most problems often depended not so much on what you knew but on who you knew.

Shortly before Christmas last year, he and a hundred and thirty-nine other officers representing the Class of '84 had graduated from the Staff College, Camberley. By the end of the year-long course, he had been syndicated with one officer in three and had been on first name terms with many others.

Seven months later, Cartwright could still recall that one of the officers he'd been syndicated with had been posted to a staff appointment at Headquarters British Forces Hong Kong.

Up front, the stewardess in charge opened the exit and smilingly stood to one side, deliberately inviting the onset of a mass exodus. Grabbing his holdall from the overhead baggage container, Cartwright stepped out into the aisle and joined the shuffling queue. A Chinese police sergeant checked his passport at Immigration and stamped one of the inside pages with the date of entry before passing him through into the Customs hall. The much-travelled suitcase he'd packed two nights ago before leaving the flat in Pelham Road was amongst the first influx on the revolving conveyor belt. Collecting it, he walked through Customs, then went over to the Bureau de Change where he exchanged half his ready cash for Hong Kong dollars. A suffocating blanket of humidity and a line of taxi drivers eagerly competing for his custom greeted him as he walked out of the airport building. Cartwright chose the one who seemed to have a good grasp of English.

"You know where this hotel is?" he asked, pointing to one of the names he'd noted down on the back of an envelope.

"Yes, very good, very cheap hotel." The driver stabbed a finger at another lower down on the list. "This one better," he said. "Also cheap."

"I only hope you're right," Cartwright told him.

A quarter of an hour later, the cab driver dropped him off at the Ambassador Hotel on the corner of Middle and Nathan Roads. The price of the single room with private bath on the sixth floor was forty-eight pounds a day but the friendly desk clerk was happy to charge the bill to American Express.

As soon as the bell boy had left after showing him up to the room, Cartwright looked up the telephone number of Headquarters British Forces Hong Kong in the directory and put a call through to their switchboard. When the military operator answered, he asked for Major Pringle.

134

"Hullo, Alec," he said when they were connected. "Remember me, Tom Cartwright?"

"Yes indeed. What are you doing in Hong Kong?" Pringle sounded guarded, like a man who'd already had his fill of visiting firemen and was hoping he wouldn't have to entertain yet another.

"I'm just passing through," Cartwright said. "Hardly got time to breathe, but then you know how it is when you're on official business."

"Only too well. All the same, Nancy will be disappointed not to see you again."

Cartwright had his doubts about that but responded to the social niceties. "Tell Nancy I'm disappointed too." He paused, then in a suitably apologetic voice he said, "I wonder if you would do me a small favour, Alec? My Brigadier has asked me to deliver a belated birthday present to his niece. Her name is Ellen Rothman and she arrived last Saturday on the Cathay Pacific flight from Gatwick. I'm afraid that's all he could tell me but obviously there would be some sort of address on the landing card she filled in. I'm hoping you can find out what it is?"

"Well, I don't know about that," Pringle said. "I mean, we are talking about prising the information out of a department of the Hong Kong Government."

"And who is better placed to do it than you, Alec? You're the staff officer responsible for personnel, logistics and liaison with the civil authority."

"Yes, but . . ."

"Look, I don't want to twist your arm," Cartwright said, interrupting him, "but my Brigadier is going to be rather peeved if I have to bring his damned present all the way back with me. And let's face it, if the worst comes to the worst, you can always tell Immigration that Ellen Rothman is a military dependant. Right?"

Pringle sighed. "All right, Tom," he said wearily. "Where are you staying?"

"The Ambassador Hotel, Room 611," Cartwright told him cheerfully and slowly put the phone down.

Hong Kong was eight hours ahead of Greenwich Mean Time but the fact that it was only four am in London did not deter him. Lifting the receiver again, he called Edgecombe at his flat in Stanmore. The girl who answered the phone sounded half asleep, so did the unfortunate Henry when he finally came on the line. At first, Alderton's name didn't register with him but as the fog cleared from his brain, he became wide awake and alert.

"The private detective," he exclaimed.

"The very same," Cartwright said dryly.

"He returned from Paris late yesterday afternoon."

"And ?"

"It seems that he and Mrs Barrington got on like a house on fire. She was particularly loquacious."

As well as being loquacious, it seemed that the former Miss Carrie Jackman was a veritable *Who's Who*. Charles Unger, the head of the South-East Asia Bureau, and Simon Faulkner, the number two man in Hong Kong and rising star whom everyone had said would be the Director General of the Service one day, were two names she had given Alderton.

For someone who was known as 'The Shark' amongst the gold market fraternity, Lance Havelock Kimber was surprisingly frail. Round-shouldered and hollow-chested, he was six feet one tall and weighed exactly one hundred and thirty-eight pounds. An accident of birth had left him with one leg slightly shorter than the other and a deformed left foot which resembled a child's hand. Being physically handicapped didn't bother him greatly; what the surgeons had been unable to rectify, a skilful shoemaker concealed, so that only a few intimate acquaintances were aware of his deformity. No one, however, really knew Lance Kimber. He had surfaced in Hong Kong in 1948 at the age of thirty, a cripple without a past and, in the view of some people, a man without much of a future either. Less than a decade later, the same people were saying that Lance Kimber never forgot a favour, never forgave an enemy.

The foundation stone of his business empire had been laid at the Gold and Silver Society, the local bullion market located in a noisy but colourful hall in Mercer Street, where he had made a small fortune wheeling and dealing. The capital he'd swiftly acquired had enabled him to set up his own house and move into the Loco London Market which, unlike the Gold and Silver Society, operated on a US dollar per ounce price geared to delivery in London. The delayed settlement introduced a futures element and Kimber had been one of the first to realise that Hong Kong's geographical position on the international time clock could be used to advantage in volatile price situations when the New York and London positions couldn't be left uncovered overnight.

By 1968, Kimber had branched out and was trading on the floors of the Far East, Kam Ngan, Hong Kong and Kowloon stock exchanges. He had also secured a foothold in the Hong Kong commodity exchange dealing in gold, sugar and soya bean futures. Along the way, he had acquired a mansion on The Peak, a Rolls-Royce Corniche and a devoted wife, a blonde, highly sophisticated German divorcée who had rapidly presented him with two daughters of his own to supplement the ready-made family she had brought to the marriage. Finally, a grateful government had awarded him an OBE for services to commerce in the New Year's Honours List for 1975.

His contacts amongst the Chinese business community were legion. Many of them dated back to his earliest days in Hong Kong and included a number of front men for the various Triads. One such long-standing acquaintance was Mr Chan Tsai, barrister-at-law and legal representative for the 14K Triad. As was invariably the case when they had business to discuss, the Chinese lawyer had telephoned Kimber's secretary and made an appointment to see him at his suite of offices on the 56th floor of the Connaught Centre.

Chan Tsai arrived promptly at 1215, immaculately attired in a lightweight single-breasted suit which had been made for him in Savile Row the last time he was in London. From his equally smart executive-style briefcase he

137

produced a small, unsealed brown envelope and passed it across the desk.

"I believe this is the Bill of Exchange you wish to discount, Lance," he said primly.

Kimber raised the flap and looked inside to satisfy himself that the envelope contained an Australian passport. "You can guarantee no one else has title to this promissory note?"

"But of course. We have also included an appropriate metal die so that the document may be franked in the usual way."

"Excellent," Kimber said enthusiastically.

"What clearing house will you be using in Bangkok?"

"The President on Rama I Road."

"And the name of the broker?"

"We still have several names in mind but rest assured we'll let you know our final choice in good time." Kimber placed the envelope on one side. "Would your associates consider fifty thousand US dollars in bearer bonds a reasonable fee?" he asked.

"My clients," Chan Tsai said, correcting him.

Kimber smiled; the situation could not be resolved without some unpleasantness and, true to form, the lawyer was already distancing himself from any involvement. "My apologies," he said, "just a slip of the tongue."

"Quite so." Chan Tsai inspected his well-manicured fingernails. "My clients have instructed me to say that there will be no fee. They feel this is merely a continuation of the previous transaction which they failed to conclude satisfactorily."

"And the Vietnamese – Le Khac Ly?"

"He is a man of small account, unworthy of our consideration."

Payment was merely being deferred. At some future date, the Triad would remind him of the debt and he would be asked to provide some sort of financial expertise.

"Then there's nothing more we need to discuss." Kimber stood up and shook hands with the lawyer. "Please tell your clients that I'm very grateful and will remember their generosity."

"You have shown them many kindnesses in the past, Lance. I'm sure you will do so again in the not too distant future."

Kimber saw him to the door, then went over to one of the porthole windows in his office, which were a feature of the Connaught Centre, and gazed at the high-rise building on Canal Road East near the Excelsior shopping complex in Wanchai. There were those who would have him believe that the source of their trouble was there in a small apartment on the twelfth floor, but he was beginning to have his doubts.

Cartwright looked round the room, uncertain for the moment where he was. Jet lag had caught up with him and he felt heavy-eyed and listless. There was also a curious buzzing noise in both ears as though the inner drums were full of water. He fingered the hotel bathrobe he was wearing, vaguely recalled standing under the shower to freshen himself up and wondered how long he had been asleep. He yawned several times but still his ears refused to pop, then glancing at the telephone on the bedside table, he realised where the buzzing noise was coming from and slowly lifted the receiver.

"Tom?" The caller sounded irritable.

"Yes. Who's that?"

"Alec Pringle. You phoned me a couple of hours ago inquiring about a Miss Ellen Rothman. Remember now?"

"Yes, of course." Cartwright rubbed a finger across his lips to remove the mucus gumming the corners of his mouth. "Sorry, I didn't recognise your voice, I was only half awake."

"The police want to have a word with you," Pringle said bluntly.

"What?"

"Your Ellen Rothman is a bit of a mystery, Tom. According to the landing card which Immigration is holding, she's supposed to be staying at Hebe Haven View, Marina Cove in the New Territories."

"Are you telling me there's no such address?"

"No. It's a private house which belonged to a Mr Donald Macready, an Australian gentleman who was murdered the night before last. Until I asked Immigration to look up their records, the police weren't aware that anyone was staying with him."

Pringle's voice grated on, waxing plaintive and indignant in turn. The Commissioner of Police had been on to the General Officer Commanding British Forces Hong Kong and, as a result, he'd received an almighty rocket from the 'Old Man' and had also been threatened with an adverse report for obtaining privileged information by deception.

"The police wanted to know where they could find you, Tom, so I had to tell them you were staying at the Ambassador."

"I guess you had no option."

"You can say that again."

Cartwright heard him slam the phone down and slowly replaced the receiver. Whatever else had happened at Hebe Haven View, Sarah was still alive. He had to believe that, otherwise there was no point in going on.

Cartwright rolled off the bed, went into the bathroom and sluiced his face with cold water to freshen himself up. He didn't know how much time he had before the inevitable knock on the door, but Pringle was unlikely to have been over-generous with the amount of warning he'd given him. Returning to the bedroom, he put on a clean shirt and a pair of Daks which didn't look as though they'd been slept in.

The bell rang only once, an imperious summons which drew him towards the door just as the sixth floor concierge unlocked it with a pass key. All three policemen were dressed alike in khaki drill uniforms with silver buttons. The black Sam Browne belts and pistol holsters had been polished until each one gleamed like patent leather. The European officer in charge towered head and shoulders above the Chinese sergeant and the incredibly young-looking police constable. The pot belly and mottled complexion suggested he was a man who liked his beer and frequently drank too much of it.

140

"Major Cartwright?" he asked, squinting at him with baleful eyes.

"Yes. What can I do for you?"

"Chief Superintendent Samuels would like to have a chat with you. I think you've a pretty fair idea what it's about."

Cartwright asked them if they would mind waiting while he collected his jacket. With the temperature hovering around 92 degrees Fahrenheit, he certainly didn't need it but the inside pocket contained his wallet and passport and he wasn't going anywhere without them.

The lift stopped at the fifth floor and again at the second. On each occasion, the other hotel guests took one look at the uniformed police officers standing either side of Cartwright and declined to join them. Their stately progress through the lobby towards the Land-Rover parked outside the entrance made them a focal point of interest and provoked a low buzz of speculation.

Once his passengers had clambered inside, the driver continued on down Nathan Road, turned right into Salisbury Road and went past the Planetarium. Just short of the Star Ferry Terminal, he turned right again and headed north on Canton Road. The police station was opposite Ocean Central, part of the vast Harbour City condominium.

Chief Superintendent Samuels was a small, neat-looking man of indeterminable age whose most notable features were his black hair, sallow complexion and gleaming white teeth which had obviously been capped. He was softly spoken and had a curiously muted accent that was hard to place.

"You're not American, are you?" Cartwright asked.

Samuels had obviously answered the same question many times before. "No," he sighed. "I come from Vancouver BC."

"I was born in Reading, Berks," Cartwright told him pokerfaced, "and not too many people know that either."

"Except perhaps Ellen Rothman?"

"Yes, she'd know; it's on our marriage certificate."

"Ellen Rothman was your wife's maiden name?"

Here we go, Cartwright thought, and prepared himself

141

for the glazed eyes and incredulous expression his story inevitably drew. "Actually, it's Lucas and furthermore her Christian name is Sarah. She and this other woman switched identities at Heathrow."

"Why?"

"I wish I knew. I think my wife left Hong Kong under a cloud the last time she was here and maybe she came back to settle some unfinished business."

"With the late Mr Donald Macready?"

Cartwright shrugged his shoulders. "I'd never heard of the man until a few minutes ago. Was he with the Foreign Office?"

"Was Mrs Cartwright?" Samuels countered.

"Nominally."

"What am I supposed to gather from that?"

"I believe Sarah was an Intelligence Officer in the SIS before we were married."

"I think we'd better have a description of the lady, Sub Inspector," Samuels said, looking past him to the plump officer.

"I can do better than that." Cartwright extracted the last remaining snapshot of Sarah from his wallet and passed it to the Canadian Chief Superintendent. "This was taken last year and it's a good likeness."

"Definition's certainly very clear." Samuels studied the photograph from all angles. "I'm sure our people can do something with this. Do you mind if we borrow it for a while?"

"By all means."

"Great." Samuels waved the snapshot at the plump Sub Inspector. "Get this along to the photo lab, Barry, and ask them to do a rush job, the usual number of prints for maximum distribution. Then question those houseboys again. I want the truth from them this time."

"I may have to slap them around a bit."

"Don't let me catch you doing that, Sub Inspector."

"You won't, sir, believe me."

"Just so long as we understand one another, Barry."

142

Samuels waited until his subordinate had left the office, then said, "He's a good police officer, Major, but sometimes gets carried away by his enthusiasm."

"He'd be well advised to contain it should he question me," Cartwright said.

Samuels stared at him, seemingly amazed. "Good God, what do you take us for – the KGB?"

"Let me ask you a question. What would happen if I walked out of your office here and now?"

"Nothing."

"It's been nice meeting you," Cartwright said and got to his feet.

"Now, hold on a minute; what about your wife's photograph?"

"You know where I'm staying, send it round to the hotel."

"I don't think I can send Roger Ingram round to the Ambassador."

"Who's he?"

"The SIS man in Hong Kong."

"You've just talked me into staying," Cartwright told him.

The SIS cell in Hong Kong was tucked away in the government office building directly behind St John's Cathedral on Gordon Road. As Head of Station, Ingram had been allocated a south-facing room with a view of The Peak. Also within the same vista were the official residence of His Excellency the Governor and the US Consulate, which cynics maintained were two very good reasons why the incumbent should have an extra pair of eyes in the back of his head.

Faulkner couldn't see how Roger Ingram had progressed as far as he had in so short a time unless he possessed some sort of human radar. A first in Maths was highly commendable of course, but a good degree, especially one from Sussex University, was not a passport to instant stardom and yet Ingram had been appointed Head of Station Hong Kong at the age of thirty-four. In his own mind, Faulkner was

143

convinced the younger man owed his rapid advancement to an uncanny knack of being in the right place at the right time, and that didn't happen by accident. When working at Century House, he had obviously crept round the PAs to find out what was going on, then sucked up to the high-priced help, anticipating their every wish.

As the big white chief in Hong Kong, he now expected every Intelligence Officer to dance attendance on him and it annoyed Faulkner intensely that Ingram should summon him to his office as he would a subordinate. The fact that the younger man didn't even wave him to a chair before he came straight to the point only rubbed salt into an already sore wound.

"I've just had a rather odd conversation with the Assistant Commissioner of Police," Ingram said, frowning at the telephone. "He seems to think I should drop everything and rush over to the central police station in Kowloon to see a Major Cartwright."

"Who's he?"

"I was about to ask you the same question, Simon."

"Cartwright." Faulkner repeated the name to himself and looked blank for several moments, then with the consummate skill of a born actor his face suddenly lit up. "Wait a minute, I seem to remember that Sarah Lucas, one of our bright young linguists married an army officer when she left the Service. I think his name was Cartwright."

"Was she attached to the mission in Vietnam?"

Faulkner nodded. "She was misemployed. Field operations weren't her forte but in addition to having an ear for languages, she was a damned good collator and we weren't in a position to pick and choose. We had to make do with local resources because the Left Wing of the Labour Party was making trouble for Harold Wilson and things had to be done quietly. At least, that's the story London gave us; personally, I don't believe the Prime Minister was ever told about the mission."

"Never mind about Harold Wilson. What else should I know about Sarah Cartwright before I see her husband?"

144

His attitude reminded Faulkner of the sort of commanding officer who confused brusqueness with efficiency. Ingram even looked the part with his square, clean-cut features and trim military moustache, though he thought the army would have frowned at his rather curly hairstyle.

"She was a failure in Vietnam," Faulkner told him reluctantly. "As I said before, field ops were not Sarah's forte and the job got on top of her, especially towards the end when a large number of ARVN units were abandoning their positions before the enemy had even fired a shot at them."

"ARVN?" Ingram said, interrupting him.

"Army of the Republic of Vietnam. Anyway, with everyone else up-country, Sarah found herself acting as Chief of Staff back in Saigon with just one operator to man the transmitter and a telephone network that only functioned intermittently. As a result, Gage never received my instructions to get out and was left behind, a lot of Top Secret documents fell into enemy hands and the greater part of our treasure chest went missing. Back in England, an unofficial Board of Inquiry decided Sarah was partly to blame and an adverse report was lodged in her file. I heard later that her security clearance was also withdrawn."

"Any idea what her husband is doing in Hong Kong?"

"I haven't the foggiest notion. You'll have to ask him."

"Quite." Ingram frowned at his wristwatch. "Could you brief the night duty officer if I'm not back in time?"

"When does he come on watch?"

"1800 hours."

"I'm waiting for a cable from Bangkok," said Faulkner. "What have you got in the offing?"

"Nothing, as far as I'm aware."

"Then it shouldn't take more than five minutes to brief him."

Faulkner was a hundred per cent correct. At 1805, he left the government offices and made his way to The Landmark on Des Voeux Road Central where the Helena Rubinstein representative was only too pleased to help him choose a whole range of make-up ostensibly as a birthday present for his wife.

12

Up till now, everyone who'd heard Cartwright's story had either expressed total incredulity or they'd started quizzing him long before he'd given them all the facts. Ingram was different inasmuch as he had listened attentively without once interrupting him. Whether he believed his account was, however, another matter altogether. The proposition that a young woman had been murdered merely in order to incriminate him was hard to swallow; the questions Ingram had subsequently asked about Bergitta Lindstrom suggested he certainly entertained a considerable number of doubts.

"Let's talk about your wife's former colleagues," Ingram said, abruptly changing the subject.

"In Bonn or Hong Kong?"

"Oh, I don't think we need concern ourselves with the girls from the typing pool in Germany."

"All right, let's start with Carrie Jackman. What can I tell you about her?"

"I don't know."

"Of course you don't." Cartwright forced a smile and did his best to sound affable, which wasn't the easiest thing in the world to do. It was the second time in less than a minute that he'd presented Ingram with an opportunity to put him down and he was feeling anything but friendly towards the man. "Carrie Jackman is now Carole Barrington, the wife of the Assistant Military Attaché in Paris. She and Sarah worked in the same section out here, became good friends and have kept in touch with one another ever since."

"Because they have similar interests," Ingram said, suggesting a reason why the friendship had stood the test of time.

146

"Partly. Sarah also told me how supportive Carrie had been when she was going through a bad patch."

"At work, or in her personal life?"

"Both." Ingram was trying to draw him out to see how much he knew, and it wasn't a lot. All he'd really got up his sleeve was a lot of office tittle tattle from the former Carrie Jackman. About the only reliable piece of information was Sarah's love affair with a Simon Faulkner and then only because it had been substantiated in part by Fay Lucas. What he had to do was establish what professional relationship, if any, had existed between them. "Sarah had an unhappy love affair with her boss and he subsequently dropped her in the shit with Head Office."

"You mean her annual report ceased to be a eulogy once they'd gone their separate ways?"

"It wasn't like that," Cartwright said, playing a long shot. "There was a major foul-up and her boss made sure that she ended up carrying the can."

"What sort of foul-up?"

"Sarah never let on but I do know the breach of security was serious enough for her vetting status to be withdrawn." Cartwright held up a hand, silencing Ingram before he had a chance to say a word. "And before you ask, Sarah didn't tell me that either, I simply put two and two together. Bright girls who hold the highest clearance in the land aren't usually assigned to the typing pool, especially when they're talented linguists to boot. Right?"

"It would be an awful waste of talent if they were."

"Your Service lost a first rate Intelligence Officer, but that didn't bother Simon Faulkner, did it?"

"I wouldn't know about that. My only information is that Faulkner was once your wife's superior officer."

At last. Just when it had seemed he was getting nowhere, Ingram had confirmed that Simon Faulkner had been Sarah's commander in Hong Kong. If he pushed his luck a little bit more, there was a chance he might pick up some more information.

147

"The best laid plans often come unstuck," he said. "Ten years on and Faulkner is feeling insecure again."

"Who says so?"

"I do," Cartwright told him. "It's the reason he's here in Hong Kong. Someone or something Faulkner thought was dead and buried has surfaced and he's going to use Sarah to protect himself, just as he did the last time."

"You're a clever man, Major Cartwright, perhaps a little too clever for your own good." Ingram stood up, walked over to the door and told the police constable outside that he wanted to see Chief Superintendent Samuels.

"I'm right though, aren't I?" Cartwright persisted.

"I wouldn't know, you'll have to ask the people in London who sent him out here." Ingram produced a pipe from his jacket pocket and began to fill it from a tin of St Bruno, a task which he seemed to find totally absorbing. He had just reached the stage when he was ready to strike a match when Samuels joined them.

"That was a long half hour," the Canadian said cheerfully. "I trust it was worthwhile?"

"We had a very interesting talk." Ingram struck a match and held it over the bowl. "Major Cartwright will be returning home on the first available flight tomorrow," he added between puffs.

"Like hell I will . . ."

"I don't have to remind you that the Major is the subject of police inquiries in the UK," Ingram said, talking him down. "In my opinion, the Hong Kong government will say they have enough problems of their own to cope with as it is without importing any more. I suggest you hold him overnight in the detention centre at Kai Tak."

"Are you proposing to have me expelled?" Cartwright asked him icily.

"I certainly am."

"I trust you've got a deportation order on you?"

"Of course I haven't," Ingram said irritably, "but it won't take me long to get one."

From the moment Sarah had gone missing, Cartwright

had lived with the secret fear that the next time he saw her would be in the morgue. And at every turn, he had been frustrated and harassed by the very people he'd looked to for help. Now, just when he was perhaps only a stone's throw away from Sarah, this stupid son of a bitch was going to send him home. The pent-up emotion bubbled to the surface and he rounded on Samuels, his face white with rage.

"You'd better make sure everything's nice and legal before one of your men lays a hand on me. You make one false move and I'm going to have you crucified, the way I'm going to nail this pipe-smoking idiot."

"I'm going to have to charge you with Common Assault," Samuels informed him gravely.

"What the hell are you talking about?"

"You wagged a finger at me, that's enough to justify a charge of Common Assault."

Ingram smiled happily. "How long will it take you to file charges?" he asked.

"An hour and a half, maybe two by the time we've found a lawyer to represent Major Cartwright."

"I'll be back with a deportation order long before then," Ingram said.

Sarah picked up one of the pair of false eyelashes and deftly fixed it to her right lid before inspecting her appearance in the mirror.

"You look different already," Faulkner told her.

"You think so?"

She had trimmed her eyebrows with a pair of nail scissors, thinning them out until only a few hairs remained and had then used a black pencil to change their colour. She had also altered their shape with a few neat strokes, but the face in the mirror still looked very familiar.

"You won't know yourself by the time we've finished," Faulkner said, as though reading her thoughts.

"Whose confidence are you trying to bolster?" Sarah asked. "Yours or mine?"

Opening the packet of kirbigrips he'd brought her, Sarah

149

pinned her hair up and kept it firmly in place with a net. The wig began the transformation, the rubber pads which filled out her cheeks completed it.

"What did I tell you," Faulkner said triumphantly. "You're a new woman."

"I don't feel like one." Her voice sounded terrible, as though she had a mouthful of marbles. "This is stupid," she mumbled, "no one's going to understand a word I say."

"Don't worry about your voice, Sarah; it'll be okay once you get used to the pads." Faulkner steered her over to the ladder-back chair he'd positioned against a bare wall and invited her to sit down. "What we're going to do now is take a few snapshots with this polaroid. Okay?"

"Where did you get the camera?"

"I borrowed it from the office." He backed off a few paces, then crouched down and peered through the aperture. "Look straight ahead and try to relax. Passport photographs are never flattering but we don't want you looking like a zombie."

"You're all charm, Simon."

"I know," he said, "it's the secret of my success. Now hold it just as you are and watch the birdie."

Despite the warning, the flashlight still caught her unawares and she flinched. "Sorry."

"It's not the end of the world," he said cheerfully. "I put a new cassette of film in the camera; we're bound to get it right sooner or later. How about a cigarette while we wait for this exposure to develop?"

"I've given up smoking."

"Maybe I will after we've heard the last of Matthew Gage."

"Has he got in touch with our embassy in Bangkok yet?"

"No." Faulkner blew a smoke ring towards the ceiling. "He hasn't tried to contact the French either, which surprises me considering how pally he was with their Consul General in Saigon."

"I suppose he is coming home?"

Faulkner stared at her, his eyes narrowing in anger. "Just

what are you implying – that everything I've told you about Matthew Gage is a pack of lies? Hell, Sarah, you know damned well I can't show you the signal we received from London, but why do you suppose MI5 put their watchdogs on to you again after all these years? You were aware of their renewed interest, weren't you?"

"I was once Peter Wentworth had tipped me off."

Exactly a month ago Wentworth had telephoned her and during the course of a rather odd conversation, had jocularly asked her if she had been behaving herself. It was only after he had rung off that his veiled speech had finally made any sense and she'd realised that MI5 had been to see him.

"How did they know where I was living, Simon?"

"Wasn't your husband PV'd before he went to the Staff College?"

"Yes."

"Well, there you are then; MI5 asked to see his security file and found your address on the next-of-kin proforma. Nothing could have been simpler for them."

And a fortnight after Wentworth had telephoned, a worried Bergitta had told her how she had been picked up in Salisbury and questioned about her employer by a man claiming to be a police officer. Their methods had become even more heavy-handed with the appearance of the Telecom engineer who'd called to rectify a fault on the line when Bergitta had been alone in the house.

"Did you know the Security Service had bugged my house?" Sarah asked.

"No, I merely presumed they had." Faulkner smiled grimly. "That's why I wrote to you instead of phoning."

"Letters can be opened, Simon."

"So what? I didn't tell you that Gage was coming home. I just said that one of your former colleagues had nominated you as a referee and could we please arrange a suitable date and time when we could interview you. As your one-time superior officer, they would have expected me to get in touch with you and my devious approach would have met with their approval. In their eyes, I would be showing a proper regard for security. Of course, I was banking on you being smart enough to ring me from a public call box, which you were."

"Bully for me."

"Well, I always figured you had more brains in your little finger than most people have in their heads." Faulkner stubbed out his cigarette, then crouched down to line up the camera. "Let's see if we can't do better this time," he said and tripped the shutter.

The flashlight still made her blink but not so noticeably as before and the likeness was up to the usual standard of a passport photograph even though her face did look as though it belonged on a 'Wanted' poster.

"Who am I this time?" she asked.

"I don't know, you think of a name."

"How about Susan Lamidy?"

"I think you just made a small Freudian slip. When choosing an alias, nine out of ten people use their own set of initials, but your choice of surname appears to be identifying with Lucas. Can it be that you hanker after the old days when you were single?"

"You'd never earn a living as a psychologist," Sarah told him. "Ellen Rothman isn't married, so it's only sensible to continue the charade in the same vein."

"What do I put for date and place of birth?"

"24 November 1949, Canberra." She smiled fleetingly. "It's always best to stick to the truth. I remember Canberra as a child when my father was a member of the British Army Liaison Staff."

He worked swiftly, first bonding the photograph to the page opposite her physical description, then die-stamping the passport to show which office had issued it and when. There were other stamps on other pages which fleshed out the legend, amongst them the date Miss Susan Lamidy had arrived in Hong Kong and how long she was permitted to remain in the Colony. For a forgery, Sarah was impressed by its seeming authenticity.

"Where did you get the passport, Simon?"

"That's a trade secret. But I'll tell you this, it'll get you past any officer in the Hong Kong Immigration Department, which is just as well, the way things are going."

"What's happened?" she asked him quietly.

"Ingram had a phone call from the Assistant Commissioner of Police earlier this evening. I don't know what they said to each other, but shortly afterwards, our Head of Station called me into his office and I found myself answering a lot of tricky questions about Ellen Rothman. I suppose the police must have leaned on Macready's houseboys and they must have told them about the Missy Ellen who'd been staying at the house since she'd arrived from England on Saturday."

"Well, you expected as much." Sarah frowned. "The thing that puzzles me is why the Assistant Commissioner should have phoned Ingram. He wasn't to know that Don had performed one or two errands for us in the dim and distant past."

"Macready wasn't the most discreet of men. Shortly after you left Hong Kong, he was arrested for drinking and driving and I had to go down to the central station and bail him out." Faulkner avoided her eyes, gazed instead at the Australian passport in front of him. "I can't be there at the airport when you leave tomorrow."

"I never expected you to."

"I haven't been able to make a reservation with Thai International either."

"There's no need to apologise, Simon. It's not as though I'm short of money."

"I've got change for three hundred pounds."

"What?"

"You're supposed to be an Australian; the airline might think it odd if you pay for your plane ticket in sterling." Taking a bulging wallet from the inside pocket of his jacket, he gave her a wad of US, Hong Kong and Australian dollars in various denominations. "One thing I can do is make sure there's a reservation for you at The President in Bangkok."

"I've never been the helpless little woman, Simon. I can find my own hotel."

"The hell you will. Gage could surface at any moment and I don't want to waste valuable time looking for you when he does. The international code for Hong Kong is 010852; as soon as you've checked into The President, call me on 65539 and give me your room number, then act surprised and pretend you must have misdialled."

"I thought that old routine had gone out with the Ark."

"Just do as I tell you. Okay?"

His vehemence surprised her and she wondered what had happened to the man who enjoyed a reputation for being cool under pressure. "Hey," she protested, "I'm not a mutinous subordinate."

"Sorry." A rueful smile appeared and he shook his head as though perplexed to know what had caused the outburst. "Can't think what's getting into me these days."

"It's understandable with the kind of worries you have on your mind."

"And I'm not thinking straight either." He snapped his fingers in a slightly theatrical gesture. "We can't have you walking around with a passport saying you're Ellen Rothman and a cheque book belonging to Sarah Cartwright. An Immigration Officer might think it a little strange."

"I guess he would." Sarah unzipped her shoulder bag and gave him the passport, then stared at the slim green book with the Lloyds Bank motif, reluctant to part with it.

"Don't worry," Faulkner told her, "I promise I won't forge your signature."

She had surrendered her own passport on Friday when they were driving from Heathrow to Gatwick; now, at Simon's insistence, she was about to hand over her cheque book. It made her feel as though Sarah Cartwright no longer existed.

"One final point, make sure you leave that flick knife behind. We don't want the metal detectors bleeping when you go through the security check at Kai Tak."

The lawyer the police had found for Cartwright arrived a few minutes before seven thirty. The white sharkskin dinner jacket he was wearing suggested the timing of their phone call could not have been more inconvenient; his attitude and general demeanour confirmed a suspicion that his one concern was to fulfil his legal obligations in the shortest possible time. The horse trading which followed was conducted in a manner befitting the market place; the police dropped the charge of common assault and served Cartwright with a deportation order instead; the lawyer read it and informed him it was pointless to contest the decision.

"We like to do things properly around here," Samuels said, his capped teeth bared in a dazzling smile.

"Are you referring to this piece of legal chicanery you call an expulsion order?" Cartwright asked.

"I'm referring to your passport, wallet, credit cards and loose cash." Samuels opened the bottom drawer of his desk and took out a large brown envelope. "Just put all your valuables in this and I'll give you a receipt for them."

"When do I get them back?"

"At the airport, before you board the plane. The conducting officer will hand the envelope to Immigration for safe keeping when he takes you to the detention centre at Kai Tak."

The conducting officer turned out to be the overweight Sub Inspector who answered to the name of Barry. He had a different sergeant with him on this occasion, a taller man whose muscular biceps led Cartwright to think he did a bit of weight-lifting in his spare time. The incredibly young-looking police constable had been replaced by a wizened veteran who'd grown old in the service. Their red shoulder badges indicated that both Chinese officers were fluent in English.

Before they left, Barry took it upon himself to deliver a small homily to the effect that he wouldn't hesitate to handcuff Cartwright like a common criminal if he didn't behave. The speech over, the Chinese officers ushered Cartwright into the back of the armoured Land-Rover, then climbed in after him and locked the rear door. This time they took the most direct route to the Ambassador Hotel, turning

155

right on Peking Road outside the Central Station and continuing on across Kowloon Park Drive and Ashley Road. At the T-junction beyond the Regency Hyatt Hotel, they turned south on Nathan Road and stopped outside the front entrance two blocks further down.

"Do me a favour," said Barry. "Try not to take all night packing your gear. I come off duty at 2000 hours and I don't want to keep my date waiting."

"How about a quid pro quo?"

"Such as?"

"I'd rather not walk into the Ambassador with half the police force of Kowloon in tow."

"How many suitcases have you got?"

"Only the one," Cartwright told him.

"Well, okay, the constable can stay here with the driver."

One less policeman didn't make a great deal of difference. The lobby was as crowded as it had been earlier on and Cartwright was conscious of being the centre of attention while Barry collected the key to his room from the desk clerk. There was another buzz of speculative conversation when they trooped across the foyer towards the lifts which only ceased when the sergeant pressed the button and the door closed automatically.

No one was waiting for the lift when they got out at the sixth floor, nor did they encounter anyone as they walked on down the corridor to Room 611. Barry unlocked the door, told Cartwright to lead the way and then followed on behind the sergeant.

Cartwright picked up his much travelled suitcase from the luggage rack in the narrow hallway and walked into the bedroom. The bed was to his right, directly opposite the fitted wardrobe. Hefting the suitcase as if to dump it on to the divan, he wound himself up like a discus thrower and swung completely round, his left arm extended to gain additional momentum. The suitcase travelled in a vicious arc and hit the police sergeant on the right side of his jaw, felling him like a poleaxed steer.

Barry dropped the envelope he was holding and attempted

156

to draw his .38 revolver without first unbuttoning the leather holster. By the time he realised why the Smith and Wesson refused to budge, Cartwright had dropped the suitcase and was on him, clubbing away with both fists to his ribs and stomach. It was all pretty scrappy: only the first punch, a short right-hand jab, carried any weight and more by luck than judgement, it caught Barry under the breast-bone, completely winding him. His legs buckling under him, he toppled forward and tried to lean on Cartwright for support. The knee jerk to the groin wasn't scientifically delivered either but there was enough force behind it to end the fight there and then. Slowly, almost gracefully, Barry sank down on to his knees and rested his head on the floor as though praying to Allah.

Cartwright grabbed the envelope containing his passport and money and got out as fast as he could. He slammed the door behind him in the hope that this might impose some sort of momentary hold-up, then ran to the bank of lifts halfway along the corridor and jabbed the call button. The delay seemed interminable and he was tempted to use the fire escape, but resisted the impulse knowing that on the basis of Sod's Law, the lift would arrive the moment his back was turned and Sub Inspector Barry would be waiting for him when he eventually reached the lobby.

As the lift indicator pinged Barry stuck his head out into the corridor, spotted Cartwright and bellowed like an enraged bull. He also charged like one, his head lowered, his feet pounding noisily even though the floor was carpeted. When the door began to close in his face, there was still no sign of the muscular police sergeant, but a shrill blast indicated he had recovered sufficiently to put his whistle to good use.

The lift descended rapidly, giving Cartwright very little time to rip open the envelope and retrieve his passport, wallet and loose cash. When the door opened seconds later, he strolled through the lobby as if he hadn't a care in the world even though there was no way of avoiding the Land-Rover parked outside the entrance. The vehicle was facing south and he instinctively turned right to head uptown on Nathan Road. At any moment he expected the veteran police constable in the back of the Land-Rover to spot him and raise the alarm but nothing happened and within a few strides he was swallowed up in the jostling crowds.

He strode on past the Imperial Hotel, the Golden Mile Holiday Inn and crossed Mody Road. Turning right at the intersection of Carnarvon Road with Nathan, he followed the signs to the Mass Transit station at Tsim Sha Tsui, fed three dollars fifty into the ticket vending machine in the entrance hall and boarded the cross harbour train to Central.

13

Cartwright left Central Station by the exit into Connaught Road. The task of finding Sarah had now been temporarily relegated to second place behind the overriding need to get the deportation order rescinded before the police ran him to ground. But to stay loose, he needed a change of clothes, a wad of folding money and a hideaway; the American Express card in his wallet would enable him to obtain all three.

Heading west, he bought a light sports jacket and slacks from one tailor and a Thai silk shirt from another, then found a bar and did a quick change in the men's room. Retracing his steps on the opposite side of the street, Cartwright bought an expensive Pentax from a camera shop and calmly asked the proprietor if he could use the phone while the sales assistant made out an invoice allegedly for the benefit of HM Customs and Excise.

Chief Superintendent Samuels was more than a little surprised to hear from him when he put a call through to the central police station in Kowloon.

Cartwright said, "I want you to get in touch with Ingram and persuade him to withdraw the exclusion order."

"Don't even give it another thought," Samuels rasped. "Stanley Prison's the only place you'll be going to if I have my way. Furthermore, I am going to make it my business to ensure you draw a seven stretch for assault occasioning grievous bodily harm."

"Ingram won't let you," Cartwright told him coolly. "He won't want to find his name in the newspapers, nor does he want to read about Macready's involvement with the SIS. And above all, he doesn't want to see what sort of conclusion

159

the editor of the *South China Mail* will draw from the circumstantial evidence that the Secret Intelligence Service is linked to the murder of a Swedish au-pair in London."

"I'm going to hang up."

"You'll be out of a job if you do."

"A word in the right ear and the Commissioner will fire me?" Samuels chortled as if he found the suggestion vastly amusing, then reverted to a snarl in double quick time. "Is that what you're telling me?"

Cartwright recognised the ploy for what it was. The Canadian Chief Superintendent had decided to play for time, endeavouring to keep him talking while the operator attempted to trace the call.

"You've got exactly ninety minutes to set things up. When I ring back at nine thirty, you'll give me a phone number where Ingram can be reached plus an assurance that he'll be waiting at the other end of the line."

Cartwright replaced the receiver, thanked the proprietor for the use of his phone, then picked up the sales invoice for the Pentax camera and left the shop. Continuing on his way towards the Mandarin Hotel, he turned into the World Wide Plaza on the corner of Pedder Street where he sought some advice from the owner of a shop in the arcade which specialised in hi-fi equipment. Shortly afterwards, he walked out with a Japanese-made answering machine roughly the size of a pocket calculator.

By the time he found a street hawker in one of the alleys off Queens Road Central who was willing to take the camera off him at a little over a third of the original sales price, he had exactly forty-one minutes to kill. The streets were beginning to empty and he felt exposed and vulnerable. As of that moment, the cocktail lounge in the Mandarin Hotel seemed a pretty good refuge. He was also confident that it was the one place he could be sure of making a phone call in complete privacy.

A lifetime spent in the RAF had left Group Captain William Quarry, OBE, AFC, with precious few illusions. As the very

160

smooth gentleman in the Directorate of Personnel Management who'd tried to convince him that the post of Defence Attaché Bangkok represented a stepping stone to greater things had rapidly discovered to his embarrassment, he was nobody's fool. Before visiting the Personnel Branch to discuss his future, Quarry had made a few discreet inquiries and already knew that not one of the previous incumbents had been promoted. He had accepted the appointment because, at the age of forty-nine, his flying days were behind him and the other staff jobs he'd been offered after his tour of duty as Station Commander Great Driffield had been very mundane and uninteresting.

There had been other equally important considerations. Although both his daughters were married, his son had been about to go up to Cambridge, and no civilian firm had been prepared to offer him a job at a salary commensurate with his service pay. The diplomatic net had also struck him as a pleasant way to spend his last few years in the service and he'd quickly recognised that the Foreign Office overseas allowance would certainly help with the mortgage on the house he was buying in Tunbridge Wells. It had been this thought which had been uppermost in his mind during the year long struggle to master at least the rudiments of the Thai language.

At no time had Quarry seen himself as a cloak and dagger man. Military Attachés in posts behind the Iron Curtain were overt spies in uniform. In friendly countries like Thailand, their role was a combination of arms salesman, technical adviser and public relations representative. Such intelligence as they did gather was mainly concerned with the readiness for war of the host nation's forces and the quality of their senior officers. Quarry had never gone anywhere without the prior knowledge and approval of Thailand's Ministry of Defence. Tonight, however, was an exception, tonight a phone call to his private residence from a man called Matthew Gage had cast him in the role of a covert Intelligence Officer. It had also brought him to the stopping point for the 'long-tailed' river taxis

161

at the Royal Orchard Hotel near the Portuguese embassy.

The address Gage had given him meant nothing to the boatman the way Quarry pronounced it and his phonetic spelling of the place name met with an equally blank response. Gage had however given him detailed instructions of how to find the place where he was staying and, knowing the house was located in one of the smaller canals off the Klong Bangkok Noi, Quarry told the boatman to make for the inlet where the royal barges were moored.

Crouching low to duck under the canvas awning, Quarry stepped off the landing stage into the boat. Except for the conventional bows, the 'long-tailed' river taxi was shaped like a punt, the bench seats arranged one behind the other across the beam. The wooden backrest seemed to have been designed with the specific intention of causing the maximum discomfort in the lumbar region and the seat itself was so narrow that Quarry had to brace his feet in order not to slide off it. The motive power was supplied by a Packard V8 engine mounted on the stern which transmitted the drive to the propeller via a long spindle shaft that also doubled as the tiller.

The exhaust blatting, they moved downstream under the Memorial Bridge, past the church of Santa Cruz and the Temple of the Dawn. The river was mud-coloured, despoiled even further by rotting vegetation and driftwood from the wholesale fresh vegetable and fruit market adjoining the Klonghoi canal. They cruised on past the Royal Palace and the Buddhist temples of Wat Rakang and Wat Mahathat. Just beyond the Siriraj Hospital, the boatman put the helm over and turned left into Klong Bangkok Noi.

Quarry knew it was now up to him to guide them the rest of the way. Keeping his instructions simple, he directed the boatman into a narrow klong off to the left. The canals in Bangkok were completely different from those Quarry had seen elsewhere. There were no towpaths and the shacks lining the banks were built on stilts pile-driven into the muddy bottom. Each one had a veranda of sorts lit by a string of unshaded 60-watt bulbs and a pontoon jutting out into the main channel. Between the wooden shacks, Quarry could see a mass of palm fronds and occasionally the dark outline of a banyan tree.

One shack looked pretty much like any other and were for the most part unnumbered and unnamed. Obeying Quarry's instructions to go slowly, the boatman throttled right back until the engine was idling. Whenever their way fell off, he opened it up again, building the revs with a quick burst to give them steerage through the mass of lotus weed floating on the surface. As they rounded a long convex bend in the klong, Quarry spotted a small, round-shouldered European on one of the landing stages and knew from the description he'd been given that it was Gage. Ducking under the awning as they came alongside, Quarry joined him on the landing stage and told the boatman to wait.

"Don't pay the man," said Gage, "then he won't push off the moment your back is turned."

Quarry found it particularly galling that someone who hadn't been in Bangkok five minutes should presume to advise him how to deal with a Thai boatman. But he resisted a cutting retort and silently followed the more nimble-footed Gage along the bobbing pontoon into the shack. The family he was staying with were clustered round the colour TV in one corner of the room but they might just as well have been on another planet for all the notice he took of them.

"Make yourself at home, Group Captain," he said mockingly and waved him to an upright chair. "Can I get you a beer?"

"I'd rather we didn't turn this into a social occasion," Quarry said woodenly. "I've left my wife entertaining some people we'd invited to dinner and I'd like to conclude our business as soon as possible."

"Whatever you say, Group Captain." Gage went outside, leaned over the low veranda rail and fished a can of beer out of a crate suspended in the water. "The poor man's fridge," he said and laughed harshly.

"Can we get a move on?"

163

"Yes, indeed. I presume you told the Ambassador about my phone call earlier this evening?"

"Naturally."

"But not the resident SIS man?"

"I did everything you asked of me," Quarry told him.

It wasn't entirely true. Gage had insisted the SIS should be kept out of it but ten years ago he'd been one of their field officers and the Ambassador had decided the Foreign Office should be kept fully informed. Even before Quarry had left the embassy to keep his appointment with Gage, the cipher clerk had begun to encode a signal to London, copy to Hong Kong.

"Those loonies in Century House think my homecoming is the keystone of a KGB inspired disinformation exercise. If they have their way, they'll keep me locked up in one of their safe houses until they're satisfied they've picked my brain clean." Gage took a long swig from the beer can, then wiped his mouth on the back of his wrist. "Well, I'm not having that. I want you to arrange for me to be admitted to the Siriraj Hospital for a complete physical."

"A complete physical?" Quarry echoed disbelievingly.

"Blood test, smears, X-rays – every step to be monitored by a British doctor nominated by the Ambassador."

"Why on earth . . . ?"

"I have been told I have six months to live," Gage continued remorselessly, "but the SIS refuses to believe that I have cancer. As far as Century House is concerned, every X-ray the Vietnamese took is a fake, but they can't say that if the prognosis is confirmed by the doctors at the Siriraj Hospital."

"And then what?"

"The medical findings are to be laid before the Permanent Under Secretary at the Foreign Office. When he's satisfied my condition is terminal, I want a letter from the Minister of State guaranteeing I'll be left in peace when I come home."

Quarry wondered if he was dreaming. Everything was unreal, from the family sitting round the TV watching an old episode of *Kojak* to the impossible demands Gage was making.

164

"I'll convey your wishes to His Excellency," he said in a bewildered voice.

"Good." Gage made a fist, crushing the empty beer can before tossing it through the open window into the canal; then, beckoning Quarry to follow him, he walked out on to the pontoon. "There is one other small point, Group Captain," he said conversationally.

"Oh – what's that?"

"If I have to stay in hospital overnight, the embassy will have to pay for a private room and two extra beds for members of my family."

"What family?" Quarry asked.

"The people I'm staying with." Gage jerked a thumb over his shoulder in case there was still any doubt in Quarry's mind. "They're Viet Cong," he said. "The old man in the corner fought against the French, the Americans and the ARVN. When Saigon fell, he and others like him thought they would have a say in running the country, but the North Vietnamese had other ideas. I used my influence to get the whole family out of the country when things turned really sour on the old man. They feel they owe me an enormous debt of gratitude. That's why I know I'll be safe if they're around."

"Safe from whom?"

"The SIS," said Gage. "Who else?"

"Yes, of course. I should have known."

Quarry shook hands with him, then stepped off the landing stage into the river taxi. The boatman started the engine, slipped the prop shaft into drive and slowly pulled away from the pontoon.

As they approached the next bend in the canal, Quarry looked back and saw that Gage was still standing there, a frail, wizened figure in a pair of khaki-coloured slacks several sizes too large for him.

The date time group showed that the signal from Bangkok had been despatched at 1205 hours Greenwich Mean Time. With the clocks in London running an hour ahead of GMT,

Faulkner reckoned one of the cipher clerks would have spent most of his lunch hour decoding the message, which meant that it would have reached Charles Unger, the Director in charge of the Far East desk, shortly after two p.m. Unger had never been one to drag his feet but there was another reason why he would be quick to respond. All signals were given a precedence by the originator ranging from Deferred on up through Routine, Priority, Op Immediate, Emergency to Flash. The one from Bangkok carried an Emergency precedence which meant everything else would go into the pending tray until it had been dealt with.

As the information addressee, the copy to Hong Kong had been sent Priority and had therefore been received some time after London had decoded theirs. At the rate the duty cipher clerk was going, Faulkner thought it likely that Unger's response would arrive via the satellite link before he'd finished decoding the original message from Bangkok. He leaned over the clerk's shoulder. So far, only the first two of five paragraphs had been transposed but from the opening sentence of the next, it seemed they already had the main thrust. Gage had contacted the Defence Attaché and had made it very clear that although he still intended to return to the UK, he wasn't prepared to either meet or talk with anyone from the SIS. The rest of the signal looked as though the Ambassador had then indicated step by step what he proposed to do about the conditions Gage had demanded.

"I'd be grateful if you would spare me a minute of your time, Simon."

Ingram: everything about him grated on his nerves, the clipped voice, the air of self-importance and his condescension. Faulkner sighed aloud and turned slowly about to face the younger man. "Can't it wait until this signal from Bangkok has been decoded – it is rather important."

"So is this and I'm afraid it won't keep."

Faulkner gritted his teeth in an effort to contain his anger, then followed on. Closing the door to Ingram's office behind him, he leaned back against it, both hands thrust deep into his pockets. "Before we go any further," he said coldly, "I'd

166

like to remind you that while you may be the Head of Station out here, you're not my superior, nor are you ever likely to be. I'm answerable to Charles Unger and no one else; so don't you ever speak to me again the way you did just now."

"I wonder how Unger would react if the press got hold of your name?"

"Why should they?" Faulkner asked, genuinely puzzled.

"Because Cartwright proposes to give the *South China Mail* an exclusive story about his wife and how you used her to protect yourself ten years ago when an operation you were running went sour."

"That's ridiculous. I didn't shelter behind Sarah; if anything, it was the reverse. Furthermore, Cartwright doesn't have a story; the Saigon business still carries a Top Secret classification and for all we booted her out of the service, Sarah knows what would happen to her if she opened her mouth."

"I slapped a deportation order on him."

"You did what?"

Ingram avoided his eyes. "When I saw Cartwright earlier this evening, he told me that less than three days after his wife had disappeared, the body of their Swedish au-pair had been found in a junkyard at Brentford. She had been strangled."

"Was she attractive?"

"Very."

"Yes, well, no doubt the press will get a lot of mileage out of a juicy murder." Faulkner took out a packet of cigarettes and lit one. He was pleased to see that his hands were just as steady as his voice. "All the same, they can hardly make a big production out of the SIS angle. As far as the Foreign and Commonwealth Office is concerned, Sarah was a career diplomat and their official spokesman will say so loud and clear. He will have the Blue Book of 1975 to prove it."

"You think we should brazen it out?"

"I'm saying we can prove the allegation is pure fiction. On the other hand, you seem to be implying that we've got something to hide."

167

"Cartwright says his wife travelled to Hong Kong under the name of Ellen Rothman and was staying with Macready." Ingram busied himself with his pipe, filling it slowly and deliberately from a tin of St Bruno. "Two murders and an exceedingly attractive ex Foreign Office young wife and mother who's gone missing? I'd say the press would latch on to that as a hell of a good story."

"And in their eyes, the deportation order you've slapped on Cartwright will clinch it." Faulkner shook his head. "That's got to be the mistake of the year. What on earth made you do it?"

"There's a strong American press corps out here," Ingram said heatedly. "I didn't want the story syndicated in every newspaper in the States."

"There's more than a couple of American correspondents in London – or hadn't that occurred to you?"

"We can issue a 'D' notice in London and the newspapers will respect it because Cartwright is caught up in a murder inquiry. The whole case is therefore sub judice."

"Let's hope the press barons agree with you. Still, with Cartwright safely under lock and key, it's too late now for regrets."

"That's just it, we haven't got him locked up in the detention centre at Kai Tak."

"You mean he's escaped from custody?" Faulkner saw the look on the younger man's face and dissolved into laughter; ever since he'd arrived in Hong Kong, everything that could go wrong had gone wrong, even the things over which he had no control.

"I don't see what's so damned funny. Cartwright assaulted two police officers; now he's demanding I withdraw the deportation order and persuade the Commissioner of Police to drop the charges. Samuels is about to give him my office number and he'll be ringing me any minute now. When he does, I either cave in or I tell him to go to hell and we receive a lot of unwelcome publicity in the *South China Mail*. Now, what's it to be?"

"It's your decision."

"I'm asking for your advice, damn it," Ingram said irritably.

"I suppose you could always double-cross him, but he's probably smart enough to have foreseen that possibility and will have taken steps to protect himself." Faulkner moved forward and stubbed out his cigarette in the ashtray on Ingram's desk. "In the circumstances, my advice is to cancel the expulsion order."

"He'll come looking for you, Simon."

"He won't find me. Gage has surfaced in Bangkok and that's where I'm going first thing in the morning. I suppose Cartwright might run around looking for the mysterious Ellen Rothman and making a damned nuisance of himself in the process but if the police can't find her, he certainly won't." Faulkner started towards the door, then suddenly turned about. "I've just had a thought: if you think Cartwright will make himself a pain in the ass, you could always get the army to deal with him."

"How?"

"Easy," said Faulkner. "Get Land Forces to ask the Ministry of Defence if they know he's out here. Ten to one he didn't tell his superiors where he was going."

Jimmy's Bar had no connection whatever with Jimmy's Kitchen, the fashionable restaurant in the Central District. For one thing, it was located in Wanchai, for another it was a decidedly seamy night spot which attracted a totally different sort of clientele. Amongst the neon signs displayed above the entrance was one which said, 'Welcome Guys, Girls and Gays' in both English and Chinese. Inside, the music was loud, the décor even louder. The centrepiece of the oval-shaped bar consisted of two naked Filipino girls sitting back to back on a large pedestal that was just out of reach of the clientele, an attraction which had been copied from the much more plush 'Bottom Up' club in Kowloon. The hostesses were predominantly Chinese but amongst the other nationalities, there were a surprising number of Swedish and West German girls.

Quite a few of the most attractive hostesses were transvestites.

The only relatively quiet place was the manager's office next to the men's room. A fifty-dollar note pressed into the right hand enabled Cartwright to secure its exclusive use for a quarter of an hour. Locking himself in, he plugged the answering machine into the telephone and rang the number Samuels had given him when he'd called the central police station from the Mandarin Hotel a short while ago. The man who answered the phone was definitely on edge.

Cartwright said, "Your voice doesn't sound as familiar as it should; would you please identify yourself?"

"If you think you've got the wrong number, you'd better hang up."

"Just do as I ask, Mr Ingram."

"It's a bit pointless, isn't it, when you already know who I am?"

Ingram was fighting a rearguard action, determined to be as awkward as he could but the tape was running, recording his every word, and Cartwright knew he had him cold. His next step was to get the essential facts on record before the police traced the call. In a few terse and previously rehearsed sentences he said enough to incriminate the SIS and whet the appetite of a news-hungry editor.

"No one has to know about this can of worms, Mr Ingram," he said, winding up. "All you have to do is cancel the deportation order and square things with the Commissioner of Police."

"Yes."

"Does that mean we have a deal?"

"I'm still thinking about it."

"Would it help if I played our conversation back to you?"

"That won't be necessary," Ingram said woodenly. "I will arrange for the deportation order to be rescinded and I will talk to the commissioner about dropping the other matter you referred to."

"Good. I'd like that in writing, delivered by you in person

tomorrow morning at ten a.m. in front of a neutral witness at a pre-designated meeting place in the open air."

"What?"

"There's nothing wrong with your hearing, Mr Ingram. Just name the place."

"Victoria Peak, the car park near the tramway station."

"I'll look forward to meeting you again," Cartwright said and hung up.

All he had to do now was find a lawyer who would be willing to represent him and figure out a way to ensure a copy of the tape reached the editor of the *South China Mail* if Ingram tried to double-cross him. He also needed a place to rest his head and lie low for the next few hours. The very petite Chinese girl in a traditional cheongsam who accosted him as he left the manager's office was only too eager to provide that and a whole lot more besides, but she had only just emerged from the men's room and the shadow on her upper lip looked as though it would become a moustache by morning.

Le Khac Ly left the mass transit station at Tsun Wan and walked slowly towards the high-rise building where he lived with his wife and four children in a tiny four-room apartment on the eleventh floor. He had returned from Macau on the hovercraft departing at 1800 hours and had gone straight to his shop in Harbour City to check on the takings in his absence. His cousin in Macau had been in a very pessimistic mood and had succeeded in thoroughly depressing him. He had never dreamed the British would hand Hong Kong to Peking when their 99-year lease on the New Territories expired in 1997, but the impossible would be an established fact long before his only son became a man.

Le Khac Ly had no intention of staying on after the British left. There was no love lost between the Vietnamese and the Chinese and no matter how many assurances Peking might give, he was convinced the commercial heartland of the colony would soon wither and die once the Communists took over. His one aim in life now was to acquire sufficient capital in the remaining twelve years to start a new life in either England or America. Money however wasn't the complete answer: he needed someone to ease the way for his family. He wondered if Mademoiselle Lucas would be prepared to help him? Curious that he should think of her after all these years but the description of the woman whom his sales assistants said had called at the shop inquiring after him had sounded very much like her.

There was a marker on Le Khac Ly and the reception committee waiting for him in the hallway of the apartment block had learned of his return from Macau shortly after he'd walked into his shop. Including the look-out on the street, there were four of them, young men in their early twenties who were enforcers for the 14K Triad and had done this kind of thing before. Le Khac Ly sensed danger the moment he saw them and turned about to leave, but the look-out was behind him blocking the way. He took a hard blow on his spine and gasped in pain; then the look-out punched him in the stomach. Someone forced a ball gag into his mouth, a hood was pulled over his head and his elbows were bound together behind his back. Then they hustled him into the lift and forced him to sit down on the floor in one corner, his back against the wall.

He heard the door close; seconds later his stomach seemed to fall away as the lift began its ascent. Two men held him fast while a third used a pair of thin leather straps to pinion his legs around the ankles and above the knees. His only chance to save himself occurred when the lift stopped at one of the intermediate floors, but the gag reduced his cry for help to an incoherent mumble. One of the enforcers also made it very clear that no one else was welcome to share the lift and it was evident the unknown, unseen Chinese residents knew better than to quarrel with the Triads.

The lift bore them relentlessly upwards. When they reached the eighteenth floor, all four men grabbed the straps around his body and carried him like a carpet roll between them along the corridor and up the flight of steps leading to the roof. They stood him up near the low parapet and swiftly

172

prepared him for his execution, removing first the hood, then the straps which held him fast. He started screaming when they pulled the ball gag out of his mouth, but by that time it was far too late, and they picked him up again and hurled him off the roof, a pathetic little bundle in a grey pinstripe suit.

14

Sarah paid off the cab, found a porter to carry her suitcase and walked into the terminal building at Kai Tak. There were two Chinese police constables on duty in the main hall near the airline desks but neither one took the slightest notice of her. There was no reason why they should; Susan Lamidy was an Australian girl with a round face and dark hair streaked with blonde highlights. Two rubber pads fleshed out her angular features and the dark sunglasses hid the false eyelashes.

She looked up at the information screen in the concourse, saw that Thai International BK 711 departed for Bangkok at 0945 hours and went over to the airline desk. Simon had suggested that if the plane was fully booked, she could always fly Singapore Airlines and pick up a connecting flight from Changi but in the event, the counter clerk was able to offer her a choice of seats in the non-smoking section. The fact that she paid for the plane ticket with Hong Kong, US and Australian dollars was regarded as perfectly natural and the only bad moment came when she went through Immigration. It seemed to her that the woman officer spent an incredible amount of time looking at the entry stamp on page three as if she felt there was something about it which was not quite right. In the end, however, she found a blank space for the exit visa and returned the false passport to Sarah without a word.

She had a fistful of loose change, time to kill before Flight BK 711 started boarding and there were several vacant pay phones in the departure lounge. She thought about Tom alone in the poky little flat in Pelham Street and the urge to hear his voice again was irresistible. Even though a tape recording of their conversation would be analysed by the Security Service later in the day, it wouldn't be the end of the world. No doubt he would be a little surprised to hear from her at one thirty in the morning, but Wentworth could hardly have omitted to mention that his phone had been tapped when he briefed him and she could therefore rely on Tom to be discreet. Arranging a pile of loose change on top of the coin box, Sarah found she had just enough money for a three minute call and punched out the international code, area and subscriber's number.

The phone started ringing and went on ringing long after she would have expected Tom to pick it up. It was there by his bedside and there was no way he could fail to hear its shrill tone unless he had fallen into bed drunk and incapable the night before, which would be totally out of character. She began to wonder if Wentworth had briefed Tom after all and whether, being unaware of the true facts, he had taken her farewell note literally. But that was ridiculous; even supposing he did believe that she had left him, he wouldn't have moved out of his flat in London.

Perhaps he was finding solace in someone else's bed? It had happened once before when she had returned to England ostensibly to supervise certain renovations to Manor Farm and Tom had been left on his own in Cyprus. What was the name of that nymphomaniac who was married to a half-colonel in the Ordnance Corps? Janet? Jennifer? Jessica? Julia? Yes – Julia. No one in trousers was safe when she was around, especially a junior officer. She should never have gone home and left the field clear because Tom had never stood a chance once that predator had begun to stalk him.

A marital squabble, which she had provoked, had paved the way for the previous affair; now it looked as though she had unwittingly precipitated another. She put the thought out of her mind and hung up. Tom was older, wiser and far more level-headed; he simply wouldn't have accepted her letter at face value. He would have questioned everything she had said in it and compared notes with Fay. Tom had always confided in her mother.

175

Sarah turned about to check the latest flight information on the TV screen before phoning Market Harborough, and froze. Although the man standing outside the duty free shop had his back to her, there was no mistaking who he was. Knowing Simon Faulkner was bound to see her the moment he looked round, she moved away from the bank of telephones and sat down in one of the easy chairs.

'I'd like to slip you into Bangkok because sooner or later, Gage is going to surface in Thailand and you'd be in place when he does.' Simon had implied that he was sending her on ahead; his sudden and last minute change of plan could only mean Matthew Gage had made contact.

The first minibus on a 'Round the Island' tour pulled into the car park on Victoria Peak shortly after nine fifty and disgorged a dozen camera-clicking Japanese. Ingram arrived by the Peak tram from Garden Road some ten minutes later and wandered over to one of the souvenir shops outside the station. He was the only man wearing a collar and tie, lightweight suit and Panama hat. Although there didn't appear to be any police officers in the vicinity, Cartwright doubted if he would have made himself quite so conspicuous unless they were keeping the car park under surveillance. Unwilling to take any chances, he waited another ten minutes, then leaving the viewpoint overlooking Happy Valley, he went over to the SIS man and tapped him on the shoulder.

"Do you get the feeling we're being watched, Mr Ingram?" he asked.

"I came alone."

"I didn't." Cartwright steered him away from the shops and out into the open where he had a clear view of the parking area. "Third row back from us, extreme left, last but one car – a red Porsche. You see it?"

"Yes."

"Good, watch this."

Cartwright raised his left arm until it was fully extended above his head, then closed the thumb and little finger.

Responding to his signal, a small dark-haired man in a pale blue shirt and tan-coloured slacks detached himself from a knot of people clustered round a soft drinks vendor and walked over to the sports car. Stopping in front of the vehicle, he looked straight at Cartwright and waved.

"My lawyer."

"But he's Chinese," said Ingram.

"You noticed."

"How much does he know?"

"Enough. He has a key to a safe deposit box which contains several tapes of our conversation and he's been given a list of people who are to receive them should anything happen to me. Putting a tail on him will get you nowhere because I've told him to assume he's being watched from this moment on. That means you won't know who is going to collect the package or where from or when."

"You fool. What makes you think he'll stick to the rules?"

"He's a lawyer and has his reputation to consider. What happens from here on is up to you."

Ingram reached inside his jacket and brought out an envelope. "I believe this is what you want," he said.

Inside the envelope was a copy of a letter from the Immigration Department cancelling the deportation order and another from the Director of Public Prosecutions to the Commissioner of Police stating there was insufficient evidence to obtain a conviction on a charge of assault occasioning actual bodily harm.

"I trust you are happy with the arrangements?" Ingram said, watching him closely.

"As far as they go."

"Are you about to renege on our agreement?"

"No, but I do need a little extra cover." Cartwright smiled. "You see, I've just remembered that it's standard practice for the police to inform the army whenever they arrest an officer or soldier."

"The military authorities have already been informed that the deportation order has been withdrawn."

"Unfortunately, that may not be the end of the problem,"

177

Cartwright replied smoothly. "I didn't put Hong Kong down as a leave address and there's a Major Pringle on the staff of Land Forces who got his knuckles rapped on my account. I could have the Military Police breathing down my neck."

"I'm afraid I can't help you there."

"You don't have any choice, Mr Ingram. It doesn't matter what colour hat he's wearing, a policeman is still a policeman so far as my friend with the Porsche is concerned. If the MPs do pick me up, I'll give the Provost Marshal your number and suggest he contacts you. Then you can tell him I'm working for Century House."

Ingram nodded, his face impassive except for a thin smile which flickered briefly. "When is your leave up?"

"Next Thursday. I suppose there's no chance of you getting me an extension if I need it?"

"None whatever," Ingram said grimly.

"All right, I'll settle for half an hour with Simon Faulkner instead."

"You'll be lucky, he left for Bangkok earlier this morning."

And Sarah would have gone with him, but not as Ellen Rothman. She had been staying with the late Mr Macready under that cover and the police were looking for her.

"Can you persuade the Immigration Department to check their records?" Cartwright asked.

"Depends on what they're supposed to be looking for."

"The name of the woman on the Bangkok flight who never arrived in Hong Kong. When you know who she is, ring me at the Ambassador Hotel."

"And then what?"

"Before I leave Hong Kong, I'll give you my friend's telephone number and a codeword he'll recognise. Then you can make whatever arrangements you like to collect the safe deposit box."

"I don't think I like you, Major Cartwright."

"The feeling's mutual, Mr Ingram, but once you give me that name, we don't have to see each other again."

178

"How right you are."

Ingram turned about and walked away from him. More and more tourists were beginning to arrive by hired car, bus, taxi and the Peak tramway. Long before he reached the station, the SIS Resident was swallowed up in the milling crowd.

Quarry glanced at his wristwatch and frowned in annoyance; 1135 and the morning almost gone. Instead of dancing attendance on a sick expatriate who wanted someone to hold his hand, he ought to be at his desk in the embassy, mugging up on the hardware the Defence Ministry's Procurement Executive were anxious the Thais should buy. The ambassador however had decided otherwise and had made it very clear that whatever Matthew Gage asked for he was to receive.

The renegade Englishman had been calling the tune ever since he had contacted him at his private residence yesterday evening and would continue to do so until all his conditions had been satisfied. Quarry had assumed the embassy would tell Gage when he was to report for a medical examination, but the old defector had had other ideas. Shortly after Quarry had arrived at his office that morning, Gage had telephoned to say that he was at the Siriraj Hospital and where was the embassy's doctor? Obtaining his services hadn't been a problem even though he had been thoroughly disgruntled when the Head of Chancery had virtually ordered him to cancel his morning surgery and get himself over to the hospital. It was the Thai medical authorities who'd proved the more awkward and it had taken all the ambassador's considerable charm to win them round.

Quarry wasn't sure what his precise role was in the scheme of things. The embassy's doctor was obviously a neutral observer and the impassive Vietnamese seated opposite him in the hospital corridor was there as a bodyguard even though he didn't appear to be armed. Head of Chancery had smilingly told him that he was to be the ambassador's personal liaison officer but the way things

179

were working out in practice, it was beginning to look as though he was simply a messenger boy at the beck and call of Matthew Gage.

Quarry heard a door open farther down the corridor, glanced to his left and saw Gage emerge from X-ray. In the course of a very thorough examination, the Thais had sounded his chest, poked, prodded and weighed him; they had also taken enough blood for several dozen slides and had practically swabbed his throat dry. Although from a layman's point of view they appeared to have covered the entire field, it had been Quarry's experience in the RAF that there was no limit to the curiosity shown by members of the medical profession and he looked to the embassy's man for guidance.

"We're finished for the day," Gage informed him and left it to the doctor to confirm his statement with a nod. "All we do now is sit back and wait for the results, Group Captain."

Quarry turned to the embassy's medical officer. "And how long is that likely to be?" he asked.

"We'll have the results of the X-rays tomorrow. If they confirm the case notes Doctor Gage brought with him, we needn't wait on the blood tests."

"There's no 'if' about it, gentlemen."

For someone who was under sentence of death, Gage was surprisingly cheerful. Like many an investigative journalist, it seemed he positively thrived on bad news.

"I'll let you know as soon as we hear from the hospital," Quarry said coldly.

"The letter from the Minister of State for the Foreign and Commonwealth Office is the only thing that interests me, Group Captain. I don't want to cool my heels in this country a day longer than I have to."

"I'll get in touch the moment we receive it."

"No. I'll contact you every afternoon at five. That will give you people almost two hours to go through the contents of the diplomatic bag after it's been collected from the airport." Gage broke off, his whole body suddenly racked by a paroxysm of coughing that left him breathless when it was over. "I can see you're bursting to say something," he wheezed, "and I can guess what it is. You're going to tell me I needn't go to all that trouble – right?"

"It does seem a little unnecessary when I know where you're staying."

"That's just it, you don't. Maybe you did last night, but not today and certainly not tomorrow." Gage poked him in the chest with a bony finger. "You understand what I'm hinting at, Group Captain?"

"Yes. You like to keep on the move."

"What a diplomatic fellow you are," Gage said and cackled mirthlessly.

"What did you expect me to say? That I think you're scared of your own shadow?"

"I've every reason to be." He turned away and hobbled off towards the hospital entrance, leaning heavily on the shoulder of the slim young Vietnamese he called 'Nephew'. Nearing the swing doors, he stopped abruptly and looked back to deliver a parting shot. "I know my days are numbered," he rasped, "but I'm in no hurry to go before my time."

It was the kind of defiant pronouncement Quarry had come to expect from him.

The Thai International Airways flight to Bangkok took a shade over two and a half hours. By the time Sarah had cleared Customs and Immigration, it was past one o'clock, the temperature had soared to 98 degrees Fahrenheit and the humidity was averaging ninety-six per cent. The air-conditioning system in the Honda taxi wasn't functioning properly and within minutes the silk blouse she was wearing had become stained with patches of sweat. The traffic which had started to build up on the two-lane highway leading into town, became a solid phalanx as they neared the President Hotel on Rama I Road. Trucks, scooters, motor bikes and Thuk Thuks, the highly manoeuvrable but noisy three-wheeler taxis, moved on down the broad avenue six abreast. On those clear stretches between the stop lights at major

181

intersections, practically every driver behaved as though they were taking part in a Formula One Grand Prix.

Nothing very much had changed since the last time Sarah had been in Bangkok. The cacophony was deafening and embraced every note from the deep pulsating throb of the juggernaut transporters to the nerve-jangling screech of the motor scooters, and the air she breathed was still the same unique blend of petrol and diesel fumes, fried noodles and jasmine.

The air-conditioned lobby of the President provided an oasis of peace and quiet; so was the room on the fourth floor which Simon Faulkner had reserved for her. Tipping the bellboy thirty-five bahts, she hung a 'Do Not Disturb' sign on the door, closed and locked it behind her; then she removed the wig and unpinned her dark auburn hair. She had discarded the ridiculous face pads soon after boarding the plane in Hong Kong and the Immigration Officer at Bangkok hadn't even given her a second glance. Passport photographs invariably bore little resemblance to the person they were supposed to identify and in a busy hotel like the President, the desk clerk was unlikely to recall there had been blonde highlights in her hair when she had checked in.

Sarah glanced at her wristwatch; Bangkok was seven hours ahead of Greenwich Mean Time and her parents would still be in bed. On the other hand, there was no Direct International Dialling facility in Thailand yet and if she didn't book a call soon, she could be faced with a long wait. She felt an overwhelming desire for some contact with her family, to hear her mother's voice and news of her children, but most of all the reassurance that Tom still cared about her.

Lifting the receiver, she buzzed the hotel switchboard only to learn there was already a forty minute delay on all calls to the UK. In fact, Sarah had just stepped out of the shower and was still towelling herself down when the operator rang back to say the Market Harborough number was unobtainable.

"Are you sure?" Sarah asked.

"Quite sure. The operator in London told me there was a fault on the line. She said she would report it."

"Is there a forty minute delay on all calls to England?"

"I think it could be longer. Do you want me to try again later?"

"I'll let you know," Sarah said and hung up.

She considered the possibility that Tom hadn't heard the telephone when she had rung from Kai Tak, then quickly discounted the notion as pure wishful thinking. Although Tom was a heavy sleeper, the phone was only an arm's length away and even if he had turned the volume right down, the residual bird-like trill was still more effective than any alarm clock. Had it been a normal working day, she could have contacted him at the Empress State Building but, as it was, she could only try Manor Farm in the hope that he'd gone home for the weekend. Buzzing the operator again, Sarah booked a call to Codford St Mary 379. But when the phone rang twenty minutes later, it was Simon Faulkner on the line.

"Giles Trant," he said, "British Council. Your plane arrived on time then, Miss Lamidy?"

"It was a very smooth flight."

"Good. So how's everything else? Are you settled in okay?"

"Yes."

"What's your room like?"

"Very luxurious. It's on the fourth floor overlooking the courtyard." Irritably, she wondered how much longer Simon was going to keep up the meaningless chit-chat for the benefit of the switchboard operator.

"I have your lecture notes in front of me," he said, abruptly changing the subject, "and it occurs to me we could provide a few visual aids which you might find useful. Perhaps we could get together and discuss things over a cup of coffee?"

"When?"

"Four o'clock would suit me. Let's meet in the cafeteria on the third floor of the Central Department Store. It's just along the road from your hotel."

183

Sarah told him she'd be there, then rang the switchboard again to inquire about her call to Codford St Mary. To her dismay, she learned there was now an hour and a half's delay on the UK link.

For the umpteenth time that afternoon, Ingram stared at the name he had printed in block capitals on his scratch pad and vowed that within the next few minutes he would make up his mind what to do with the information he had received from Immigration. Ellen Rothman had arrived in Hong Kong on Saturday the fifteenth of June and, according to their records, was still in the colony. At Ingram's request, Immigration had accepted this as an established fact and had fed into their computer the names of everyone who had left Hong Kong between the sixteenth of June and the departure of Thai International Airways Flight BK 711 that morning, and had then matched them with their respective arrival dates. Miss Susan Lamidy was the only name which had mismatched. Although the flight manifest showed that she had been on the Thai Airways plane to Bangkok, Immigration had been unable to establish when she had arrived in Hong Kong. Ingram was therefore ninety-nine per cent certain that Ellen Rothman and Susan Lamidy were one and the same person. His only problem lay in deciding whether or not he should pass the information on to Cartwright.

He wished to God that Charles Unger, the Deputy Director in charge of the Far East Division at Century House, had seen fit to brief him in depth about the Gage Inquiry. Amongst other things, he would like to have known just what terms of reference Simon Faulkner had been given. Specifically, he wanted to know if Faulkner had been authorised to smuggle Sarah Cartwright in and out of Hong Kong. If it had been done officially, then briefing Major Cartwright would be a gross breach of security. Conversely, if the normal immigration procedures had been circumvented without Unger's knowledge, he could well find himself on the mat for aiding and abetting Faulkner should things go sour.

The telephone saved Ingram from making a decision. Answering it, he found himself dealing with a very irritated Chief Superintendent.

"I've got a dead Vietnamese called Le Khac Ly," Samuels growled. "What do you know about him?"

"Nothing," Ingram assured him in all honesty.

"He took a dive off an eighteen-storey tenement block in Tsun Wan last night. The neighbours say he committed suicide, his wife claims he was murdered by one of the Triads."

"He still doesn't ring a bell with me."

"His wife had a visitor late on Wednesday afternoon, an English woman called Sarah Lucas whom the Le Khac Lys had known in Saigon when she was in charge of the Mission House." Samuels paused, then said, "What were you people trying to do – pass yourselves off as members of the Salvation Army?"

"Don't ask me, I wasn't there. That's why I can't tell you anything about Le Khac Ly. Of course, I'm not denying that Sarah Lucas was a Second Secretary in the Foreign and Commonwealth until she resigned ten years ago to marry this fellow Cartwright."

"I think we're making progress."

"Furthermore, we wouldn't stand in your way should you want to question Mrs Cartwright."

"We've got to find her first, Roger."

"Quite."

"My spies tell me you've had Immigration run a check on Ellen Rothman?"

Ingram smiled. Whatever the end result, no one could possibly accuse him of committing a major breach of security now. "Then I expect you already know that she left Hong Kong this morning, travelling under the name of Susan Lamidy?"

"Sure I do. But can I use the information?"

"I don't see how we can possibly stop you," Ingram said smoothly.

"The question of who has prior jurisdiction over Mrs

185

Cartwright will have to be settled with the Home Office in London, and we'll also have to apply for extradition, which means involving the Foreign Office."

"You must handle the situation as you see fit."

"Thanks for the green light, Roger."

"Don't mention it. I imagine you'll be having a quiet word with Cartwright about the lady before you send him on his way?"

"I can take a hint," Samuels told him.

Ingram put the phone down. Experience had taught him to leave nothing to chance and he would need to call the Ambassador Hotel to make sure Samuels had indeed pointed Cartwright in the right direction, but first things first. Taking out a message pad, he drafted a Top Secret Op Immediate signal to Bangkok, addressed Personal For SIS Resident. It read: PLEASE ADVISE FAULKNER THAT HONG KONG POLICE DEPARTMENT HAS CHECKED ALL ARRIVALS AND DEPARTURES FOR LAST TWO MONTHS WITH IMMIGRATION AND ARE AWARE THAT SARAH CARTWRIGHT ALSO KNOWN AS ELLEN ROTHMAN AND SUSAN LAMIDY DEPARTED FOR YOUR LOCATION ON THAI INTERNATIONAL FLIGHT BK 711 THIS MORNING(.) UNDERSTAND HKPD ARE APPROACHING HOME OFFICE AND FCO LONDON FOR ADVICE ON JURISDICTION AND EXTRADITION PROCEDURE(.)

186

15

The cafeteria on the third floor of the Central Department Store was merely a convenient rendezvous. From there, Simon Faulkner steered her to the Siam Centre via the footbridge spanning Rama I Road before exiting into the parallel street behind the complex, where he flagged down a passing cab. What followed was a haphazard tour of the city; avoiding the main avenues, the driver traversed China Town and subsequently headed north on Mahachai towards the National Assembly and Royal Palace. Long before then, Simon Faulkner had satisfied himself that the driver's comprehension of English was extremely limited.

"What happened to the blonde highlights?" he asked tersely.

"They didn't suit me," Sarah told him. "I may have needed a wig to get past Immigration at Kai Tak but it was becoming a positive liability in this heat. No one gave me a second glance when I checked into the hotel so I figured I could dispense with it."

"I don't suppose it matters, you'll be getting your own passport back any day now."

"You've heard from Gage?"

"Only indirectly. He's using Group Captain William Quarry, our Defence Attaché, as a messenger boy. Gage went for a complete medical check-up at the Siriraj Hospital this morning – X-rays, blood tests, the lot. We shan't know the results until tomorrow but the embassy's doctor reckons he has terminal cancer. Apparently, he can tell that just by looking at him." Faulkner clucked his tongue. "I wish I knew what Matthew is up to."

"As far as I'm concerned, Simon, the disinformation theory is no longer tenable."

"Oh really? According to Quarry, we're planning to liquidate him, which is pretty ironic considering he's a dying man. Anyway, that's why he's gone to ground again."

"He's disappeared?"

"Yes, somewhere up-country. He told Quarry he'd call him tomorrow to learn the results of his physical."

Faulkner leaned forward and with the aid of sign language, told their driver to turn right at the next intersection. Sarah thought they were circling the royal palace with the intention of doubling back on their tracks but it was hard to tell in the dark. The night had closed in rapidly, the way it always did in the Far East. There was no gradual transition: one moment the sun was sliding below the horizon, then an instant later it was pitch black as though someone had drawn the curtains and switched off all the lights in a room.

"You might not believe this, but Matthew's actually had the gall to ask for a letter signed by the Minister of State guaranteeing his safe conduct."

"It's understandable," Sarah volunteered. "After all, he has been living in a Communist country for the past ten years."

"I don't know how you can be so tolerant when Gage has it in his power to crucify you. Of course, we're all vulnerable but you're the one who's most at risk."

Sarah didn't need reminding. There had been a large question mark against her name ever since she had been captured by the Viet Cong. Losing a cool four and a half million, mislaying a Top Secret Op Immediate signal, and allowing a clutch of highly classified files to fall into enemy hands had been bad enough, but the fact that the North Vietnamese had released her a mere fourteen days after she had been put into the bag had really made the SIS sit up and take notice. To this day, there was a faction in Century House led by Charles Unger, the former head of the South-East Asia Bureau in Singapore, who were convinced she had made a deal with the Communists. But worst of all, she had been unable to confide in Tom and there had been many occasions in the past when she had despised herself for deceiving him.

"The North Vietnamese certainly didn't do me any favours," Sarah observed wryly. "I sometimes think clearing my name would have been relatively easy had I spent a couple of years in the cooler. There's nothing like a long spell in solitary confinement to arouse the sympathy of the people who are debriefing you."

"I did the best I could for you."

"I know you did, Simon, and I'm very grateful."

"And no matter how long you'd been inside, your security file would still have been marked with a grey card."

He was probably right, but it no longer mattered whether her file was black, white or grey. That part of her life was over and she had no desire to resurrect the past. Her sole concern was to bury it once and for all.

"I don't believe Matthew intends to stir things up," she said, returning to her pet theme. "He knows he's dying and there's nothing to keep him in Vietnam."

"All right, have it your way; there's no malice aforethought, he just wants to come home and live out the rest of his days in peace in some ivy-covered cottage deep in the heart of Wiltshire." Faulkner took out a packet of cigarettes, lit one and slowly exhaled. "Question is, where is he going to find the money for this idyllic existence?"

"I don't know."

"He won't be getting a pension from us and the Vietnamese certainly won't have allowed him to bring any money out of the country. Supplementary benefit won't feed and clothe him and pay the rent on the cottage, so he'll have to look elsewhere for the readies. And who's going to provide him with a nice little nest egg?"

"One of our mass circulation dailies?"

"Damn right," said Faulkner. "What press baron could resist his story? I can just see the headlines – 'Former Agent Claims SIS Raised Secret Army in Vietnam – Wilson Government Not Told'."

"Was the PM informed?" Sarah asked.

"The Director General never confided in me, so I couldn't say. But whatever did or did not happen, there'll be one hell of a storm when the story breaks. As Gage never signed the Official Secrets Acts, I don't see how we can prevent him from bursting into print, especially if he includes all the salacious bits."

"What salacious bits?"

"You and me." Faulkner laughed mirthlessly and almost choked himself on a lungful of cigarette smoke. "Field Director and Intelligence Officer involved in sex orgy after pot party," he wheezed. "Need I say more?"

The bile welled up in her throat and she thought she was going to be sick. The love affair with Simon Faulkner had finished long before the SIS had gone into Vietnam. Concerned not to bruise his ego, she had let him down gently and, as a result, they'd remained good friends. The incident he'd referred to had occurred roughly four months after they'd arrived in Saigon. They had gone up-country with Le Khac Ly to liaise with Matthew Gage at Hieu Thien and had spent several days touring the province to see how the village cadres were progressing. Although supposedly a safe zone, the roads were frequently mined by the VC and it was not unknown for the odd vehicle travelling alone to be ambushed. The knowledge that this could happen to them at any time had generated an atmosphere of unbearable tension and they had been in a mood to really unwind at the party Matthew had arranged for them the night before they returned to Saigon.

The guests had included a German correspondent, two American Peace Corps Volunteers and a Danish couple who both worked for the Westinghouse Corporation selling colour TV sets and transistor radios. The drink had flowed like water and one of the Americans had offered her a joint which she had smoked as an experiment. After that, things had got out of control and, as a dare, she and the Danish wife had ended up doing a striptease to a Billy Rose recording of 'The Stripper'. The next thing she remembered was waking

190

up to find herself naked and in bed with the Danish girl. One arm had been resting across her stomach in a possessive sort of way, but it was only after she'd staggered into the bathroom to be sick that she had seen the bites on her neck and had realised the full enormity of what apparently had happened.

"Are you feeling all right?" Faulkner inquired anxiously.

"I think I'm going to be sick."

She half turned her back on him and retched. Before she could ask him to, he stubbed out his cigarette, then leaned across to wind the window down. At the same time, he somehow managed to make the driver understand that he wanted him to pull over to the kerb and stop. She retched again and a dribble of bile escaped from her mouth and splattered the door panel.

"I'm making a mess of this car," she said feebly.

"No one's going to notice, the state it's in," he said, and gently squeezed her shoulder.

He talked to her soothingly as though she were a child who'd had a bad nightmare and was now frightened to be left alone in the dark. Even as she listened to him, Sarah realised it was a form of brain-washing which anaesthetised her guilty conscience and left her with the feeling that she had been absolved of all responsibility. Simon had used the same technique the morning they'd left Hieu Thien for Saigon, accepting the blame for what had happened the night before and asking her to forgive him. 'It was the bloody grass, it made us behave like animals. I should have put a stop to it the moment Gage encouraged those Americans to share their reefers with his guests.' She remembered his words as though it was only yesterday.

"I didn't mean to upset you, Sarah."

"I know you didn't." She wondered how many times they'd had the same conversation over the years.

"We can limit the amount of damage Matthew can do to us if we handle him carefully. We're not dealing with some disgruntled former employee who's been shabbily treated and has written his memoirs in order to get his own back.

191

We're talking about an ex part-time agent who, of his own free will, spent ten years behind the Bamboo Curtain. At least, that's the story we'll put about in London and it should make any editor think twice before chasing after him with a blank cheque . . ."

She began to feel a little better and rummaged through her shoulder bag for a tissue to wipe her mouth, only to have Simon press a large polka-dot silk handkerchief into her hand.

"Here, use this," he said, then instructed the cab driver to move on before reverting to his proposals for dealing with Matthew Gage. "If he writes a book, there are ways and means of delaying publication until after he's dead, when it won't have quite the same impact. Of course, that's a last ditch option; we must aim to get everything settled out here before the Grub Street Brigade get hold of him. We've got to make Gage an offer he can't resist and take it from there. Meantime, you must continue to lie low and talk to no one, least of all the folks back home." Faulkner reached for her hand and squeezed it affectionately. "Just hang in there, Sarah, it'll all come right in a day or two."

Simon was a little too close to the truth for comfort. It was as if he knew that she had tried to phone her family.

"I hope so," she murmured.

"Trust me, it will." He squeezed her hand again. "This is where we part company."

Sarah glanced about her, realised they had stopped in the side road by the President Hotel, and got out of the cab. She walked round the block, lifting her arm in a farewell gesture as Simon's taxi overtook her, and entered the lobby through the main entrance. Riding the lift up to the fourth floor, she took the room key from her shoulder bag, unlocked the door and reached for the light switch in the hall.

On more than one occasion, Simon Faulkner had told her that she must be clairvoyant. It had been a standing joke with him, but in fact, she did possess a curious sixth sense which sometimes enabled her brain to receive a picture a fleeting second before her eyes actually saw it. When the hall

192

remained in darkness after she had tripped the switch, she knew two men were waiting for her, one inside the bathroom immediately to her left, the other round the corner of the L-shaped suite.

The image was clear and she didn't bother to consider the possibility that the light bulb had blown; slamming the door in their faces, she ran towards the fire escape and went on down the staircase, tackling each flight at breakneck speed. The emergency exit on the ground floor opened into a shopping mall directly behind the hotel and from there she made her way into Ratchadamri Road. No less than four Thuk Thuks responded when she raised her left arm to signal for a cab. Scrambling into the foremost three-wheeler, Sarah told the driver to take her to the Victory Monument, one of the few landmarks she could remember from the last time she was in Bangkok.

The other Thuk Thuks began to pull out from the kerb, their drivers on the look-out for a fare. Tail-end Charlie didn't have to travel very far to find one. Before he'd covered more than a few yards, the shrill note of a police whistle brought him to a dead stop to pick up two men who'd surfaced from amongst the crowd of pedestrians on the pavement. They did not appear to be in a hurry, nor were they even vaguely familiar, but Sarah knew instinctively they were the same two men who had been waiting for her in the hotel room.

The driver turned left at the first major intersection, beating the traffic lights a split second before they changed to red. Lane hopping whenever he saw a gap, he tried to beat the lights just short of the Victory Monument and was baulked by a single-decker bus. By the time they changed to green, the other Thuk Thuk had caught up with them. The British Embassy was the only safe haven Sarah could think of but the duty clerical officer was the only person who was likely to be on the premises and it was doubtful if the security guards would even allow her into the compound. That however was a problem she would put her mind to once she had shaken off her pursuers. In basic English, supplemented with a mixture of every language she thought the driver might recognise, Sarah got him to circle the Monument and double back to the main centre on Phyathai Road past the Century, EMI and Athens.

Romancing the Stone was showing at the Hollywood. Amongst the crowd gathering for the five-thirty performance were four naval ratings from HMS *Birmingham*, a Type 42 destroyer on a good-will visit to Bangkok. They were in turn surprised, flattered and highly delighted when a striking redhead asked if she might join them.

Faulkner paid off the cab driver outside the British Embassy on Rama I Road, showed his temporary pass to the nightwatchman on duty in the forecourt and scarcely managed to contain his impatience while the man slowly removed the padlock and chain securing the wrought-iron gates. Gaining admittance to the embassy itself proved even more frustrating and he was obliged to keep his thumb on the doorbell for several minutes before the locally employed security guard eventually condescended to put in an appearance. The time-consuming way he subsequently examined the pass suggested that either he'd never seen one before or else he was practically illiterate and had difficulty reading it. The wireless room was on the floor above, next to the central registry in the secure area; even though he could find nothing wrong with the entry permit, the guard still made Faulkner sign the visitor's book before he would allow him to go upstairs.

The signal was classified Top Secret, carried an Op Immediate precedence and was addressed Personal for the SIS Resident. The first sentence was enough to set his pulse racing, the second made him sick with apprehension.

"When did you receive this signal?" he asked the duty clerk.

"1625 hours. The Resident saw it twenty minutes later, after it had been decoded." The clerical officer reversed the signal log so that Faulkner could check the entries for himself. "I'm sorry you weren't informed sooner but no one at the Sheraton Hotel seemed to know where you were. The only thing I could do was leave a message with reception."

"I was at Group Captain Quarry's house; there were matters we had to discuss which couldn't wait. I gave the desk clerk his home number but obviously he failed to record it."

He wondered why he should feel obliged to give the clerical officer such a fulsome explanation. In terms of their respective seniority, the man was a nobody. He just hoped he hadn't given him the impression that he was attempting to establish some sort of cover story to account for his absence from the hotel.

"Do you want me to sign for the cable?" Faulkner asked.

"You're really only an info addressee, sir," the clerical officer said diplomatically. "Perhaps it would be best if you merely initialled the flimsy to indicate that you have seen it."

Faulkner borrowed the clerk's Biro, then signed and dated the copy. If the clerical officer hadn't been quite so sharp, he could have put the clear text and encrypted message through the shredder and apologised profusely for making such a stupid mistake. Unfortunately, the damned thing was now going to be on record for ever.

"I'll have to make the odd phone call." Faulkner went over to the keyboard and removed the one belonging to the SIS Resident. "If anyone should want me, I'll be in Room 11."

The only thing which distinguished Room 11 from the offices of the other First Secretaries was the fact that the plaque outside the door failed to indicate precisely what the occupant was First Secretary of. Otherwise, the furniture was exactly the same, from the executive-style desk to the secret waste destructor. The photographs either side of the blotter were of course different: they were of a very ordinary-looking woman and two equally plain children. Even if he hadn't had more important things on his mind, Faulkner would not have found the photographs a distraction.

1848 hours. Back in England it was almost twelve noon on

a Saturday morning. Had this been a normal week-end, Charles Unger would now be approaching the 18th green, but not today. This was one Saturday when he wouldn't stray from his home in Oxford despite the bleeper and the radio telephone with secure speech facility which the engineers from Century House had installed in his Daimler Sovereign.

Faulkner was by no means clear what he was going to say to 'Fat Little Charlie' and was still undecided when the international operator connected him after a thirty minute delay. Unger was shrewd, intelligent, perceptive and a brilliant operative and he hadn't got where he was today without being a bit of a slippery customer. Whenever the shit hit the fan, he was the one person in the vicinity who never got sprayed. It was typical of 'Fat Little Charlie' that he should give the impression he was surprised to hear from him. Knowing Unger of old, Faulkner was sure that their conversation was being recorded and would be used by him to prove his innocence should the necessity arise.

"Something's come up," Faulkner said bluntly, "and I need a few answers from you. I've just been informed by Ingram that our former colleague, Sarah Cartwright, is on the way here from Hong Kong."

"Careful, Simon, this is an open line."

"I'm aware of that. The thing is, she's travelling under the name of Susan Lamidy and I just wondered if you knew anything about it?"

"Have you taken leave of your senses?"

"Yes or no?" Faulkner demanded.

"I'm going to hang up."

"What about the letter Gage wants from the Minister of State?"

There was a loud clunk as Unger put the phone down to prevent him asking any more awkward questions.

Smiling to himself, Faulkner returned the key to the Central Registry, secure in the knowledge that the damage had already been done. Slippery Charlie could expunge their conversation but he was in for the shock of a lifetime if he

196

seriously believed that that would save his hide. Obtaining the signal again from the duty clerical officer, Faulkner added a footnote to the effect that he had discussed the implications with Unger in their telephone conversation of twenty-two June at 1920 hours local time. No one would be able to dispute the veracity of his claim; within the next few days, the embassy would receive corroboratory evidence in the shape of a bill from the telephone company.

The Gage affair was bad news all round. Faulkner just wanted to make sure Charles Unger realised that they either sank or swam together.

16

The central police station in Kowloon was about the last place Cartwright wanted to see again, but Samuels had said just enough on the phone to convince him it would be worth his while to make one final visit. Although he was inclined to think that Samuels had deliberately withheld the results of the computer check until after the last flight to Bangkok had departed, it was difficult to see what the Canadian hoped to gain by forcing him to stay over one more night. Ingram knew he wouldn't get the vital codeword and telephone number until minutes before he left Hong Kong and there was no way the SIS man would allow Samuels to foul things up.

Cartwright waved his passport at the English-speaking police constable on duty outside the entrance, informed the Chinese officer that Chief Superintendent Samuels was expecting him and was promptly directed to the desk in the main hall. One internal phone call later, he was shown into the Assistant Commissioner's office on the first floor. The Canadian even acted as though he was pleased to see him.

"Can I offer you a drink?" he asked, after they'd shaken hands. "Whisky, gin, vodka, beer?" Samuels crouched in front of a free-standing bookcase and gazed at the array of bottles behind the glass sliding door. "We seem to have all the proprietary brands here."

"Whisky?" Cartwright asked.

"You got it. Soda, ginger ale, on the rocks or branch water?"

"Soda. You believe in doing yourself well."

"The Assistant Commissioner does," Samuels said, correcting him. "I'm just keeping the seat warm while he's on

198

leave in the UK." He poured two generous measures of whisky into separate glasses and then deftly uncapped a Canada Dry and a bottle of soda water which he found in the mini fridge positioned in the far left corner of the room behind the desk. "Your wife ever mention a Vietnamese called Le Khac Ly?" he asked casually.

"No."

"A small dark-haired man knee high to a grasshopper? Came here at the back end of '75 with the boat people."

"The answer's still no."

"Your wife called at his shop in Harbour City on Wednesday afternoon. One of the sales assistants told her he hadn't been in all day and directed her to another branch he owned in Tsun Wan on the outskirts of Kowloon. From there, she eventually found her way to the high-rise building where he lived with his wife and family, only to learn that he'd gone to Macau on business."

"How do you know this woman was Sarah?"

"We talked to Le Khac Ly's widow, Major; she knew your wife when she was in charge of the Mission House in Saigon back in '75. Of course, her name was Sarah Lucas in those days and the Mission House had nothing to do with the Salvation Army."

"You're telling me this Le Khac Ly is dead?"

Samuels nodded. "He took a dive off the roof of the tenement building where he lived. The neighbours say he jumped, his wife claims he was murdered by one of the Triads."

"What's your opinion?" Cartwright asked him.

"Some people can't take the pressures of living in a high-rise condominium with eight or nine thousand neighbours. In August last year, a couple of fourteen-year-old high school kids living in an apartment block on the Wong-Tai-Sin housing estate stepped off the roof hand in hand. Le Khac Ly could have jumped but I think he was helped on his way."

"So, when did it happen?"

"Last night, shortly after he returned from Macau."

Samuels raised his glass. "Here's to your continued good health," he said. "Seems to me you're going to need it."

"Thanks."

"Macready was in Vietnam the same time as your wife."

"I guessed as much as soon as you mentioned Le Khac Ly."

And now ten years later, both men had been murdered within a few days of one another. Why? Because they'd double-crossed one of the Triads and someone had decided the time had come to make an example of them? If so, it didn't explain what had prompted Sarah to suddenly take off for Hong Kong or why their au-pair had been strangled and left in a Brentford junkyard.

"Was Simon Faulkner ever in Vietnam?"

"I wouldn't know, Major. In 1975, I was a lowly Inspector in charge of the border post at Sha Tau Kok up in the New Territories. I didn't get to meet any of the SIS crowd." Samuels eyed him thoughtfully. "Surely your wife would have said something about it if he had?"

"Until yesterday I wasn't aware there was such a person as Simon Faulkner. Until you told me, I didn't know my wife had even set foot in Vietnam."

"That's a shame; I was hoping you might be able to give me a steer."

"How about Unger, the man who was in charge of the South-East Asia Bureau in those days?"

"Roger Ingram is the only SIS man I'm acquainted with and I wouldn't have met him if I hadn't been deputising for the Assistant Commissioner."

There was one other name Alderton had brought back from Paris, a Hong Kong commodity broker and general wheeler-dealer whose connection with the Foreign Office circle, according to Carole Barrington, was entirely social.

"What about Lance Kimber?" said Cartwright. "Is he still around?"

"Very much so." Samuels finished the rest of his whisky, then gazed at the empty glass as though debating whether he should have another. "Am I to assume that he and Mrs Cartwright are acquainted?" he asked.

200

"He invited Sarah and Simon Faulkner to dinner on a couple of occasions."

"They must have had an awful lot of clout between them; Kimber doesn't socialise with just anybody. You've got to be in *Who's Who* or extremely well-connected before you're invited to his house on the Peak."

"What is he, some kind of tycoon?"

"Yes. Gold, silver, sugar futures, marine insurance, property – you name it, Kimber's into it. And not only here in Hong Kong; he's a member of a Lloyds syndicate and is said to have a controlling interest in a European time-sharing consortium – holiday homes on the Costa Brava and the Côte d'Azur – that sort of crap."

Samuels appeared to have studied the relevant entry in *Who's Who* in some depth; yet, although it was all very interesting to hear about the German-born divorcee he'd married, the OBE which had been conferred upon him in 1975 for services to commerce, there was little the Canadian could really tell him about the man himself.

"Are you a fan of his?" Cartwright asked.

"Hell no, he's much too smooth for my liking. As a matter of fact, I personally wouldn't trust him an inch and it would never surprise me to learn that he's not exactly persona non grata with the 14K Triad, but don't quote me on that. Kimber is a steward of the Hong Kong Jockey Club which makes him a pillar of society and all that jazz."

"Did he have anything going in Vietnam?"

"Only he can tell you that."

"Then you'd better give me his address."

"What for? You won't even make it past the front gate."

"You don't know me," Cartwright told him, "I'm a very persistent fellow."

The Canadian sighed somewhat theatrically, then said, "You want number 5 Harlech Road; turn right outside the Peak tramway station."

"Thanks."

"A word of advice, Major. Don't push your luck with

Kimber; you've already made one bad enemy out here, don't make another."

"Your Sub Inspector's got it in for me, has he?"

"Well, let's say Barry is not the happiest of police officers. He reckons you were allowed to get away with murder, and of course he's right."

Cartwright drained the rest of his whisky soda and stood up. "And how do you feel about it?"

"I do what I'm told. The Assistant Commissioner is retiring next year and I mean to have his job." Samuels walked him to the door. "Besides," he added, smiling, "I can afford to take a more relaxed view; I wasn't the one you socked in the gut."

A senior police officer who was in his office at seven o'clock on a Saturday evening was hardly taking a relaxed view, but Cartwright let it pass. On his way downstairs, he saw Barry in the main hall and gave him a cheery wave; the Sub Inspector's venomous glare came as no surprise.

Turning left outside the central police station, Cartwright made his way through the Harbour City complex to the Star Ferry terminal and paid seventy cents to board the cross harbour service to Victoria. It was a warm, humid evening and he didn't feel like walking to the Peak tramway in Garden Road; after disembarking, he left the pedestrian walkway, descended to street level and flagged down a cab outside the General Post Office.

Number 5 Harlech Road reminded him of the large Edwardian houses which faced Hampstead Heath. There was even the same kind of lamp standard lining the drive that had been found on the streets of London at the turn of the century, but the electronic surveillance gadgets around the house and grounds were Japanese and bang up to date. A pair of TV cameras mounted on the wall covered the approach road and enabled the controller back at the house to identify a vehicle and its occupants before using the remote control to open the gates. While Cartwright was looking the place over, a Rolls-Royce Phantom VI went through the basic security check; a few

202

minutes later, a Mercedes 560 SEL pulled up outside the gates.

Although there was a notice inviting callers to use the house phone by the gates, Cartwright doubted if Kimber would agree to see him when he was obviously hosting a dinner party. Accordingly, he positioned himself in a blind spot behind the Mercedes where the Chinese chauffeur couldn't see him and followed the luxury saloon into the grounds. A dog handler who showed little inclination to control the vicious-looking Doberman he had on a long leash, intercepted him while he was still some distance from the house.

"It's all right, I'm a friend." Cartwright raised both arms shoulder high and did his best to smile in what he hoped was a reassuring manner. "My name's Major Cartwright," he said. "I'm on a secondment to the Hong Kong Government."

The handler gazed at him impassively and made no attempt to restrain the snarling Doberman.

"Perhaps I can show you my ID card?"

Cartwright lowered one hand to reach inside his jacket and promptly raised it again when the dog came within an inch of taking a lump out of his thigh. Two Filipino strongarm men appeared from nowhere and began to frogmarch him off the property. Fortunately, the older-looking one could understand English and he managed to convince him he was there on official business on behalf of His Excellency the Governor and that there would be hell to pay if he was prevented from seeing Mr Kimber. Suddenly reversing course, they marched him round to the conservatory at the side of the house where he was made to wait amongst the indoor grape vines until the financier finally condescended to see him.

Ten minutes later Kimber joined him, his cold and imperious manner more than making up for his frail appearance; something which did not tally with Cartwright's mental image of the man.

"You're Major Cartwright?" His nose wrinkled as though there was a nasty smell in the conservatory.

"Yes."

"Would it surprise you to know that His Excellency the Governor has never heard of you?"

"I'd be surprised if he had," Cartwright said. "I just thought his title would carry more weight with you than Roger Ingram's."

"You're absolutely right, though of course I have heard of Mr Ingram."

"How about Simon Faulkner and my wife, the former Sarah Lucas?"

"What exactly is it you want from me, Major Cartwright?"

"I'm hoping you will tell me the real reason why you were awarded the OBE in the New Year Honours List in 1975."

"Are you trying to be funny?"

"Depends on your sense of humour," said Cartwright. "Personally, I don't think what happened in Vietnam was particularly funny."

"What are you trying to imply?"

"Towards the end of 1974, my wife and Simon Faulkner were told to set up an Intelligence network in South Vietnam. It had to be done in complete secrecy and for that reason alone, it doesn't matter whether or not the project was sanctioned by the Wilson Government. Clandestine operations cost a lot of money and it was essential no hostile Intelligence agency should discover where the financial aid was coming from. It's my theory that you laundered the money for us and then a grateful government honoured you with an OBE."

Kimber didn't say anything. A faint smile that was clearly intended to convey both amusement and scorn etched the corners of his mouth. In the ensuing silence, Cartwright heard another limousine glide up the drive and stop outside the front door. Responding on cue, Kimber glanced at his slim but hugely expensive wristwatch, then adjusted the sleeves of his sharkskin tuxedo.

"Is there anything else you want to add to your quite remarkable hypothesis?" he inquired politely.

"I don't think so."

"Then don't let me detain you."

It was perhaps a little undignified to be escorted off the premises by two Filipino muscle men, but Cartwright was barely aware of their presence. He had taken three separate strands of information from Samuels, Carole Barrington and Roger Ingram and had woven them to make one tiny segment of a tapestry. And while the picture was still a long way from being complete, he was sure money had to be the dominating theme. It had drawn Sarah, Faulkner and Kimber together and had bought the financier respectable distinction. Ten years later, it was conceivable that the very same money had been responsible for the deaths of Macready and Le Khac Ly. He only had to prove it.

The Lotus Flower was one of the smaller discos in Patpong Lane. It was, however, one of the most popular haunts in Bangkok: the bar girls who frequented it were unlikely to give their clients a dose of the clap, the whisky was not made in Japan and a round of drinks did not cost a small fortune. On the other hand, the dance floor was minute, the décor was a psychedelic experience and the output from the stereophonic music centre was almost loud enough to wake the dead. It was the last place Sarah would have chosen to while the night away but she had foisted herself on the Navy and did not have a great deal of say in the matter.

The film had ended at seven-thirty and from The Hollywood Movie theatre they'd gone on to a Chinese meal at the Shangri La in Thaniya Road before ending up at the Lotus Flower, having stopped off at a couple of bars on the way. Somewhere between the restaurant and the disco, their numbers had been swollen by a quiet Highlander from Inverness, a somewhat amorous radar technician whose accent placed him somewhere in the Midlands and two American nurses from the Children's Hospital. Although the men now only outnumbered the women by two to one, Sarah had lost count of the number of hours she had spent gyrating about the dance floor.

She was bone tired and would have given anything to sit down and take the weight off her feet, but every time she collapsed into a chair, one of the ratings insisted on buying her another brandy sour. Thus far she had managed to stay sober but there was a limit to the number of drinks she could palm off on to the American nurses, and the rubber tree plant nearest their table looked as though it was beginning to wilt. The same could not be said for the Navy, none of whom seemed the least bit affected by the amount of alcohol they had consumed. Worse still, they were reluctant to return to their ship a minute before they had to.

Heavy Metal gave way to Procol Harum's 'A Whiter Shade of Pale' and it was no surprise to Sarah when the radar technician eased the quiet Highlander aside. The man from Wolverhampton liked any record with a slow beat because it gave him an excuse to hold her close and in the last hour or so, he'd invested a considerable amount of money with the disc jockey for that very purpose.

"Where did you say you were staying?" he asked unabashed.

"The President."

"Sounds swish."

"It is," Sarah told him.

There was no way she was going to allow him to take her back there when it was the one place the intruders were bound to be watching. Except 'intruders' was hardly an apt word for the two men who'd broken into her room. Had everything gone according to plan, they would have killed her; of that she hadn't the slightest doubt. Just who should want her dead and why were two questions she was not yet in a position to answer. And right now, her first priority was to find a safe refuge because even though she hadn't seen them for several hours, she knew the killers were still out there somewhere, waiting for an opportune moment to make the hit.

"Penny for them?"

"They're not worth it," she said. "My thoughts never are."

Somehow she had got to alert Simon, but that was easier said than done. From the moment he had first warned her that Matthew Gage was coming home, the channel of communication had always been one way. Group Captain Quarry was the only connecting link. If Matthew Gage was using the Defence Attaché as a go-between, then Simon would certainly keep in touch with him. Sarah decided she had two options: either she walked into the embassy in broad daylight and introduced herself to Quarry, or else she made her number through the Navy.

"Do you like Country and Western?"

"What?"

"Crystal Gayle – 'Don't it make my brown eyes blue'."

Another ballad, another singer, but the same seductive beat and the radar technician's wandering hand gravitating towards her right hip once more, his fingertips stroking her buttocks with a feather-light touch. The technique never varied. Despite his unwelcome attentions, she came to the conclusion that she would be safer staying with the Navy. It would be after seven before the embassy opened and the quiet Highlander had told her they had to be back on board by 0500 hours. That would leave her with something like two hours to kill in a city that would only just be coming to life again. Alone on the near-empty streets, her chances of survival would be less than evens.

Across the room, one of the nurses pushed her chair back with a loud scraping noise and stood up. Swaying unsteadily on her feet, she leaned on the table for support and managed to sweep half a dozen glasses on to the floor. A small river of brandy sour mixed with rum and Coke flowed towards the adjoining table where a party of merchant seamen from a West German freighter were being entertained by a motley collection of bar girls.

A diminutive Thai girl took one look at the liquor stain on the front of her figure-hugging gold lamé dress, jumped down from the lap of a particularly brawny seaman and gave the nurse a violent shove in the back. Unable to retain her balance, she executed an almost perfect about face and tried to cling on to her smaller adversary. In attempting to remain upright, her flailing hands grabbed the strapless lamé dress and accidentally ripped it to the waist a split second before she sat down heavily in a large puddle on the floor.

The bar girl used every obscenity in every language at her command and kicked the nurse in the ribs again and again. One of the naval ratings attempted to place himself between the two women and was promptly attacked by the brawny West German who caught him with a lucky punch which drew blood from his nose. Anticipating a full scale riot, the management and staff armed themselves with a variety of baseball bats, truncheons and wooden clubs. Leaving the radar technician stranded on the dance floor, Sarah advanced on the mêlée.

"That's enough – now sit down – all of you."

Her voice was calm but sufficiently authoritative to make it absolutely clear that she expected them to do as they were told. Her manner seemed even more commanding when she repeated the order in fluent German. Only the hooker ignored her and went on kicking the American nurse. Spinning her around, Sarah felled the diminutive Thai with a flat hand Judo blow to the jaw which left her unconscious.

"I think you'd better get your friends out of here," Sarah told the quiet Highlander from Inverness. "The police could arrive at any minute."

It was not the most dignified withdrawal in the annals of the Royal Navy: the would-be Sir Galahad was still bleeding profusely from the nose and the nurse he'd tried to protect had sobered up sufficiently to complain in a loud voice about a cracked rib. Their anger was such that World War Three could easily have started had one of the West Germans so much as raised an eyebrow. No one did because Sarah held them captive by the sheer force of her personality. When the moment came for her to leave, the brawny seaman kissed her hand and called her '*Gnädige Fraulein*', then saw her wedding ring and hastily corrected it to '*Gnädige Frau*'.

A second altercation had started on the pavement outside

the disco and Anglo-American relations were definitely strained. The amorous radar technician had evidently decided to give Sarah up as a bad job and wanted to escort the nurses back to the Children's Hospital, an offer they'd declined with some heat. The injured rating who believed he had a prior claim on their company was also more than a little put out when he was told to get lost. Between them, Sarah and the quiet Highlander sent the nurses on their way in a Honda cab and piled the others into a Thuk Thuk.

"I can't begin to thank you," he said in his soft burr.

"You don't have to, I've always had a soft spot for the Navy."

"Oh aye." He shifted his weight from one foot to the other, uncertain what to say. "You'll be going back to your hotel then?"

"No, I'm coming with you."

"Och, there's no need to do that."

"Oh yes there is," Sarah told him. "Someone's got to explain to the Officer of the Day that you weren't to blame for the fracas."

"With all due respect, m'am, I doubt he'll take any notice of you."

"I'm quite sure he will, one of my uncles is a Vice-Admiral."

"Jesus," said the radar technician, "wouldn't you just know it."

The Officer of the Day was the *Birmingham*'s electronic warfare specialist, a twenty-four-year-old university graduate from Manchester who was more at home with his computers than he was with Navy Regulations and such everyday matters as Ship's Harbour Routine. Until Sarah informed him otherwise, he hadn't realised that the programme for the goodwill visit to Bangkok had largely been organised by the Defence Attaché, nor was he aware that the appointment was currently being filled by Group Captain William Quarry, OBE, AFC. After he had found Quarry's name, home address, official and private telephone numbers in the special addendum to the standing orders for the

OOD, he was inclined to believe that Susan Lamidy was indeed a Foreign Office official.

The Petty Officer who was standing duty with him had never entertained any doubts about her. From the moment she had stepped on board, he had known instinctively that Susan Lamidy was well-connected. There was an indefinable aura about her and the air of easy confidence that came with money, position and influence. You only had to take one look at the ratings who came aboard with her to realise they had been involved in a punch-up and instead of making difficulties, he thought the OOD ought to have been grateful that she had been on hand to sort things out with the Thai authorities. For the life of him, he couldn't understand why the Officer of the Day had made such a song and dance before he allowed her to use the ship's landline to call the Defence Attaché at his home to put him in the picture.

Quarry wasn't at his best at five o'clock in the morning and couldn't understand why some young woman whom he'd never met, never even heard of, should rouse him from a peaceful slumber. Convinced she had dialled the wrong number and wanted the consular officer, he advised her to telephone the embassy at eight o'clock or go there in person half an hour later when it would be open to the public. It was only when she mentioned Simon Faulkner and Matthew Gage that he really sat up and began to take notice. Thereafter, he was rapidly persuaded that in order to ensure her continued survival, he should collect Miss Lamidy from HMS *Birmingham* without further delay.

17

Quarry's house off the Sukhumvit Road in the residential area of Bangkok reminded Sarah of the typically French villas she'd seen in Saigon. It even had the same faded look, the sunblistered paint flaking off the windowsills and dark green shutters to expose the bare wood. Bougainvillaea grew in profusion everywhere, against the house, in circular beds dotted higgledy-piggledy in a brown-coloured lawn, and on three sides of the property where it formed an impenetrable hedge.

The sitting room was at the back of the house, farthest away from the main road and the perpetual drumming noise of the traffic. The furniture had been purchased locally and was mostly bamboo. The knick-knacks on the mantelpiece above a stone fireplace and on the occasional tables placed strategically around the room provided visible evidence of a lifetime spent travelling the world. There were also reminders of home, watercolours of the English countryside executed by an unknown artist.

"My wife did them," Quarry told her before she could ask. "Most of them are local views not far from our house in Tunbridge Wells."

"They're very good," Sarah murmured.

"Yes, Eve's a talented painter." Quarry retired to the darkest corner of the room and returned with a painting depicting a formation of delta-wing planes in level flight above the towering cumulus. "This is my favourite, Miss Lamidy," he said proudly, " 'Vulcans at Forty Thousand'. I was flying one of those beauties when I was stationed at RAF Scampton up in Lincolnshire."

"The best days of your life?"

"They were certainly the happiest. But you haven't come here to listen to me wittering on about myself. You want to get in touch with Simon Faulkner?"

"Yes. Do you know where he's staying?"

"Don't you?"

She could tell at a glance that it was no use trying to bluff Quarry. The Defence Attaché might give the impression that he was half asleep but he didn't miss much, and anyway, she was tired of lying.

"I'm no longer with the SIS and I've no right to be here." Sarah smiled. "And while I'm being honest with you, my name isn't Susan Lamidy either."

"Who are you then?" Quarry asked with a bemused expression.

"I'm Sarah Cartwright. My husband's a Major in the army and there are facets of my life even he doesn't know about. The Security Service has been keeping an eye on me ever since my vetting status was withdrawn ten years ago. Simon Faulkner smuggled me out of England under their very noses, and that's why I have to stay in the shadows until he wants me to make an entrance. Officially, I don't exist."

"Am I allowed to know what this charade is all about?"

"I think I've already told you more than I should have done."

"That's what I thought you'd say." Quarry rehung the painting then stepped back a pace and looked at it with a critical eye to satisfy himself it wasn't lopsided. "Faulkner is staying at the Sheraton Hotel," he said abruptly. "The number is 4519886."

The way Quarry was able to reel off the number suggested to her that he must have called Simon Faulkner on several occasions. Although anxious to know the latest on Matthew Gage, she thought it best not to raise the matter. "Would you mind if I also booked a call to England?" she asked.

"Of course not."

"Naturally, I'll ask the operator to let me know the cost so that I can reimburse you."

"Oh, I don't think a few pounds is going to break me, but

212

as you wish." Quarry smiled. "I'm going to make a pot of tea and take a cup up to Eve. Would you like one?"

"Thank you, that would be nice."

Sarah waited until he had left the room before she raised the operator and booked a call to Market Harborough. This time she was told there was a fifteen minute delay on calls to the United Kingdom. Satisfied the girl on the international switchboard had made a note of Quarry's phone number, she broke the connection, rang the Sheraton Hotel and asked to speak to Mr Simon Faulkner.

It was still only seven o'clock and she had never known Simon to be at his best at that hour of the morning. On this occasion, however, he seemed particularly slow to grasp the situation, and she virtually had to repeat every little detail before the penny finally dropped and he realised she had broken cover.

"What have you told Quarry?" His voice was matter-of-fact and so lacking in emotion that he might have been inquiring about the weather.

"As little as possible, but he knows I have no official status."

"That's unfortunate."

Sarah began to count to ten to give herself a chance to cool down, but it didn't work. With every reason to believe that she had barely managed to avoid what probably had been a second attempt on her life, all he could think of was that she had let the cat out of the bag.

"I'm sorry if I've made life somewhat difficult for you," she snapped, "but we wouldn't be in this embarrassing position if I'd known how to contact you in an emergency."

"Now I've made you angry," he said contritely. "Just hang in there, Sarah, and leave everything to me. I'll figure out a way to limit the damage."

"Whatever you say." The adrenaline, which had acted like a stimulant, stopped flowing and left her feeling listless.

"That's the style. I'll be with you in no time."

Sarah heard a faint click as he replaced the receiver and slowly put the phone down. She couldn't remember

213

experiencing such exhaustion since that last terrible day in Saigon when she had worked through the night in a vain attempt to destroy the card index and Top Secret files before the Viet Cong arrived. Leaning forward in the chair, she folded her arms and rested them on her knees to form a pillow for her head. Presently, her eyelids began to droop and she didn't hear Quarry enter the room. Nor did she hear the door close quietly behind him as he left again on tiptoe. Then the phone started ringing and she sat up, suddenly wide awake and conscious that her heart was thumping like a runaway train.

There was no back echo or rushing noise on the line to Market Harborough and Edwin's voice was so loud he could have been in the same room. Sarah had caught him just as he was about to retire for the night and his mellow tone was a sign that he had consumed several more whiskies than was good for his blood pressure. Once Edwin had got over his incredulity, the questions came thick and fast. 'What was she doing in Bangkok?' 'Why had she lied to her mother?' 'Who had she run off with?' 'Hadn't she read the newspapers?'

It was only when Fay came on the line after plucking the phone from his grasp that Sarah began to understand what had precipitated her father's hysterical interrogation. The news that Bergitta had been murdered shocked her so much that she felt physically sick with horror and apprehension.

"Had she been raped?" Sarah asked in a voice she scarcely recognised as her own.

"Do you honestly think Tom is capable of doing something like that?" Fay said coldly.

"No, of course I don't."

"I should hope not. In any event, the pathologist could find no evidence of a sexual assault, nor were there any indications that intercourse had taken place twenty-four hours prior to her death."

But it wasn't difficult to understand why the police had viewed Tom with jaundiced eyes and how they could make a case against him. Husband and wife living separate lives for most of the week, the woman wealthy in her own right, the man frequently hard up with no expectations from his family and probably ripe for a love affair with the Swedish nanny. She threatens to tell his wife he's cheating on her, he can't let that happen and decides to rid himself of a tiresome mistress. His intricate plan goes wrong because the crusher breaks down and his wife leaves him after discovering he's hopping into bed with the au-pair.

"Do I gather the police have cleared Tom?" Sarah asked after learning the salient facts.

"Well, let's say they didn't prevent him from going to Hong Kong."

"Where?" Sarah gasped.

"Hong Kong. He's looking for you, darling."

A dozen questions sprang to mind but she asked only one. "When did Tom leave?"

"Thursday morning. He was hoping someone called Simon would know where you were staying."

"Someone called Peter should have told him that and a whole lot more."

"I don't follow you, Sarah."

"I'm not surprised, I'm more than a little confused myself." Sarah rubbed the sleep from her eyes, then said, "Would you phone the police, Ma, and tell them I'm all right?"

"They may want to know what you're doing in Bangkok."

"I can't tell you; it may sound crazy but that's the way it is. You'll just have to convince them I'm alive and well."

"I'll do my best."

"And if you should hear from Tom before I make contact, tell him I'm staying with the Defence Attaché and give him my love."

"As you have ours."

Sarah told herself that she was a grown woman but the lump in her throat refused to go away. From the earliest days of her childhood, her mother had always been there when she'd turned to her in a crisis. She just wished she had

215

confided in Fay ten years ago, then none of this might have happened.

"I love you and miss you all," she said huskily, and slowly hung up.

Sarah felt the small pot of tea which Quarry had left on a tray with a jug of milk and a sugar bowl while she was asleep and found it was now only lukewarm. For the sake of appearances, however, she poured herself a cup, added a dash of milk and gulped it down.

A bell pinged and presently she heard voices in the hall. Then Simon Faulkner walked into the room looking very spruce in a pale blue suit that had been tailored to fit him perfectly. The absence of Group Captain Quarry suggested he had asked the Defence Attaché if he could have a few minutes in private with her. He made to kiss her and seemed genuinely perplexed when she retreated from him.

"Are you all right, Sarah?" he asked.

"No, as a matter of fact I'm not. I've just learned that Bergitta Lindstrom was murdered shortly after I left England."

"What?" His jaw dropped and he looked completely bewildered. "When did this happen?"

"I've just told you – shortly after I left England. Don't tell me you didn't know."

"Of course I didn't. There was no mention of it in the newspapers on Saturday when I flew out from Heathrow, and the *South China Mail* certainly hasn't carried the story. I don't know about the *Bangkok Post* or *The Nation*; you'd have to ask Bill Quarry."

"Are you telling me you haven't seen an airmail edition of *The Times* or the *Daily Telegraph*?"

"When do you think I've had time to read an English newspaper?" he asked, his voice brittle with exasperation. "Jesus Christ, Sarah, I've been far too busy looking after you and dancing attendance on Matthew Gage."

"Peter failed to brief my husband," Sarah told him, launching an attack on another front.

"So I guessed when Tom showed up in Hong Kong."

"When was that?" she snapped.

"The day before yesterday. I didn't tell you because he was making such a damned nuisance of himself. Believe me, Sarah, if ever there was the proverbial bull in a china shop, your husband was it."

"That's no reason for not telling me."

"Isn't it? Christ, Sarah, have you forgotten how far out on a limb I've gone for you? Charles Unger might have initialled the requisition for those additional blank passports but I've always known he would never stand by me if the Security Service learned about our little escapade. And that would have happened for sure if you two had met up in Hong Kong."

He went through his pockets, found a packet of cigarettes and lit one. There had been occasions in the past when Sarah had seen him resort to this ritual in order to gain time and she wondered if his addiction was really genuine.

"Anyway, it's all so much water under the bridge now. Your husband's on the way to Bangkok; we can expect him some time later this morning."

"I don't understand."

Faulkner smiled lopsidedly. "He's a pretty clever fellow, your Tom. First he discovers you have travelled to Hong Kong under the name of Ellen Rothman, then he gets the Immigration authorities to match arrival and departure dates and learns you've changed your name to Susan Lamidy."

"When did you hear this, Simon?"

"Last night; Ingram cabled the Head of Station, copy to London." He saw her eyes narrow and guessed what was passing through her mind. "It arrived after we parted company outside your hotel. This is the first chance I've had to tell you."

"So what do we do now?"

"You might as well come out into the open. Everyone who matters between Hong Kong and London knows that Susan Lamidy and Sarah Cartwright are the same person. I may not be in charge of this assignment much longer, but if you

217

want to stay on to hear what Matthew Gage has to say, I'll try to square it with Charles Unger."

"Thank you, Simon. I think I'll talk it over with Tom first."

"You do that. Meantime, you'd better stay here with Bill Quarry while I check what plane he's on and sort things out with the embassy."

Sarah gazed at him thoughtfully. "What's going to happen to you, Simon?" she asked.

"Oh, I expect I'll be moved sideways again. You have that effect on people."

Like Tom, she thought. Every fellow student who knew Tom at Camberley had told her he was one of the high fliers on the course but when the appointments had appeared on the notice board, he hadn't been given one of the plum jobs. And she knew why. Because of the cloud hanging over her, the Security people had made sure he wasn't sent to a post which would give him access to highly sensitive information.

Cartwright finished dressing, collected his shaving tackle from the bathroom and packed it into the hold-all containing the rest of his hand luggage, then sat down at the writing desk. Leafing through the brochure, he looked up the name of the chain hotel in Bangkok and wrote a brief note to Ingram. That done, he rang Ingram on his home number to let him know that he would be leaving Hong Kong on Thai Air International Flight 824 departing at 0920 hours.

From his apparent lack of interest, he knew the SIS Head of Station had got airport security at Kai Tak to set up a screening operation with the various airline desks. Consequently, shortly after he'd made the booking yesterday evening, Ingram had known his flight and departure time.

Cartwright picked up the phone again and put a call through to Edgecombe in London. The chances of finding him at home on a Saturday evening at eleven thirty seemed fairly remote but it transpired that having spent the day painting and decorating, Henry and his live-in girlfriend hadn't felt like going out. Instead, they'd decided to retire early and Edgecombe wasn't best pleased to be dragged out of bed, nor was he at his brightest.

"Who is this fellow, Lance Kinder?" he asked, getting the surname wrong.

"Kimber," Cartwright said, then spelt it out using the phonetic alphabet. "His corporation is based in Hong Kong but he's also a member of Lloyd's and is said to have a controlling interest in something called Euro Time Sharing."

"What am I supposed to do with the information?"

"Brief Alderton and put him on to Kimber. I want him to look up Euro Time Sharing in the Register of Companies and find out when it started trading and the names of the other directors. Tell Alderton I'd like him to drop everything else and get on to it first thing on Monday morning. Short of it costing my in-laws an arm and a leg, he can write his own cheque."

"I don't think Bream, Cotton and Roose will go along with that," Edgecombe said. "They're handling the financial arrangements and they weren't at all happy when I told them how much Alderton proposed to charge for the time he'd spent in Paris on your behalf."

Edwin was probably making difficulties; he hated parting with money even when it wasn't his. Fortunately, when it came to the crunch, Fay was the one who had the last word.

"I'll talk to Mrs Lucas," Cartwright said.

"I'll hang fire then until I hear from you again."

"No, you go ahead and get in touch with Alderton. I guarantee there won't be any problem about his expenses."

Cartwright hoped Fay wouldn't ask him why he was anxious to discover the extent of Kimber's financial interests in the UK. Although he'd never asked Sarah about her private income, he couldn't help noticing some of the dividends which came through the post. At the back of his mind, he had a hazy notion that Sarah had received a handsome dividend from Euro Time Sharing towards the end of October '84. Twenty-four hours ago, he would not

219

have given it a second thought; however, having met Kimber he could see all kinds of sinister possibilities.

"What are your plans for the immediate future, in case I need to get in touch?" Edgecombe asked.

"I'm just off to Bangkok. The best thing is for me to keep in touch with you."

"Try to make it during normal office hours," Edgecombe said and made sure his yawn was loud enough for Cartwright to hear.

"What about Nuri Assad? Have the police managed to trace him yet?"

"I don't think it would be politic to inquire, they might get the wrong impression."

"You could have a point, Henry," Cartwright said, then wished him goodnight and hung up.

Room Service sent up his order for coffee, fresh orange juice, rolls and butter at seven forty-five, the time he'd stipulated on the card he'd hung on the door the previous evening. The management had thoughtfully provided a copy of Sunday's edition of the *South China Mail* but there was nothing in the headlines to catch his eye and he didn't have time to do more than glance at the inside pages. Reception had the bill ready for him and the desk clerk had already been forewarned he was going to charge it to his account with American Express. By the time Cartwright had signed and received his copy of the invoice, the bellboy had a cab waiting for him outside the main entrance.

Cartwright encountered the same kind of efficiency with Thai International Airways when he arrived at Kai Tak. His plane ticket was ready for collection at the airline desk and there was no delay at the check-in counter. It didn't come as any surprise to him that Ingram was the first person he saw when he walked into the departure lounge. In his panama hat, linen suit and college tie, he was more than somewhat conspicuous amongst the more informally dressed travellers. For the benefit of any onlookers who might be remotely curious, he greeted Cartwright as though he was the last person he expected to see.

220

"I think you have something for me," he said, the smile still there on his mouth, his lips barely moving.

"You mean this?" Cartwright took the envelope out of his inside jacket pocket and gave it to him.

Ingram glanced at the crest on the back, then inserted a thumb under the flap, ripped the envelope open and extracted a sheet of notepaper folded in half. What was left of his friendly smile died instantly and he looked up, his eyes narrowed in anger. "The Asia Hotel or the Defence Attaché's office?" he hissed. "What the hell do you think you're playing at?"

"Those are the two places in Bangkok where you can get in touch with me. You'd better warn the embassy, otherwise they might not allow me to cross the threshold."

"We had an agreement . . ."

"You didn't really expect me to give you the phone number and codeword here and now, did you?" Cartwright shook his head. "If I was that stupid, I'd deserve to find myself under arrest and on the next plane back to England. At least you can't touch me in Thailand."

"You bastard."

"So long as we're name calling, let's talk about Kimber and the special relationship he seems to have with the SIS."

"I don't know what you're talking about."

"You should do," Cartwright said calmly. "He smoothed the way for Century House to set up shop in Vietnam."

A desire to dispel the notion that one of Hong Kong's leading businessmen had been involved in a covert Intelligence operation vied with Ingram's natural curiosity and lost out. "Perhaps I was being a little hasty," he conceded, "but you have my undivided attention now."

Cartwright wasn't too sure how long he was going to keep it, but in a few brief sentences, he told Ingram about the phone call he'd had from Samuels and how, quite by accident, he'd discovered there had been an SIS involvement in South Vietnam during the mid-seventies.

"Kimber's not whiter than white," he said, winding up. "What is more, it's said he's a front man for the 14K Triad."

221

"And now you can't wait to give me the benefit of your advice," Ingram said derisively.

"It's no skin off my nose," Cartwright said, shrugging, "but if I were in your shoes I'd want to distance myself from Kimber. Like I said, he helped your lot to set up a wildcat Intelligence operation in South Vietnam and the way things are going just now, he may think you owe him."

For all that he was Head of Station, it was apparent that Ingram knew very little about the operation and when all was said and done, there was no reason why he should. The Vietnam affair was ancient history and the relevant files would have gone to the shredder long ago. Furthermore, its existence had only been known to those actually involved; even the former Carrie Jackman who'd been Sarah's flatmate and had worked in the same office had been excluded from the inner circle. Ten years on, the need-to-know principle was still being rigorously applied.

"They didn't take you into their confidence, did they?" said Cartwright.

He was fighting a losing battle; Ingram refused to be drawn and time was running out for him. The Thai International flight to Bangkok was boarding at Gate 3 and any moment now the final call for Flight 824 would be paged over the public address system.

"When something happened to resurrect the whole sorry business, they sent Simon Faulkner out here to cool it and told you to give him all the support he needed."

Cartwright searched for something to say that would spark an angry response from the other man and perhaps give him another piece of the puzzle. The last of the passengers for his flight were leaving the departure lounge and the indicator arrow on the TV screen was flashing alongside the 'Now Boarding' sign.

"But perhaps you don't mind being kept in the dark?" he said. "And even if you do, it's so much water under the bridge now that the showdown is going to happen in Bangkok instead of on your own doorstep."

222

"That's because of Matthew Gage," Ingram retorted. "He always was unpredictable."

"Who's Matthew Gage?" Cartwright asked.

"The Prodigal Son," said Ingram, "though I doubt my colleagues are planning to kill the fatted calf to celebrate his homecoming."

18

Kimber opened the tailgate, dumped his golf clubs in the back of the car, then got into the Volvo hatchback and went on down The Peak Road to the cross-harbour tunnel. Roughly twice a month he attended morning service at St John's Cathedral with his wife and family, but the pattern was not so regular that his absence this particular morning would be noticed. Nor would anyone who knew him think it odd that he should choose to leave the Rolls-Royce in the garage and motor out to Fanling in the modest Volvo. Although one of the richest men in Hong Kong, Kimber had never been one to flaunt his wealth and he secretly despised those mandarins who arrived at the golf course in their chauffeur-driven limousines.

He had telephoned Chan Tsai shortly after Cartwright had left his house the previous evening and had arranged to meet the Chinese lawyer on the first tee at nine forty-five. If he'd then had a pressing reason to meet the front man for the 14K Triad, it had become even more vital to settle the Gage affair once and for all in the light of the news he'd subsequently received from Bangkok.

Unless decisive remedial action was taken, there was a real possibility his financial empire would be destroyed and that was something Kimber was prepared to do everything in his power to prevent, no matter how many lives it cost. He had arrived in Hong Kong with little more than the clothes he stood up in and at a time when the colony had scarcely begun to recover from World War Two. He could remember the influx of refugees when Marshal Lin Piao at the head of the Chinese Communist Army had come down from the north and the days when Tai Po had been a tiny fishing village in the New Territories, and the racecourse which now existed at Sha Tin had been under the sea. He had watched the strong pick themselves up off their knees to make a fortune and having prospered with them, Kimber was damned if he was going to let anyone take it away from him now.

The road climbed out of Kowloon, snaked through the hills, then descended to sea level near Sha Tin. Less than half an hour after emerging from the cross-harbour tunnel, Kimber arrived at the Fanling golf course eighteen miles away.

Chan Tsai was waiting for him on the first tee with two caddies in tow. The Chinese lawyer was dressed for the occasion, though the loud check pants he was wearing were altogether too garish for Kimber's conservative taste. No one was waiting to play off the tee and the fairway to the first green was clear. The course was usually crowded on a Sunday morning but most of the members of the Fanling Golf Club were Chinese and as the legal representative of the 14K Triad, it was only necessary for Chan Tsai to have a quiet word with the steward for the club pro to rearrange the order of play.

The lawyer spun a coin, Kimber called 'heads', won the toss and asked his opponent to go first. Although both men played off a twelve handicap, Kimber was the more talented golfer and often showed flashes of brilliance. He demonstrated it by placing his ball dead in line with Chan Tsai's. Side by side, the two men then set off down the fairway, their caddies some twenty yards behind them and out of earshot.

"Your people have failed again," Kimber said without any preamble.

"As I've pointed out to you before, Lance, they're not my people."

"Clients, business associates, I don't care what you call them, the fact remains the sub-contractors in Bangkok bungled the job."

"No one regrets that more than my clients."

"I think it would be more accurate to say that they know

225

why they have lost face. A mere woman has outwitted them, not once but twice."

"Truly, she is a very lucky person, Lance."

"Luck has precious little to do with it," Kimber said scathingly. "But incompetence most certainly has. Mrs Cartwright was supposed to disappear without trace; now everyone who matters knows she's in Bangkok and we also have to contend with her husband."

"You can't blame my clients for that."

"I don't, but his presence does complicate matters." Kimber broke off, watched the lawyer play his approach shot, then walked on to where his ball was lying and taking a number 5 iron, lofted it on to the green. "The Major may well persuade her to forget Gage and catch the next plane to England."

"Would that be so very bad, Lance?"

"I don't believe in leaving things to chance; it cost me a small fortune to learn that lesson."

"When was this?"

"Before you were born, Chan Tsai. I was rash enough to carry part of the insurance on certain capital assets belonging to a Mr Claire Chennault. He was an American aviator who raised a volunteer group to fight for Chiang Kai-shek against the Japanese before Pearl Harbour. They called themselves 'The Flying Tigers' and formed the nucleus of the US Army's 14th Air Force after the Americans came into the war. Anyway, Chennault stayed on in China after World War Two to run some kind of military air transport command for the Generalissimo. When Chiang was forced to leave the mainland for Taiwan, he came to Hong Kong with his Chinese wife and a fleet of C74s. The Government didn't want any trouble with Mao Tse-tung so they impounded the planes at Kai Tak. Then they looked round for people who were willing to insure the aircraft against all risks including war, civil insurrection, sabotage and just about every other catastrophe known to man. Although the premiums on cach C47 had to be competitive, the Hong Kong government realised they'd have to dig deep into their

226

pockets. I drove out to Kai Tak and took a look at the planes. They were parked close to the perimeter fence on the landward side and appeared to be guarded by the RAF Regiment. I put in a tender to insure up to six C47s and was allocated half the original bid."

Kimber sank his putt, watched Chan Tsai do the same to halve the hole and then walked over to the next tee, subsequently resuming his anecdote after they'd both driven off.

"One Saturday afternoon a few weeks later, two P51 Mustangs fitted with drop tanks flew in from Hainan, which was still in Nationalist hands, and violated Hong Kong's air space to shoot up an oil tank farm the other side of the border at Shenzhen. Our soldiers manning the observation post on Sandy Ridge thought it was the best firework display they'd seen in years; the Communists didn't think it was at all funny and wanted to know why we hadn't fired on the Mustangs. Like I said, it was a Saturday afternoon, there was no special alert, and all the troops were downtown enjoying themselves, but of course the Communists refused to believe our anti-aircraft batteries were unmanned. I had a gut feeling that I ought to unload the insurance but I hung on, hoping for the best. Within a week, Communist sympathisers had cut their way through the perimeter fence and blown a hole in every C47. It nearly cleaned me out."

"That would have been most unfortunate," Chan Tsai said politely.

"It's not going to happen again."

Kimber heard the distant noise of jet engines and looked up, shielding his eyes against the glare. Way beyond Tai Mo Shan, he could see a 737 climbing out of Kai Tak and wondered if Cartwright was on board, then recollected that the Thai International flight to Bangkok would have left some time ago.

"The woman had to be eliminated because we couldn't allow her to meet Matthew Gage," he continued in a low voice. "Even if Cartwright persuaded his wife to go home tomorrow, it wouldn't change anything. I know this woman

227

and she is a very determined lady. Sooner or later, she would run Gage to ground in England because there are some questions she wants him to answer."

"What are you asking us to do, Lance?"

"The woman is now untouchable, she has acquired a very high profile . . ."

"We appear to be going over the same ground again . . ."

"We have to tackle this problem from a different angle," Kimber continued unruffled. "That's why I now want you to kill Gage."

"This is madness . . ."

"Gage is hiding up-country with one of his Vietnamese friends. Finding him should not be too difficult; money talks and the Thais, especially their police, are not incorruptible."

Kimber studied the lie of his ball. It was a long hole and he was still a good two hundred yards from the green. Wordlessly, his caddy handed him a spoon and then moved away.

"Seek, locate and destroy, Chan Tsai. Do you think your friends could manage to do it right for once?"

"I'm sure they can, Lance."

"Good."

Kimber addressed himself to the ball, taking infinite pains to get his stance exactly right. He put a lot of power behind the swing but he looked up too soon and instead of hitting the ball cleanly, uncharacteristically he hooked it high and wide into the rough. It seemed very much like an omen to Chan Tsai.

Sarah was the last person Cartwright had thought to see in the main concourse at Bangkok Airport. Taken by surprise, he felt his jaw drop, then swiftly recovering, he almost ran towards her. A knowledgeable fellow traveller had told him the Thais were essentially a modest people and easily embarrassed by any outward show of affection, but as of that moment he wasn't in the mood to observe the niceties of local etiquette. Nor was he inhibited by the presence of the blond, elegant-looking man standing beside her. Sweeping Sarah into his arms, he planted a lingering kiss on her mouth. After a while, he felt a hand press lightly against his chest and let her come up for air. There were a million things he wanted to say to Sarah but all of them would have to wait until they were alone.

"This is Simon Faulkner," Sarah said quickly as though anxious to pre-empt the inevitable question.

"Hello." Cartwright shook hands. "I've heard a lot about you," he added and managed to smile.

"Really? May I ask from whom?"

"Carole Barrington, your colleague Roger Ingram, an entrepreneur called Kimber and of course Sarah's mother."

"Goodness me, I hadn't realised I was quite so popular."

"No, I bet you hadn't."

"Simon's booked us into the Erawan Hotel, Tom."

"I'm sure that's very kind of him," Cartwright said in an offhand manner, "but unfortunately, Ingram and I have some unfinished business to conclude and I told him I would be staying at the Asia."

"If you know his home number, you could always phone him from the Erawan," Faulkner said, not unreasonably.

"I could, but it's not that simple. I've pulled a couple of fast ones with Ingram and I'd like him to feel he could begin to trust me."

"Whatever you wish. There's an embassy car outside; just tell the driver where you want to go and he'll take you. I'll make my own way back to town."

Cartwright wasn't inclined to argue with him, nor was Sarah. However, his absence didn't alter the fact that they still had to contend with the chauffeur and it didn't take Cartwright long to discover that he had a pretty good command of the English language. Their conversation therefore remained on an impersonal level until they'd checked into the Asia Hotel and the bell boy had shown them up to their room.

"You want to tell me why you left that cock-eyed note for me?" Cartwright asked her quietly.

229

"It was for the benefit of the Security Service. Wentworth was supposed to have told you what it was all about."

"Wentworth? Now there's a name I haven't heard before. Was he with you in Saigon?"

"Yes." Sarah gnawed at her bottom lip. "You know about our involvement in Vietnam then?"

"Not the whole story, I was hoping you would tell me that."

"I'm not sure where to start."

"The beginning is usually as good a place as any."

"I guess it is." She smiled wanly. "I could do with a drink though."

"So could I." Cartwright inspected the array of miniatures inside the mini-bar. "We have gin, whisky, brandy or rum," he said.

"Any ginger ale?"

"One small bottle of Schweppes."

"I'll have a brandy and ginger ale then."

Sarah had always been lucid and blessed with a sharp, incisive brain which enabled her to sort the wheat from the chaff; the drink merely gave her time to compose her thoughts. Although she gave him only the bare facts, he could imagine what those last forty-eight hours in Saigon must have been like for her alone in the Mission House with the Viet Cong closing in on a doomed city.

"So there you have it," Sarah concluded. "Over four million in gold and US dollars went missing, a vital signal disappeared, I failed to destroy most of the Top Secret files and then, to cap it all, the North Vietnamese let me go in double quick time after I'd fallen into their hands."

"This vital signal," Cartwright said, "did it have anything to do with Matthew Gage?"

"Yes. There had been a last minute change of plan and London wanted every UK national out of the country before the Communists took over. I don't know what happened to the original signal which was despatched a week before Saigon fell. I only saw the follow-up that had arrived after I'd left Bien Hoa on the morning of the twenty-eighth of

230

April. Wentworth had left a note for me saying he was going up-country to bring Gage out and when he failed to return, I didn't know what to think. The telephone lines to Hieu Thien where Gage was living were down, the wireless transmitter was out of action, and there was no alternative means of communication. I did the best I could."

"But they expected a miracle, so they crucified you for failing to deliver one."

Sarah finished the rest of her drink, then said, "At the time, I felt very bitter about the way they treated me but with hindsight, I eventually realised they had no option but to withdraw my security clearance. The money had nothing to do with their decision, it was the loss of the Top Secret documents coupled with my sudden release from detention which led them to believe I might have been recruited by a hostile Intelligence Service. They sent me to Bonn to work in the Consular Office where I didn't need any access to classified material. I think they were waiting to see if the KGB would try to establish contact, instead of which, I met you."

"And in due course, Sarah Lucas became Sarah Cartwright."

She gazed at him lovingly. "You may find this hard to believe, Tom, but that was the best thing that ever happened to me even though we may have had our share of ups and downs."

And Sarah had allowed Faulkner to smuggle her out of England because she was convinced Gage had it in his power to destroy their lives. Maybe he was doing the man an injustice, but as far as he could figure out, Faulkner hadn't lifted a finger in her defence when it had mattered most. Now, more than ten years after the event, he was willing to put his neck on the block for purely altruistic reasons. It simply didn't make sense to Cartwright.

"Do you still trust Simon Faulkner?" he said.

"Why do you ask?"

"How far do you think he'd go to save his own skin?"

"Self-preservation is the name of the game in his line of

231

business, Tom, and in that situation I've no doubt that Simon would be completely ruthless."

"Ruthless enough to have someone killed?"

"What?" She shook her head. "I don't think Simon would harm me."

"How about Matthew Gage?" Cartwright asked, forcing her into a corner.

"Under certain circumstances he might be ready to advocate extreme measures, but someone else would have to make the decision."

"And Le Khac Ly?"

Sarah froze. "What's happened to him, Tom?"

"He was thrown off the roof of the high-rise apartment building where he was living. This was on Friday night, just after he'd returned from Macau. The police claim you tried to see him on the Wednesday?"

"Yes, I did."

"What was his job at the Mission House?"

"A little bit of everything – driver, general handyman, interpreter. In the last few weeks before the Republic collapsed, he was employed as a radio telegraphist and was doing an eight hour shift like Peter Wentworth and myself."

A radio telegraphist. Cartwright wondered if Sarah was thinking what he was thinking. "That Top Secret signal which no one could find," he said. "Who should have logged it in?"

"Me. At least, according to the follow-up signal, I would have been standing watch at the time it was despatched from Hong Kong by Simon Faulkner."

"What precedence did he give it?"

"Op Immediate. The flimsy was produced at the official Board of Inquiry chaired by Charles Unger. He also questioned Peter Wentworth and Simon at length and was satisfied that no blame could be attached to them."

"And what did Le Khac Ly have to say for himself?"

"The Inquiry was held after the fall of Saigon and he was one of the Vietnamese we left behind. He eventually got out with the boat people some months later but I guess the SIS

232

were no longer interested in questioning him. In their own minds they were satisfied they knew who was responsible for losing the Top Secret signal."

Sarah spoke without bitterness. There were, he thought, two possible reasons for this: either she acknowledged the fault was hers or else she had ceased to care.

"You didn't lose the signal recalling Gage."

"Thanks for the vote of confidence, Tom, but you're prejudiced."

"I don't believe there was any such cable. I think Le Khac Ly knew this and that's why he was killed. He was a dead man the day Gage decided to come home."

"That presupposition would only make sense if Matthew had voluntarily stayed on in Vietnam and had made his intentions known beforehand."

"Is that so impossible?"

The telephone rang while Sarah was still trying to make up her mind. Answering it, he knew it was Ingram when the switchboard operator announced she had a call for him from Hong Kong. What followed was short and not entirely friendly. Cartwright gave him the codeword and phone number of his Chinese lawyer; Ingram repeated both and then hung up.

"I've been thinking," Sarah told him. "Maybe there was a reason why Matthew would have stayed behind of his own accord. He had a Vietnamese wife and they're very strong on family. It's possible she refused to leave the country unless her parents, grandparents, brothers, sisters, aunts, uncles and cousins came too. The British Government would never have agreed to that; hiding one or two Vietnamese away wouldn't have been a problem but questions would have been asked the moment we started bringing them out in droves." Sarah broke off, frowning, then said, "But you don't kill a man just because he knows there wasn't a signal."

"You might if there's a lot of money at stake, and well over four million did vanish. Kimber laundered the money on behalf of the SIS before they went into Vietnam; perhaps he did the same thing coming out."

"Are you implying that Wentworth arranged for Military Police to hijack the money?" Sarah gave it a moment's thought before shaking her head emphatically. "I can't accept that. Wentworth had no way of knowing the Vietnamese paratroopers at the New Port bridge would accuse me of being a spy for the Viet Cong."

"I think he got lucky. Had everything gone according to plan, the senior NCO in charge of the MPs would have told you he knew another route to the airbase at Bien Hoa which would bypass the Viet Cong at the bridge. Needless to say, you would have 'disappeared' along with the money. To all intents and purposes, you would have been one of the many victims who'd died following the complete breakdown of law and order which preceded the final collapse."

He had only given Sarah a brief outline of what he believed was the full scenario. The rest however took a bit of swallowing and he wasn't sure whether she was ready to digest it yet.

"What am I going to do, Tom?"

He had never seen Sarah looking so vulnerable and his heart went out to her. "I want you to come home with me. There's a British Airways flight to Heathrow this evening and I can't think of a single reason why we shouldn't be on it. Gage, Wentworth, Kimber, Faulkner; none of them can hurt you now, too many people are in the know."

"I can't leave."

"Can't or won't? You've got two bewildered children at home – don't you care about them?"

"Please don't be angry with me, Tom."

"How much longer is your mother expected to go on pretending we're in Paris?"

"You don't understand . . ."

"I'd like to, but you're right – I don't."

"I told you I was taken prisoner on Tuesday the twenty-ninth of April, the day after the battle at the New Port bridge. But the Americans didn't complete the evacuation of their people from the embassy compound until 7:45 a.m. on the thirtieth and there's incontrovertible proof that neither the Viet Cong nor the North Vietnamese Army entered Saigon until after the last helicopter had lifted off."

Sarah was still in control of herself, but only just. Her voice was subdued and all the colour had gone from her face.

"Don't you see, Tom, there's a twenty-four hour gap I can't account for."

Sarah had told him that one of the ARVN paratroopers at the bridge had butt-stroked her with his Armalite rifle and like most people who'd been badly concussed, she had probably lost all account of time.

"Matthew Gage was a VC sympathiser."

"I don't believe that, Sarah, and neither do you."

"It's true, damn it, he told Bill Quarry so. All his wife's family were active Viet Cong."

Cartwright guessed what was coming and knew there wasn't a bloody thing he could say which would calm her very real fears.

"The SIS lost four and a half million in gold and US dollars. What if Matthew tells them I handed it over to the VC? How the hell do I prove he's lying?"

"We'll find that Australian reporter, Mike Kent, who took you to the Caravelle Hotel after you'd been injured . . ."

"They're going to put me in jail, Tom. I'm going to lose you and the children and . . ."

"No one is going to do anything of the kind." He went to Sarah and took her into his arms. "No one is going to lay a finger on you," he said fiercely. "I've got a very loud voice and I'll make sure it's heard all the way from Fleet Street to Parliament Square."

19

Nuri Assad unlocked the door of his flat in Bayswater, picked up the tan-coloured suitcase, the zipper hold-all and the carrier bag containing the duty-free gifts he'd purchased from the stewardess on the British Airways flight and stepped inside the hall. A cleaning woman came in on Mondays, Wednesdays and Fridays to tidy up the flat and he could see at a glance that she had continued to do so in his absence. The carpet looked as though it had been recently vacuumed and the letters and circulars which had been left in the PO box on the ground floor had been collected and placed on the hall table to await his return. Ignoring the pile of envelopes, he carried the suitcase and holdall into the bedroom and unpacked his clothes. It was only after he'd placed the empty suitcase on the top shelf of the fitted wardrobe that he noticed the key on the chest of drawers.

He wondered why Bergitta should have left it there and was immediately angered that she should have the nerve to walk out on him. Usually, it was the other way round and his sense of grievance was fuelled by the fact that Bergitta was the only girlfriend who'd ever had a key to his flat. An English Police Inspector from the Anti-terrorist Squad had talked him into doing that and, in a moment of pique, he wished he'd never met the man. Consoling himself with the thought that he'd already found a replacement for the Swedish girl in the blonde stewardess he'd met on the plane, Assad picked up the key and returned to the hall.

Amongst the circulars and junk mail on the hall table was a small brown envelope without a stamp which had obviously been popped into his mail box downstairs. Opening the envelope, he found it contained a handwritten note from a Detective Inspector Dalton who wished to have a word with him and had thoughtfully listed two phone numbers where he could be contacted. The area code meant nothing to Assad; he simply assumed that Dalton was a member of the Anti-terrorist Squad like Wentworth. Dialling 577-1212, he was vaguely surprised when he got straight through to him.

"My name is Nuri Assad," he said. "I have just returned from Baghdad. You left a note at my flat asking me to call you."

Dalton thanked him for getting in touch so promptly, then said he had reason to believe he was acquainted with a Miss Bergitta Lindstrom.

"We are what you would call good friends," Assad said, then suddenly aware of Dalton's sombre tone, realised that something was wrong. "Miss Lindstrom hasn't come to any harm, has she?" he asked.

"I'm afraid she's dead."

"Dead?" Assad gripped the handle tighter, his knuckles turning white as the blood drained from them. "Dead?" he repeated hoarsely.

"Murdered. Her body was found in a junkyard at Brentford."

"You were supposed to protect her from the Israelis. Inspector Wentworth said that if we helped the police, he would see to it that Bergitta would be guarded night and day. Now you tell me she is dead." His voice rose in fear and anger. "Had I known the Israelis had killed her, I would never have returned from Baghdad. Now my own life is in danger."

"We're not in possession of all the facts yet," Dalton told him, "but no one is going to kill you. There will be a policeman on your doorstep within ten minutes and I'll be with you shortly."

"Don't be surprised if I'm not in," Assad shouted.

"Try to keep calm, sir. Getting yourself into a lather won't help matters."

"I'm going home . . . ."

"I'm afraid we can't allow that," Dalton said quietly.

"Just try and stop me."

Assad slammed the phone down. He had to get away before the Israelis discovered he was back in London and decided to come after him. In a state of extreme agitation, he went into the bedroom, dumped the entire contents of the wardrobe and chest of drawers on to the king-size bed and feverishly started packing. Then it suddenly dawned on him that the police would probably intercept him at Heathrow and he scuttled back to the hall to telephone the Iraqi Embassy in Queens Gate.

Sunday morning wasn't the best time to get hold of anyone; although Moslem, the diplomatic staff believed in conforming with local custom as far as office hours were concerned. By the time Assad succeeded in contacting a senior official, a police constable from the local station was already on his doorstep.

The Dalmatian was eight months old and very lively. Moving with the speed of a greyhound, the dog set off downhill in pursuit of a tennis ball thrown by his young owner. It was a game they always played whenever they were out walking and with almost contemptuous ease, the Dalmatian caught the tennis ball well inside forty yards and while it was still bouncing. Full of energy, the dog turned about, ran back to the boy and dropped the ball at his feet. Then he stood back, tail wagging, and waited for him to pick it up.

From the Thiepval Ridge, they went on down the forward slope towards the road to Miraument, a narrow overgrown copse on their left partially concealing the war memorial to the 36th Ulster Division, a cornfield on the right covering the site of the Schwaben Redoubt. For the umpteenth time, the boy wound himself up, broke into a short run and performing a number of sidesteps as he approached some invisible mark of his own choosing, hurled the ball into the air with all his might. The dog watched the trajectory of the tennis ball for a moment or so as if to calculate where it would land, then

238

scampered after it. On impact, the ball struck a large stone and bounced off at a tangent into the cornfield beyond the low hedgerow.

The Dalmatian changed direction, jumped the obstacle and disappeared from sight a few strides farther on. Unbeknown to the boy, he lost all interest in the ball the instant he saw the rabbit. The subsequent chase was frenetic: the rabbit petrified with fear, twisted and turned, sometimes doubling back on its tracks until at last it reached the hollow fenced in with barbed wire. The Dalmatian was in no mood to call it a day; lying flat on his belly, he wormed his way under the bottom strand and followed the rabbit into what, almost seventy years ago, had been one of the entrance shafts to the Schwaben Redoubt. The dog slithered, fell all of twenty feet and, landing awkwardly, broke his hind leg.

The boy heard his dog howling in pain and ran through the cornfield as fast as his legs would carry him. The barbed wire surrounding the shaft was about chest high and a warning sign placed inside the perimeter spelt out the danger of proceeding any farther, but the fence itself had never been intended to keep anyone out. In places it was possible for an adult to step over it, but the boy had to wriggle under the fence on his stomach and even then the barbs snagged and tore his shirt.

The shaft had served a twofold purpose. It had ventilated the underground chamber where the garrison, except for those sentries on duty in the trenches above, had lived, eaten, slept and sheltered from the almost continuous artillery bombardment of the redoubt. At the same time, the shaft had also enabled the defenders to reach their fire positions in time to cut down the assaulting infantry whenever the barrage had lifted. The shaft had been sunk at an angle of forty-five degrees from the perpendicular. Instead of going straight down, the engineers who'd dug the fortification had made a sharp bend some twenty feet below the surface in order to minimise the blast effect from a direct hit.

Very little light entered the hole and visibility was extremely poor. The boy could not see the Dalmatian but he was sensible enough to realise that the shaft was in a dangerous condition and that anyone who attempted to climb down it in the pitch dark without proper equipment could meet with a serious accident. He called to the dog, tried to calm his fears and promised he would be back to collect him in no time. Then he crawled under the wire again, got to his feet and started running uphill towards the village of Thiepval where he lived.

His father happened to be the Mayor; consequently, there was no shortage of volunteers to make up a rescue party even though it was getting on towards Sunday lunchtime. The equipment, which consisted of ten fathoms of half-inch rope, a flashlight, two lightweight extending ladders, a sledge-hammer and a block and pulley, was provided by a jobbing builder. It was carried to the scene by those patrons of the local *estaminet* who were still sober and the man who elected to go down the shaft was a scaffolder by trade. The village gendarme came along because he had nothing better to do and wished to impress the Mayor.

The scaffolder inspected the hole, decided the extending ladders were not required, and directed the other villagers to anchor the block and pulley to the ground with a number of metal spikes. That done, he passed the rope through the pulley, tied himself on and organised the necessary manpower to lower him down the shaft under the supervision of the gendarme. When he touched bottom, he discovered that in addition to the injured Dalmatian, there were two suitcases and the dead body of a woman in the shaft. He was not a squeamish man but the sickly smell made him gag and it was several moments before the nausea passed and he was able to carry on.

He sent the dog up first, then the pair of matching Vuitton suitcases. Getting the dead woman out proved more difficult than he'd imagined and appreciably more distasteful: rigor mortis had set in and the body had started to decompose. One of the villagers, who wanted to prove he had a stronger stomach than the others, took one look at the ivory-coloured satin slip which had been tied above the head and remarked that the corpse reminded him of a giant tulip that had rotted on the stalk.

According to the luggage labels, the deceased was an Englishwoman called Sarah Cartwright. In reporting the facts to his superior in Albert, the gendarme was bold enough to suggest that the British Embassy in Paris should be informed without delay and wondered why the Inspector should vent his spleen on him.

Nuri Assad, Iraqi national, born 18 March 1953, Baghdad. Height five foot seven, weight one fifty-three pounds, trim, well-proportioned torso, olive skin, dark wavy hair, pencil thin black moustache. Good looking, undoubtedly fancies himself as a ladies' man, married with three children – female 8, female 6, male 5. Wife and family resident in Baghdad. Professes to be a businessman.

Dalton glanced at the profile of Nuri Assad which he'd jotted down in his notebook and felt like adding, 'Is also evasive and probably a compulsive liar'. He thought it significant that Assad had refused to answer any questions before one of the First Secretaries from the Iraqi Embassy arrived.

"This Inspector Wentworth," he said. "When did you say you first met him?"

"One evening around the beginning of May, the second or third – I forget precisely when."

"He just appeared on your doorstep and you invited him inside?"

"Only after I was convinced he knew a great deal about Miss Lindstrom and myself. He also showed me his warrant card which looked exactly like yours."

"Miss Lindstrom wasn't present at the time?"

"No, it was during the week; she was down at Codford St Mary with her employer, Mrs Cartwright."

"Whom Mossad, the Israeli Intelligence Department, were planning to kidnap?"

"So Inspector Wentworth told me."

"I take it you'd heard of the Mossad before?"

Assad looked to his counsellor from the embassy for guidance. Out of the corner of his eye, Dalton saw the Iraqi official nod his head as if to confirm it would be okay for him to answer the question.

"Everyone has heard of those Jewish terrorists," said Assad.

"So when this Inspector Wentworth informed you that you had been targeted by the Israelis, you naturally took his advice and returned to Baghdad a fortnight ago today?"

"I don't understand why you keep asking me the same questions," Assad complained. "As I've already told you, I had some business matters to attend to at home and elsewhere in the Gulf, so it wasn't altogether inconvenient for me to leave this country when I did."

And the Iraqi had allowed Wentworth to have a copy made of his own door key because the Anti Terrorist Squad wanted to lie in wait for the Israelis. Dalton pursed his lips; it was all down there in his notebook and it was pointless taking Assad through his story again because he wasn't going to change it. Furthermore, 'the minder' from the embassy might be tempted to claim diplomatic immunity on his behalf if he thought his fellow countryman was being subjected to a form of police harassment.

"Could you describe Inspector Wentworth?" Dalton thought it unlikely that Assad would be able to help him much there but at least the question had the merit of breaking fresh ground.

"He's taller than me and much broader, has light brown hair and regular features." Assad gave the matter some further thought, then said, "I would think he must be in his early forties."

Dalton couldn't begin to compute the number of man hours they'd spent tracing Assad on the basis of the information Cartwright had given the police through his lawyer. Given the end result, it hardly seemed worth all the effort. But somehow in thanking Assad for assisting them, he even managed to sound as if he meant it.

On his return to Brentford, he looked up Wentworth in the

242

Police and Constabulary Almanac for 1985 and found there was such an Inspector listed under the Anti-terrorist Squad. Further inquiries however elicited the information that Wentworth had died of a heart attack shortly after the almanac had been published.

The Police Sergeant was wearing the same kind of para-military uniform Gage associated with the private security guards he'd seen on the streets of Bangkok. The khaki drill shirt had been starched with rice water, the sleeves folded neatly above the elbow to a regulation width of three inches and pressed with a hot iron. The knife-edge creases in his pants looked sharp enough to draw blood and retained their rigidity even when he was relaxing in a bamboo armchair. The Sam Browne and cutaway pistol holster gleamed like patent leather and the hand-made copy of the Colt .45 automatic which had been turned out in some backstreet workshop in the Philippines had been smeared with a light film of oil and then polished with loving care. It was a typically humid summer evening and the bungalow where Gage was staying could only be approached by a mile long dusty track through the jungle. Yet there wasn't a speck of dust on the working parts of the pistol and the Sergeant somehow managed to look as cool as a cucumber.

Gage had made his acquaintance the previous afternoon not long after he and 'nephew' had arrived from Bangkok. Just how the Sergeant had known that he was staying at 'great uncle's' bungalow near Namtok village was something of a mystery which Gage accepted he was unlikely to solve. Relations between the Thais and the Vietnamese refugees were invariably antagonistic and he supposed one of the locals must have tipped off the Sergeant that an Englishman had moved in with them. It was also far from clear why the policeman was apparently concerned to keep an eye on him.

In the absence of a common tongue, they were obliged to communicate by sign language and the Sergeant's hand signals were open to various interpretations. If Gage understood him correctly, the Thai wanted to know how long he

243

would be staying with 'great uncle', and that was one question he wasn't prepared to answer. Whenever the sergeant raised it, he simply shrugged and made an expansive gesture with his hands as if to say, who knows? As had been the case yesterday, Gage had to repeat the mime umpteen times before the policeman finally gave it up as a bad job and settled back to enjoy the can of beer he'd been given. When he'd completely drained it, he stood up and solemnly shook hands with 'nephew' and 'great uncle', then got into his jeep and drove off, a thin dust cloud rising slowly into the sky behind him.

"I made a mistake coming here, 'nephew'," Gage said quietly. "I'm too conspicuous."

"The fault is mine," the young man told him. "I thought no one would notice your white face amongst all the others."

Gage knew what he meant. Every day, several coach loads of tourists left Bangkok to visit the bridge on the Kwai, stopping off on the way to walk round the war cemetery with its neat rows of headstones set amongst bougainvillaea bushes and jacaranda trees at Kanchanaburi before boarding a four car diesel train for the ninety minute ride to the end of the line. But the bungalow where he was staying was off the beaten track for the tourist and he couldn't have been more obvious.

"You weren't to know the police would be looking out for me, 'nephew'," Gage said and squeezed the young man's shoulder.

For all his fine promises, Group Captain Quarry had briefed the SIS and they in turn had persuaded the Thai authorities to run him to ground. It was the only logical explanation he could think of for the Sergeant's unwelcome appearance late yesterday afternoon and again only a short while ago.

"At least they haven't come for me yet," he said aloud.

"Who haven't?"

"My so-called friends." Gage pushed a hand through his thinning hair. "And speaking of them, they should have the results of my physical by now."

244

"Perhaps they will have some good news for you."

"Depends what you mean by good news. Still, it's time I phoned the Group Captain again. You want to run me down to the store, 'nephew'?"

"I would be honoured to do so," the young man said.

The family owned a Honda scooter that had seen better days and looked as if it was about to fall apart. The saddle had been repaired so many times it resembled a patchwork quilt and there was hardly any stuffing left in the pillion seat. The engine lacked compression, leaked oil and had acquired a thick coating of dust. The clutch was shot to hell and the gearbox sounded as though it was in mortal agony, and if that wasn't enough, the tyres were bald and down to the canvas in several places. The fact that the machine was still more or less in running order was something of a miracle.

The track to the main road followed a tortuous path through tall buffalo grass and the headlight which only functioned intermittently in the gathering dusk was more of a hindrance than a help. Straddling the pillion seat, Gage hung on to the younger man for grim death as they made their way to the highway where there was a filling station and a general store with the only telephone for miles around.

It was the chill from the air conditioner which roused him rather than the dull nagging throb of a headache. Always a restless sleeper, Cartwright had ended up with the lion's share of the bedclothes, leaving just a small triangular flap to cover Sarah's legs as far as the calves. She was completely still and breathing shallowly but although her back was towards him, he knew instinctively that she was wide awake.

"What time do you make it?" he asked her quietly, peering at his wristwatch.

"It's coming up to seven fifteen."

"Check. For a moment, I thought my watch was running on wheels. Do you want to get dressed and go down to dinner?"

"I think I should phone Bill Quarry; Matthew was supposed to call him at five o'clock."

245

"On a Sunday evening?"

"The Sabbath doesn't mean anything to Matthew. He wants a letter signed by the Minister of State at the Foreign Office guaranteeing him immunity from prosecution and he intends phoning every night at five until Quarry confirms that it has arrived from London."

Sarah reached for the telephone and drew it towards her. Then, utilising the full length of the extension cord, she turned over on to her back and placed it between them so that he could listen in. Lifting the receiver, she obtained an outside line and dialled Quarry's number. When he answered, she greeted him like an old acquaintance and asked if he'd heard from Matthew.

"About ten minutes ago," Quarry told her. "He didn't say why he hadn't called at the prearranged time and I didn't bother to ask him. Gage wanted to know if we'd had the results of his medical and I said the doctors at the Siriraj Hospital had confirmed the previous diagnosis. Then he asked if there'd been any word from London yet and I told him the Ambassador had produced a draft on the Minister's instruction which we wanted him to okay."

"Whose idea was that?" Sarah asked. "Simon Faulkner's?"

"Gage was very co-operative," Quarry said, neatly avoiding her question. "I must say it made a welcome change."

"I think you'd better let me talk to Simon. I imagine he's breathing down your neck?"

There was a momentary silence which seemed much longer than it was. Although Cartwright had his ear close to the receiver, he couldn't hear any background noise and presumed Quarry had cupped his hand over the mouthpiece while he and Faulkner hurriedly conversed. If Faulkner had been reluctant to talk to Sarah, he was careful to hide it when he eventually took the phone from Quarry.

"Hello, Sarah," he said coolly. "I was about to phone you with the good news that Matthew has agreed to meet us. I've been in touch with Charles Unger and he's authorised me to offer Matthew a package deal we're sure he'll be unable to resist."

"You mean you're going to buy him off?"

"Only if it's necessary."

"So where and when are you going to see him?"

"Tomorrow morning, some time after eleven," Faulkner said, "but we don't know precisely where just yet. We're to wait at a rendezvous until Matthew sends a guide to collect us."

"Good. What time are we leaving, Simon?"

"Well, there we have a problem. I didn't warn Matthew that you'd be coming too and his guide might walk away from us at the sight of an extra body in the car. Anyway, I rather hoped you'd be going home with Tom. I mean, there's no reason for you to stay on now that we know Matthew isn't in the business of spreading disinformation."

"I'll believe that when he tells me to my face that I didn't give the missing four and a half million to the Viet Cong."

"Hell, Sarah, everyone knows you didn't. Wentworth told the Inquiry he knew the MP sergeant had hijacked the money when he came across the bullet-riddled army truck down by the coast at Can Duoc."

"I'd still like to hear it from Matthew," Sarah told him.

"I'll get him to put it in writing if you like," Faulkner said, then chuckled as if to warn her not to take his offer seriously.

"I want to see Matthew," Sarah repeated stubbornly. "Not sometime maybe never, but tomorrow." She drew a deep breath, then added, "You owe me that much, Simon."

"You're absolutely right," he said, "and if it was up to me, I'd take you with us. But I'm answerable to London if anything goes wrong and there's no way I can get in touch with Gage."

Faulkner sounded as though he was genuinely sorry, but in the short time they had been acquainted, Cartwright had already summed him up as a talented actor with a smooth tongue. Almost leisurely, he removed the phone from Sarah's grasp.

"Let me tell you something, Mr Faulkner," he said icily, "I've had enough of your crap. You've got exactly one minute to give me the location of the rendezvous, otherwise

247

I'll give the *Guardian* a story which will do nothing for you or Mr Charles Unger."

The seconds ticked away, each man waiting to see who was bluffing who. Then, just as Cartwright was about to put the phone down, Faulkner caved in.

"I'll need some time to prepare the ground with Gage."

"We'll arrive at noon," Cartwright told him. "That'll give you an hour."

"The RV is opposite a filling station six miles south of Namtok."

"Where's that?"

"You're in the army, Major," Faulkner said acidly, "I'm sure they must have taught you to read a map."

Cartwright heard him hang up and slowly replaced the receiver. "Somehow, I don't think Simon likes me very much," he told Sarah.

"Never mind, I do."

Sarah picked up the phone and, still facing him, placed it behind her. Then she unravelled the sheet which cocooned his body and proceeded to demonstrate what she meant.

20

Quarry pulled off the road on to the uneven dirt shoulder opposite the filling station and wayside store where Gage had said a guide would meet them. Shifting into neutral, he left the engine running; with the temperature soaring into the high nineties, the Toyota saloon would become hotter than an oven unless he kept the air conditioning on full blast.

"Ten minutes early," Faulkner said, looking at the clock in the instrument panel. "You made good time."

"The traffic was much lighter than I'd expected. How long do you suppose we'll have to wait for the guide?"

Faulkner chuckled. "Matthew has a thing about punctuality, as anyone who works for him knows only too well. In his book, eleven o'clock means exactly that, not a minute after, not a minute before. I don't know how he's managed to keep his sanity all these years considering time doesn't mean a damn thing to the average Vietnamese. They nearly drove me crazy those few months I was in Saigon."

A jeep came down the road from the direction of Namtok village and skidded to a halt opposite one of the pumps on the forecourt of the filling station. A spruce-looking sergeant in khaki drill uniform that still looked as though it had been freshly laundered, got out of the vehicle and stood there staring at them from behind dark sunglasses while the attendant filled the tank.

"Do you suppose he's trying to tell us something?" Quarry said drily.

"No, I just think he's a frustrated movie star."

The attendant removed the nozzle, hooked it into the pump and then replaced the filler cap before returning to the shed in rear of the forecourt which served as his office. Leaving him to make out the sales invoice, the sergeant turned away and strolled over to the roadside store, his right hand brushing the leather pistol holster on his hip.

"See what I mean?" Faulkner continued. "He's been watching too many Clint Eastwood films."

Quarry glanced into the rear view mirror, spotted two cyclists in the far distance and watched them draw slowly nearer. Still riding abreast, they overtook the parked Toyota and eventually disappeared into the shimmering heat haze which lay across the road farther on. A little while later, a bullock cart emerged from the jungle on a narrow track that was not marked on Quarry's map and made a leisurely right-hand turn before trundling off in the same direction as the cyclists. At exactly eleven o'clock, the Vietnamese guide, who had been keeping them under discreet observation from the moment they had arrived, left the roadside store and approached their vehicle. He closed on them cautiously, using the blind spot between the wing and rear view mirrors so that neither man noticed him until just before he tried the rear offside door.

Quarry opened his window a fraction and twisted round to face the stranger.

"Doctor Gage send me," the Vietnamese told him before he could ask.

Quarry nodded, reached past his shoulder and raised the locking catch. "You'd better get in then," he said.

"Sure." The diminutive Vietnamese opened the offside rear door and slid across the bench seat until he was sitting exactly midway between them. "My name Lam Phuong but Doctor Gage, he call me Charlie, say I'm like all VC."

"Is that a fact?" drawled Faulkner.

"You also call me Charlie. Okay?"

Quarry released the handbrake and shifted into drive. "All right, Charlie, suppose you show me the way."

"You go on little bit, then we see track this side of road."

Quarry checked the road was clear behind and pulled off

250

the dirt shoulder. After driving less than a quarter of a mile, he suddenly spotted the track and was forced to put the wheel hard over in order to make the turn.

Tall elephant grass, palm fronds and bamboo hemmed them in on either side, restricting visibility to just a few feet. The track itself was full of potholes and meandered this way and that like a sluggish stream. Occasionally, when they breasted a slight rise in the undulating ground, they could see clumps of bougainvillaea amongst the sea of grass and, forward of the barren hills in the background, a dark blur on the horizon marked the limit of the tree line.

"Nice country for an ambush," Faulkner observed casually. He caught Quarry's eye and smiled ironically. "Reminds me of Vietnam."

"Yes? Well, I'm happy to say that's one experience I missed."

"Truth is, you never knew where or when Charlie was going to hit you. The Yanks built this four-lane highway to their air base at Bien Hoa, fifteen miles north-east of Saigon, and cleared the scrub on either side of the road as a deterrent to snipers, yet it didn't stop the local VC taking potshots at the passing traffic in broad daylight. Usually they missed the target by a mile and their efforts were more of a nuisance value than anything else but come nightfall, things were very different. No one, unless he was a complete idiot, moved along that road after dark."

Quarry tried reminding himself that they were in Thailand not Vietnam but he couldn't suppress an involuntary shudder. The private armies of the warlords who controlled the heroin coming out of the Golden Triangle frequently clashed and sometimes the bloodshed spilled over into Thailand. He glanced at the reflection in the rear view mirror and wondered if the placid Vietnamese sitting behind them was carrying a revolver under the traditional black pyjama suit. Although Quarry couldn't think of one good reason why Charlie should want to kill them, the fact remained that he was ideally placed to take both of them out

251

with a bullet through the head. The sight of the ramshackle bungalow in a jungle clearing therefore came as something of a relief.

"We here," Lam Phuong informed them unnecessarily.

As if to confirm his announcement, Gage appeared on the veranda leaning heavily on the shoulder of the 'nephew' Quarry had seen him with at the Siriraj Hospital in Bangkok. If he didn't seem all that pleased to see him, he looked grimmer still when Faulkner got out of the car carrying a government-issue briefcase. A spark of anger flared in his sunken eyes and he rounded on Quarry.

"Your word isn't worth a lot, is it?" he said furiously. "You promised me you would keep the SIS out of this."

"You're not being fair to him, Matthew." Faulkner smiled. "You might have guessed the Foreign Office would consult us the moment you made your demands known."

"Maybe so, but they didn't have to send you."

"Oh yes they did, Matthew. I knew you better than anyone else in the Service, with the possible exception of Sarah Lucas."

"Sarah's here in Thailand?"

"Yes, with her husband. As a matter of fact, she's due to arrive at the RV in less than an hour's time. She wants to have a word with you."

"What about?" Gage asked, immediately suspicious.

"Vietnam finished Sarah's career and she's got it into her head that you were partly to blame for that because you elected to stay behind when we pulled out."

"I made my position very clear the day you recruited me. I told you then that I would never leave the country unless my whole Vietnamese family could accompany me."

"You couldn't have made the point more forcibly. But Sarah has got this fixation and nothing I can say will convince her she's got it all wrong." Faulkner advanced towards the veranda. "Don't look so worried, Matthew. If you don't want to meet Sarah again, just say the word and I'll send her packing."

Although Quarry's knowledge of what had happened in Saigon ten years ago was decidedly sketchy, it did seem to him that Faulkner was distorting the facts to present Sarah Cartwright in the worst possible light.

Gage pursed his lips. "Can you do that?"

"No problem, Sarah doesn't have any official status."

"Then how come she's fastened on to you again?"

"Because she's a Lucas and that family has a lot of influence." Faulkner raised his briefcase and put on an even more dazzling smile. "Can't we go inside out of the sun?" he asked cheerfully. "I've got a draft letter here I'd like to discuss with you."

"I asked the Minister of State to guarantee me immunity from prosecution. So long as he's put that in writing, we've nothing to discuss."

"There's the little matter of your pension."

"What pension?"

Gage hadn't retreated an inch and was still blocking the way at the top of the short flight of steps leading to the veranda. Glancing over his shoulder at the Vietnamese guide, Quarry saw that Charlie had folded his arms across his chest in a half-hearted attempt to conceal the small automatic he was now holding in his right hand.

"Century House is empowered to make discretionary awards from a special contingency fund," Faulkner explained patiently. "Charles Unger, who used to run the South-East Asia Bureau in your day, persuaded the Director General that you should receive a pension of six thousand in recognition of past services."

"What's the catch?" Gage demanded.

"We'd rather you didn't publish your memoirs. Leastways, we don't want you to include any anecdotes about the SIS should you be invited to write a book about your experiences in Vietnam."

"How about the CIA?"

"Oh, you can rubbish them as much as you like," Faulkner said airily. "They deserve a few brickbats for the dog's breakfast they sold us."

253

"You're quite a character, Simon."

"I have my moments."

"Like the time at Hieu Thien when you introduced your Girl Friday to Pot?" Gage looked past them to the guide, gabbled something in Vietnamese, then said, "I've decided to send Charlie back to the RV on the family moped." Beckoning Quarry and Faulkner to follow him, he slowly turned about and led them into the bungalow. "It'll be nice meeting Sarah again after all these years."

"I've always been very fond of her too," Faulkner told him.

The bungalow had been subdivided by a hardboard partition to form a communal living room and an equally communal sleeping area. The living room was furnished on spartan lines with cushions scattered about the floor, three assorted home-made bamboo chairs and an ice chest in lieu of a refrigerator. Quarry's nose told him that some highly spiced dish was simmering on a wood-burning stove next to the sleeping quarters where he presumed the rest of the family were hiding themselves.

"You wouldn't kid an old man, would you, Simon? I mean, is it really true that the SIS is prepared to grant me a pension of six thousand a year?"

A motor cycle engine coughed into life and ran unevenly, backfiring at least twice before it finally settled down. Faulkner waited until the rider moved off, then said, "Our insurance assessors thought it was a fair sum."

"Especially when they took the state of my health into account," Gage said bitterly.

The car was parked somewhere off the dirt road in a small clearing halfway between the bungalow and the highway to Bangkok. The vehicle was hidden from view by the tall elephant grass and Lam Phuong would never have known it was there had it not been for the fresh tyre marks on the dusty surface of what was a game track made by a herd of water buffalo. He did not find it hard to justify why his curiosity should take precedence over the task he'd been given. The car represented a potential threat and, in his opinion, checking it out was more important than guiding two more visitors to the bungalow. Cutting the engine, Lam Phuong left the Honda lying on its side by the dirt road and followed the game track into the elephant grass, a 6.35mm Tokarev automatic pistol in his right hand.

The driver of the grey-coloured Mercedes had followed the game track for roughly forty yards, then made a U-turn to leave the car facing the dirt road leading to the main highway. The way the elephant grass had been trampled underfoot in the immediate vicinity of the vehicle suggested that the driver had been accompanied by three other men. It was also apparent that all four had moved off in single file towards the bungalow.

He wondered how long they had been gone; the car felt warm when he touched it but with the sun directly overhead, that was only to be expected. Lam Phuong tried the front offside door, found it wasn't locked and quietly opened it. Locating the appropriate catch, he released the bonnet, then walked round to the front of the car to check the radiator. The header tank and hose connections were still hot, proof that the strangers had arrived only a few minutes ago. They would have heard the Honda and realised the rider had stopped some distance from the highway. It was also logical to assume that they would therefore send one of their number doubling back on their tracks to investigate.

A shiver ran down his spine and he sensed someone was watching him. But instead of trusting his instincts, Lam Phuong merely stood there rooted to the spot, immobile as a statue. He heard the intruder break cover and turned round, but he'd already left it far too late and the knife slid between his ribs to pierce the right lung. A bloody froth trickled from the corner of his mouth and spattered the front of his black high-necked jacket. His legs buckling, he somehow managed to face his attacker and even contrived to aim the Tokarev automatic at him, only to discover he lacked the strength to squeeze the trigger.

The Chinaman struck again and buried the hunting knife deep into the left side of his chest. Lam Phuong grunted in pain, sank down on to his knees and rolled over, his eyes glazed and already sightless before his head struck the ground.

21

The highway was an uneven black stripe that cleaved through the jungle in a dead straight line to Namtok and beyond. The village had existed long before the surveyors had plotted its position on a map and, without knowing the facts, it was difficult to see what had persuaded Caltex to build a filling station two miles south of the nearest habitation. Despite its weather-beaten appearance and ramshackle construction, Cartwright thought the general store was very much an afterthought and had been erected by some local entrepreneur who'd hoped to cash in on its proximity to the highway and the adjoining filling station. Neither establishment was doing much in the way of business: there was just a solitary jeep on the Caltex forecourt and in the quarter of an hour they'd been waiting there, four coachloads of tourists had swept past without stopping.

"It's beginning to look as though Matthew has refused to see me," Sarah said, breaking a lengthy silence.

"Not yet it isn't; you forget we arrived here well ahead of time."

Privately, Cartwright wondered if Faulkner had decided to shelve their arrangement in the confident belief that he couldn't give the story to the *Guardian* without putting Sarah in the firing line. But to get away with that, Faulkner would have to pull the wool over Quarry's eyes and from what Sarah had told him, the Defence Attaché was no slouch, for all his placid ways. In the end, it all came back to Gage.

"What's Matthew like?" he asked.

"He was always very kind to me – and thoughtful too. He was also a fine doctor. Mind you, as a resistance leader, he was next to useless, like all the other so-called guerilla fighters we inherited from the CIA." A whimsical smile appeared on Sarah's lips. "Of course, I may be doing Matthew an injustice; I mean, we know now that all his in-laws were Viet Cong sympathisers and it's possible he deliberately set out to create the impression he was incompetent."

"Where did Wentworth come from?"

"The CIA. They took him on after he was discharged from the New Zealand Army."

No one could say Wentworth was incompetent. A highly professional soldier, he would have realised the Government forces were cracking up long before the final showdown. Cartwright also believed he was the man who had been the driving force behind the plan to steal the four and a half million in gold and US dollars belonging to the SIS mission. And poor communications wasn't the reason why Faulkner had left Saigon: he had returned to Hong Kong in order to give himself the perfect alibi and finalise the arrangements with Kimber for laundering the stolen money. In which case, it was likely that Kimber had also provided an ocean-going boat to collect the proceeds of the hijack. Although Macready had been waiting down-river from the port of Can Duoc the day the money had been hijacked, Cartwright was pretty sure the Australian hadn't been involved in the conspiracy. According to what he had told Sarah, a fast patrol boat had passed him heading out to sea shortly before he'd picked up Wentworth. Then, too, Macready would have made sure he wasn't at home the night the hit team came looking for Sarah.

"How long have you known Ellen Rothman?"

Sarah looked faintly amused. "What is this, Tom – an interrogation?"

"Sort of."

"Our one and only meeting took place in the departure lounge at Heathrow when we swapped plane tickets. I didn't really pay much attention to her at the time, but looking back, she did seem a bit on edge, as though it was her first assignment."

258

"I wonder how Faulkner got his hooks into her?" he said idly.

"Search me." Sarah caught her breath. "Wait a minute though, Simon is now the Assistant Director in charge of Personnel and Administration. He's responsible for internal recruiting and would see all the applications from Foreign Office personnel who consider they have a special skill to offer and would like a transfer to the SIS."

Sarah had just given him one of the missing pieces from the jigsaw he had been looking for. Ellen Rothman was undoubtedly one such applicant and Faulkner had chosen her because she'd happened to be available and no one else in the Service had ever laid eyes on her.

"'Ellen Rothman won't talk out of turn,'" Sarah said bitterly. "That's what Simon told me when I asked him if she would be okay."

"Well, he would, wouldn't he?"

"They've killed her, haven't they?"

"They had to. If they hadn't screwed it up, you were going to disappear without trace and I was going to be charged with Bergitta's murder. If you accept that premise, there was no way they could allow Ellen Rothman to walk away."

A trim-looking policeman in khaki drill appeared in the doorway of the general store and stood there gazing in their direction. Then, as if to see them more clearly, he removed his dark sunglasses and tucked them away in the breast pocket of his shirt. Finally, having apparently given the matter some considerable thought, he sauntered towards them.

"How's your Thai, Sarah?"

"I can't even say good morning."

"Terrific. Let's hope he understands English."

It did not take them long to establish that he had no comprehension whatsoever. Although there was a Chinese community in Bangkok, the Sergeant was an up-country policeman and Sarah's Cantonese was wasted on him. He also proved equally unresponsive to their attempts to communicate by sign language.

259

"I've had enough of this." Sarah opened the door on her side and got out.

"Where do you think you're going?" Cartwright asked her.

"The general store. Seems to me it's the only place with a telephone and I've a hunch Matthew used it to get in touch with Bill Quarry. And if I'm right about that, he must have obtained the owner's permission somehow."

Sarah walked round the back of the car, beckoned the sergeant to follow her and crossed the road. When she returned some ten minutes later, he could tell Sarah was secretly pleased with herself even though she tried to hide it.

"Well?"

"The man who owns the place has his entire family living on the premises – parents, aunts, uncles, cousins – the lot. One of the girl cousins could speak a little English. She described Matthew and said he and a young Vietnamese had been in there yesterday. She also told me that about an hour ago she'd seen two men sitting in a car where ours is parked now. A guide was waiting for them in the store and after he'd got into their car, they drove off towards Namtok. There's a track on our left just up the road which she says leads to a bungalow occupied by a large number of refugees from Vietnam."

"What do you want to do, Sarah? Wait for a guide who may not show up or take a chance that the track she spoke of is the right one?"

He hoped Sarah would tell him to turn round and go back to Bangkok, but that was like asking for the moon.

"The sergeant behaved rather strangely. I got the distinct impression he was angry with the girl cousin for telling me where I could find Matthew."

The sergeant had returned to his jeep and was leaning against it, arms folded across his chest. The sunglasses were back in place again and it was difficult to tell if he was still angry, for the rest of his face below the eyes was about expressive as an image of Buddha.

"He looks harmless enough." Cartwright pursed his lips,

then said, "Gage seems to have an absolute mania for privacy and it wouldn't surprise me if he'd paid the sergeant a retainer to discourage visitors."

"I expect you're right, Tom."

"So what do we do?"

"Let's go and see Matthew," she said.

The more Quarry got to know Matthew Gage, the more convinced he was that the man lacked stability and was as changeable as a weather vane. When Gage had phoned him at home soon after disembarking at Bangkok, he'd insisted the SIS should be kept in the dark and had hinted his life would be in danger if any of his former colleagues should catch up with him. He had also wanted a letter from the Minister of State for the Foreign and Commonwealth Office guaranteeing him immunity from prosecution under the Official Secrets Acts. Now it seemed he was prepared to accept a draft the Minister hadn't even seen and was ready to sit down with Simon Faulkner despite the hostility he'd shown him just over an hour ago.

There was, Quarry thought, only one possible explanation for his strange behaviour. For all his outward show of bravado, Gage had never really accepted that he had terminal cancer. Deep inside him, he had nursed a hope that the tests he'd undergone at the Siriraj Hospital would show the disease was still operable. The fact that they had confirmed the original prognosis he'd received from the Vietnamese doctors had brought him up with a jolt and made him realise he might well die in Thailand if he persisted with his impossible demands. In his present state of mind, Gage was ready to clutch at any straw and the pension of six thousand a year had been the final clincher.

"Do I get a copy of this offer?" Gage asked.

"Of course you do," Faulkner assured him.

"It would look better with your signature on it, Simon."

"So long as you're happy with the terms." Faulkner took out a gold-plated Parker, uncapped it and signed the original and three carbon copies with a flourish.

261

"You wouldn't mind witnessing it, would you, Group Captain?"

Quarry couldn't see what good it would do Gage to have his signature on the document. If the SIS decided to renege on the agreement, a memorandum drawn up on a single sheet of uncrested notepaper was unlikely to deter them, but he reckoned the doctor was old enough to look after himself.

"Why not?" he said genially.

"That's the ticket."

Quarry couldn't remember the last time he'd heard anyone use that old-fashioned expression. In his attitude, even in his speech patterns, it was obvious that Gage hadn't seen England for a very long time.

"I believe in travelling light," Gage continued, "so it won't take me long to pack. Meantime, help yourselves to another beer."

Faulkner stared at him, mouth open in surprise. "You mean you're returning to Bangkok with us?"

"I haven't the time to let the grass grow under my feet." Gage stood up. "I figure 'nephew' and I will travel with you in the Group Captain's car and Lam Phuong can bring up the rear with Sarah and her husband." The usual lopsided smile made yet another brief appearance. "I don't see me taking in the bright lights of Bangkok, so my friends will be keeping me company until I get on the plane to London."

"I've got a better idea," Faulkner said casually. "Why don't you stay here until I've made all the necessary arrangements? Tomorrow evening is the earliest we can get you on a direct flight to the UK."

Gage ignored the suggestion. His attitude as he stood there completely motionless in the middle of the room reminded Quarry of an alert gun dog.

"Car's coming," he said tersely.

Quarry heard it too and moved to the open window. Away to his left a thin plume of dust rose into the still air like an Indian smoke signal. Then a Mazda saloon entered the clearing, its driver making for the only patch of shade near a spindly tree at the side of the bungalow.

"Where the hell has Charlie got to?" Gage asked in a querulous voice, then answered his own question before anyone else could. "Damned scooter must have broken down."

He stepped out on to the veranda, the 'nephew' providing a shoulder for him to lean on. Faulkner was still moving towards the door when someone armed with an automatic rifle opened up with a long burst of twelve to fifteen rounds from a fire position in the elephant grass at left ten o'clock from the bungalow. A second gunman directly to the front added to the lethal cacophony and was rapidly joined by a third positioned on the right flank. The combined firepower of three Kalashnikov assault rifles began to reduce the ramshackle bungalow to matchwood.

Quarry threw himself flat on the floor and crawled out of the zone of fire, seeking what cover he could find in the near corner of the room. A bullet shattered his left ankle, all but severing the foot. Although in a state of extreme shock, he somehow managed to undo and remove the narrow leather belt from his slacks and use it as a tourniquet to stop the arterial bleeding. Over by the open doorway, Faulkner was lying on his right side, knees drawn up to his stomach like a foetus in the womb. There was a blank look of total incomprehension in his eyes and all the colour had drained from his face.

Cartwright was half in, half out of the Mazda saloon when the ambush was sprung. The gaunt-looking European whom he assumed must be Gage, had just started down the short flight of steps from the veranda when he was hit by the initial burst of fire. The impact lifted him off his feet and he almost made a complete revolution in mid-air before coming to rest in a crumpled, untidy heap at the foot of the steps. The young Vietnamese he'd been leaning on was lying face down on the veranda, one arm reduced to a bloody trunkated stump above the elbow.

His brain registered the carnage with the shutter speed of a camera and instantly moved on to another plane. Realising Sarah would make a plum target for the rifleman on the right flank if she got out on her side, he twisted round and, crouching down, reached inside the car to pull her across the front seats. Sarah was already inching her way towards him in a semi-prone position on her side, both feet still on the floor, head, right shoulder and hip bridging the seats. Grabbing her arms, he hauled Sarah out of the car, then shielded her on the ground with his body as the nearest gunman raked the Mazda from nose to tail.

The windscreen exploded like a bomb, exit holes appeared in the rear door and a ricochet punctured the fuel tank. A pool formed underneath the rear axel, failed to drain away in the sunbaked earth and began to spread outwards. Although none of the Kalashnikovs were loaded with one in five tracer, Cartwright knew the exhaust system was still hot enough to ignite the petrol should it drip on to the tail pipe. There was also the risk that a high velocity bullet striking the chassis would produce a flash on impact capable of detonating the vapour.

"We've got to make a break for it," he told Sarah. "Soon as I give the word, run like hell and go to ground in the elephant grass."

To reach it, they would have to cross roughly fifteen yards of open ground. Although both of them were reasonably fit, they weren't exactly in training and with the best will in the world, they were unlikely to cover the distance in less than three seconds starting from a prone position. That would give the gunman on the right flank plenty of time in which to pick them up in his sights and aim off for a moving target. The Kalashnikov stuttered again, then stopped abruptly. While he didn't hear the weapon being re-cocked, Cartwright reckoned there was a good chance the thirty round magazine was empty.

"Go – go – go."

Sarah responded automatically and was up and running like a hare before he was. Still a good arm's length ahead of him when they reached the tall elephant grass, she instinctively veered to the right to distance herself as much as possible from the unseen gunman before she dropped flat.

Cartwright followed her example, caught his foot in a pothole and went sprawling. When he looked up, she was nowhere in sight, nor could he hear her moving about.

Another rifleman started blasting away somewhere behind the bungalow, but after ripping off four quick bursts, he ceased firing. Moments later, Cartwright heard the hollow whoof of a petrol bomb and a mushroom-shaped cloud of black smoke appeared above the corrugated iron roof. As the fire took hold, there was a frantic exodus from the rear of the shack.

The gunman on Cartwright's right started to advance towards him, putting down suppressive fire as he came on. The fact that he had put the selector switch on to repetition suggested a need to conserve ammunition. Retreating before him as quietly as he could, Cartwright moved deeper into the jungle with the intention of circling round behind him in a wide outflanking movement. Someone the other side of the bungalow called out in a high-pitched voice and was answered by two other men who sounded as though they were to his left and right. The high-pitched voice called again and this time got a reluctant monosyllabic grunt from the gunman advancing in Cartwright's direction. Then, in what seemed a gesture of defiance, he squeezed off two more rounds in rapid succession before obeying the command he'd been given to cease firing.

Although the brief verbal exchange hadn't meant a thing to him, Cartwright was sure the intruders were about to pull out. No one had spooked them into springing the ambush prematurely; on the contrary, they had decided when was the most opportune moment to open fire, and therefore Gage had to be the target. Their mission accomplished within a matter of seconds, they'd then sought to eliminate anyone who might prevent them from making a clean break. The cease-fire had come about because the man in charge had realised no one was capable of lifting a finger to stop them.

But neither side had reckoned with Sarah. Above the noise of the fire, Cartwright could just hear her moving stealthily through the elephant grass. She had waited until the gunman had passed the spot where she had gone to ground and was now closing on him from the rear. He couldn't think what the hell she was playing at; the hit team was leaving and with her knowledge of Cantonese, she ought to have known that better than anyone else. But that was beside the point; if he could hear her, so could the man with the Kalashnikov and unless he did something pretty damned quickly, Sarah would be dead.

"I'm over here," he shouted.

Cartwright leapt up and clapped his hands for good measure, then threw himself sideways and rolled over on one shoulder. The Chinaman fired from the hip, traversing in a clockwise direction as he ripped off four rounds. One was a little too close for comfort and ploughed into the earth inches from his head. Cartwright bobbed up again and this time broke into a fast jinking run to present a tempting yet fleeting target. It was in fact a variation of Russian Roulette and very nearly as suicidal.

Sarah went in fast. She had trusted Faulkner implicitly because she had been brought up to be unswervingly loyal to her superiors no matter what, and in return, he had done his level best to have her killed.

In his absence, the hired killer was an acceptable substitute on whom she could vent her rage. His back was still towards her as he fired round after round into the swaying grass completely oblivious of the danger behind him. Judging the distance to perfection, she suddenly pirouetted like a ballet dancer and delivered a high, side-step kick to his spine. She caught him with the heel and sole of her foot, her right leg, initially bent at the knee, the pile-driving force behind the blow as she straightened it out.

There was a sharp cracking noise followed by an agonised grunt; then the man toppled forward over the Kalashnikov. His index finger was still inside the trigger guard and the barrel was pointing upwards at his chin when he involuntarily fired the last shot. The high velocity bullet shattered his jaw and removed the greater part of his skull as it exited. Numb with horror, Sarah stood there on the edge of the clearing in full view of the enemy looking down at the fine spray of blood, fragments of bone and grey matter which had spattered her sweatshirt, cotton slacks and trainers.

Cartwright sprinted towards her, took off in a headlong dive and knocked Sarah flat, his left shoulder catching her above the knees as he folded both arms around her legs. She hit the ground hard and lay there on her back, dazed and winded. Leaving her to recover, he crawled back to the dead man and retrieved the Kalashnikov. A bullet passed low enough over his head for him to feel the physical displacement it made in the air before he heard the crack, thump of a high velocity round travelling at 2330 feet per second. More importantly, he spotted the muzzle flash from the weapon and was able to pinpoint the marksman. Still lying in a prone position, he pulled the butt into his shoulder, closed his left eye and taking deliberate aim, squeezed the trigger. On the opposite side of the clearing, a man dressed in a Hawaiian shirt and dark trousers tumbled out of the elephant grass and lay still.

"Tom?" Sarah's voice rose a fraction. "Where the hell are you?"

"Between you and the bungalow," he told her.

"Thank God. I was sure you'd been hit."

"No, that was the other fellow." Cartwright thought he could detect signs of movement in the dense undergrowth the far side of the clearing. "I think maybe the survivors have had enough," he added.

"They're going?"

"Looks like it."

He told Sarah to stay put until he was absolutely sure, but she wasn't in a mood to listen. Hugging the ground, she crawled forward to join him.

"Are you okay?" he asked.

"I'm fine. I must have gone into shock back there, but I'm okay now."

"Good." Cartwright jerked a thumb in the direction of the bungalow. "Do you think you can cover me while I take a look in there?"

"Are you mad? The whole place is ablaze."

"I think Quarry and Faulkner are still inside. I can't walk away not knowing whether they're dead or alive."

Sarah took the rifle from him. "Be careful then," she said.

A lot of the roof had already fallen in and those sheets of corrugated iron that were left were glowing. Even as Cartwright approached the veranda, the intense heat began to singe his hair. Holding his breath, he scrambled through the open window and lay down on the floor. It was impossible to see anything in the dense black smoke, but a few feet to his right he could hear someone choking and crawled over to him. He reached out and grabbed hold of an arm, then crabbed his way to the door, dragging the injured Quarry with him. It was then he came upon Faulkner curled up in a tight ball, knees and arms hugging his stomach as though he was trying to close a gaping wound.

Cartwright thought he was probably dead but couldn't stop to make sure, nor could he abandon him on the strength of a cursory glance. With his free hand he seized Faulkner by the waistband of his Daks, got to his feet and keeping his head and shoulders well down, began to haul both men out on to the veranda. The smoke attacked his eyes, nose and throat, got down on to his lungs and brought on a paroxysm of coughing. A tongue of flame licked his head and set the hair alight. On the verge of collapse, he made it through the doorway, fell down the veranda steps in a jumbled heap, and blacked out. When he came round, Sarah was pummelling his chest.

"My God, Tom, that's the second time you've frightened the life out of me."

"I thought I'd had it too," he gasped. Bouts of coughing racked his whole body and he leaned over on to his left side to spit out the mucus he'd brought up from his lungs. Gradually his chest cleared and he was able to breathe more easily. "How's Quarry?"

"Bill's alive, but only just. He's in shock and has lost a lot of blood."

"And Faulkner?"

"He's dead." Sarah paused, as though surprised at her

268

own composure then said, "Bill's the one we should be worrying about. Do you think you can look after him while I go back to the highway and phone the embassy?"

"Of course I can. You get moving."

"Right. HMS *Birmingham* should still be in port and she has a Lynx helicopter on board . . ."

Sarah broke off and tilted her head on one side to listen intently. Cartwright thought she was imagining things and was just about to say so when he too heard the vehicle.

"It's coming this way."

Sarah nodded, picked up the Kalashnikov she had placed on the ground within easy reach and moved back into the elephant grass. He asked her where she was going but instead of answering him, she merely waved a hand as if to say no more questions. A few minutes after she had disappeared from sight, a jeep pulled into the clearing and the immaculate Sergeant got out. He glanced left and right as if sizing up the situation and slowly undid the leather flap of his pistol holster.

"Don't even think about it," Sarah screamed at him.

The sergeant jumped, spun round to face her and nearly had heart failure when she put a round into the earth inches from his left foot.

"You heard me," Sarah yelled at the top of her voice.

"For God's sake," Cartwright told her, "the man doesn't understand English."

"Oh yes he does. That's why he was so angry with the girl at the store when she told me how to find this place. He didn't want us to see Matthew because he knew what was going to happen."

Somewhat tentatively, the sergeant raised both hands shoulder high. Whether this proved that he understood English was a moot point. In his place, Cartwright thought most people would do the same, especially after someone had fired a shot at them.

"Don't you see, Tom? Money talks, and someone in Bangkok took a backhander to locate Matthew Gage and the sergeant was in on the deal."

269

The Kalashnikov was equally persuasive. At Sarah's command, the Sergeant removed his Sam Browne and pistol holster and laid them on the ground, then obediently waited, hands clasped together on top of his head while she exchanged the assault rifle for his Colt .45 automatic. Sarah then climbed into the back of the jeep and ordered him to get in and drive her to the general store.

The afternoon wore on. About an hour after Sarah had departed, some members of the Vietnamese family returned and, using sign language, Cartwright got them to cut down enough palm fronds to build a makeshift shelter to protect Quarry from the sun. He did the best he could for him, periodically loosening the tourniquet to prevent the onset of gangrene, but the Defence Attaché kept slipping in and out of consciousness and was delirious most of the time.

The Lynx helicopter arrived with Sarah on board shortly after four o'clock and was the best sight Cartwright had seen all day. The medical evacuation team consisted of a Surgeon Lieutenant Commander and a Leading Sick Berth Attendant, both of whom knew their jobs backwards. Quarry, the surgeon announced cheerfully, would be almost as good as new by the time they had finished with him, and Cartwright was inclined to believe it. Within the space of a few minutes, they had given Quarry a shot of morphine, patched him up for the journey, and were on their way to Bangkok.

"You did a great job, Sarah," Cartwright said when they were alone.

"Oh, sure," she said wearily, "I'm a regular heroine."

Cartwright reached out for her and wondered why she flinched as he seized a wrist to draw her into his arms. When he inspected her hands, he saw that both palms were blistered.

"How . . . ?"

"Your hair was on fire, Tom, and I didn't want you to go bald on me."

Cartwright smiled and kissed her tenderly.

"I want to go home, Tom."

"So do I."

"I mean right now."

"I'm afraid the authorities in Bangkok may want to question us first," Cartwright said.

It proved to be something of an understatement. The police interrogation and their subsequent debriefing with the SIS Resident at the embassy lasted until Wednesday the twenty-sixth of June.

1985

FRIDAY 28 JUNE

22

Cartwright tried to concentrate on the file that had been marked up for his urgent attention, but the case was as dull as ditchwater and he felt himself nodding off again from the effects of jet lag. He shook his head in an attempt to suppress a cavernous yawn and made a determined effort to keep his eyes open, but to no avail. The words became even more blurred and his chin finally met his chest; then the phone rang and he woke up with a start. Lifting the receiver, he found he couldn't remember the number of his extension and had to peer at the disc in the centre of the dial before answering.

"2198, Cartwright," he said in a voice that sounded far away.

"Lionel Alderton."

"Who?"

"The Sentinel Inquiry Agency."

"Sorry, Mr Alderton," he said apologetically, "I'm just not with it this morning."

"That's all right, Major." Alderton cleared his throat. "I phoned Mr Edgecombe twice yesterday evening but couldn't get a reply and it seems he's in court this morning. I only tried your office number on the offchance you might be in." He cleared his throat a second time. "I've finished my investigation into the business interests of Euro Time Sharing," he continued. "A full report is in the post but I can give you the salient points now if you're not too busy."

"There's nothing on my desk that can't wait."

"Well then, the first thing you should know is that Euro Time Sharing is merely a subsidiary of Eurcom Enterprises. The parent firm is a highly diversified company; their

registered offices are in Lichtenstein and they're into everything – insurance, banking, commodities, tourism, property,
warehouses, scrap metal and land. I think they've developed
asset-stripping to a fine art."

"What's this about scrap metal?" Cartwright said, interrupting him.

"That comes under the heading of land speculation.
About a year ago, Eurcom acquired a junkyard in Brentford
to go with the wharf belonging to the defunct East India
Tea Company which they already owned. Apparently, that
whole area down by the river is scheduled for redevelop-
ment."

The junkyard was also the place where Bergitta Lindstrom's body had been found. Cartwright had often
wondered how the man who'd stolen his Mini and reduced it
to a heap of junk in the crusher could have been so confident
that no one would disturb him. Now he knew the answer.

"Is a man called Peter Wentworth on the board of
directors?"

"You know him, Major?"

"No, but his name has cropped up a few times in the past
week. When did Eurcom Enterprises start trading?"

"October 1975. Euro Time Sharing was formed twenty-
one months later in July '77. Both companies are co-located
in the New Providence office block near the Baker Street
Underground."

Kimber's timing had been perfect; the SIS had finished
their internal inquiry and the Wilson government had got
the result they wanted from the referendum on the Common
Market. The business world was looking to Europe and
amongst the many other holding companies which were
being formed to exploit this new opportunity, the emergence
of Eurcom Enterprises would not have caused a stir.

"Do they hold an annual general meeting?" Cartwright
asked.

"Yes, and a very cosy affair it is too; there are very few
shareholders and they all seem to vote by proxy."

There was a whole lot more but he listened to Alderton

276

with only half an ear, his mind busy grappling with what he was going to do with the information. The obvious answer was to pass it straight on to Dalton, but things were never that simple. Everything that had happened in Thailand was taboo and the SIS Head of Station in Bangkok had made it very clear what would happen to them if the press ever got hold of the Matthew Gage story. Even supposing the Attorney General proved reluctant to prosecute them for offences under the Official Secrets Acts, Cartwright knew the army would come down on him and there were any number of ways they could finish his career if they really put their minds to it. And although it was difficult to see what the Establishment could do to Sarah when it was evident they weren't prepared to charge her, she had wanted the Foreign Office to know that she wouldn't rock the boat.

"I'm glad I managed to have a word with you," Alderton said, winding up. "I wouldn't have been very happy if the police had learned what was in my report before you did."

"Why should they?"

"I sent them a copy, Major. Naturally, I consulted Mr Edgecombe first."

"I thought you said you couldn't get in touch with him yesterday evening?"

"This was on Wednesday. I'd just finished drafting my report and had popped out of the office to have a bite of lunch when I saw this paragraph about Ellen Rothman in the *Standard*."

He knew what was coming before Alderton told him. Ellen Rothman was a dead woman the day she agreed to pass herself off as Sarah. The precise manner of her death and what they had done with her body were the only things he hadn't been able to work out for himself.

"You did the right thing," Cartwright told him.

"I didn't have much choice, Major. I hung on to the report until yesterday evening hoping you would phone me."

"Where did you send my copy?"

"To your flat in Pelham Street."

In truth, it wouldn't have made a jot of difference where Alderton had sent it. Their flight from Bangkok had arrived shortly before eight thirty yesterday morning and they had only dropped by the flat so that he could pick up a clean change of clothing; then they'd gone straight on to Market Harborough to collect Helen. Nolan had ordered him to report for duty immediately when he'd called the office from Edwin's house, but after a lot of argument he'd reluctantly agreed to extend his leave for a further twenty-four hours. This morning he had travelled up to London on the first train and hadn't gone anywhere near his flat.

"What are you doing about your account?" Cartwright asked.

"I've already sent it on to Mr Edgecombe under separate cover. I hope that's all right, Major?"

Cartwright said it was, thanked Alderton for everything he'd done on his behalf and put the phone down. He could nip back to the flat during the lunch hour for the report but that really wouldn't solve anything. He needed to discuss the finer implications with Sarah and she was on her way to Manor Farm at Codford St Mary. Torn with indecision, he rubbed the frizzled patch where the fire had burned his scalp, then hesitating no longer, he looked up the number he'd recorded in his diary and rang the police station at Brentford. When the desk sergeant answered, he asked to speak to Detective Inspector Dalton and was put straight through.

Dalton said, "I can guess why you've called."

"You've received your copy of Alderton's report then?"

"It's on my desk now. Mind you, it would probably have ended up in the wastepaper basket if Mr Alderton hadn't enclosed a note drawing our attention to the various assets owned by Eurcom Enterprises. Then I noticed that a man called Wentworth was one of the directors and became even more interested."

"Enough to arrest him?"

"And charge him with what?" Dalton snorted. "Because Eurcom owns the junkyard in Brentford and a Mr Wentworth called on Nuri Assad claiming to be a Detective Inspector in the Anti-terrorist Squad, it doesn't follow that he killed Bergitta Lindstrom. We have to place him at the scene of the crime or in Assad's flat in Bayswater and we're a long way from doing either."

The description Assad had given him of Wentworth in no way resembled the man who worked in the New Providence building. And since the Iraqi had returned to Baghdad the day after Dalton had interviewed him, the police could scarcely put Wentworth on an identity parade. Dalton's only hope of linking him to Bergitta Lindstrom lay in obtaining forensic evidence which would prove he'd visited Assad's flat in Bayswater. Every room, every surface, every stick of furniture, every glass, every knife would have to be dusted for latent fingerprints. But first, they needed a search warrant and getting one was proving unexpectedly difficult.

"The Home Office is involved," said Dalton. "So is the Foreign Office."

"You'll be eligible for the old age pension before they withdraw their objections. On the other hand, I can give you Wentworth today."

"How?"

"By forcing him to cut and run."

"You're not to go anywhere near the man."

"Wentworth thinks he's sitting pretty," Cartwright said, talking him down, "which is why he hasn't left town. And there's nothing you can do about it except keep him under surveillance and hope that some day something will turn up."

"I'm going to say this just once more," Dalton said angrily. "You're not to go anywhere near Wentworth. If you so much as set foot in Baker Street, I'll have you arrested for obstructing the police."

"Then you'd better circulate my description," Cartwright said and hung up.

Nolan called him on the squawk box as he walked out of the office but he ignored the tetchy summons and took the lift down to the ground floor.

There was no mistaking the New Providence office block. A steel, glass and concrete structure faced with imitation black marble, it was completely at odds with the other buildings near the Underground station in Baker Street. The foyer, with its modern impressionist paintings, fitted carpets and piped music seemed to Cartwright more reminiscent of a hotel than a business house. Glancing at the list of companies displayed on the notice board behind the reception desk, he noted the appropriate floor for Eurcom and nipped into the nearest lift before either of the two commissionaires could intercept him.

The lift bore him swiftly and silently upwards. Alighting at the second floor, he walked along the corridor checking the offices on either side and discovered that Wentworth occupied the one at the far end. The smartly-dressed PA in the outer office looked as though she was very adept at protecting her boss from people who hadn't made an appointment to see him.

"My name's Lucas," Cartwright told her. "I'm with the Kimber Corporation in Hong Kong, and no, Mr Wentworth isn't expecting me." He walked on past her desk and opened the inner door. "This is a surprise visit," he added.

Wentworth didn't act as though it was. In the middle of a telephone conversation when Cartwright walked in on him, he told someone called Alec that an important client had just arrived and promised to call him back as soon as he could. Waving Cartwright to a chair, he informed his agitated PA that he didn't want to be disturbed and asked her to close the door.

"Now – do you mind telling me who you are and what this is all about?" he asked coolly when they were alone.

"I'm Sarah's husband," Cartwright told him, "and this is all about four and a half million and a man who wanted to die in England. Charles Unger thought it was some

Machiavellian plot by the KGB to spread disinformation, but for you and Faulkner it was a personal thing. You knew that if Gage ever ran into my wife again they were bound to compare notes and then the shit would really hit the ceiling. You couldn't touch Gage; too many people in the Foreign Office knew he was coming home, but Sarah didn't enjoy that kind of protection."

"Are you saying we decided to take her out?"

"Yes."

"Can you prove it?"

Wentworth was ice cool and the same faintly amused smile was still there on his mouth after Cartwright had finished telling him how and why the police would eventually do just that.

"Giving Assad your real name was idiotic; you should have used an alias."

"And you should take a look at the *Police and Constabulary Almanac* some time; there's a DI Wentworth listed under The Met. A warrant card wouldn't necessarily satisfy a man like Assad; he's the sort who'd get his friends in the Iraqi Embassy to check out the name. The *Almanac* is the first place they'd look. Of course, it could be said that Faulkner was simply taking out a little insurance; there's nothing like stitching a man up to ensure he stays loyal."

Cartwright listened to him in amazement. Either Wentworth had lost touch with reality or his supreme confidence was founded on the belief that he had a trump card up his sleeve.

"Did you pull the same stunt on Faulkner?"

"Well, there was always a chance Ellen Rothman would look up the name of the man who'd interviewed her in the Diplomatic Blue List."

"That's tantamount to an admission of guilt."

"It's my word against yours, old son," Wentworth said cheerfully, then reached for the vest pocket lighter which was lying on his desk. "Of course, it would be a different matter if you were wired for sound but this little gadget tells me you

281

aren't. It can sniff out a bug at thirty paces and the Japanese turn them out by the barrow load."

"You're crazy."

"Wrong, I'm merely cautious. I've been protecting myself against electronic surveillance ever since I learned that Matthew Gage was coming home."

"The police are watching you."

"I'd be surprised if they weren't; the cat and mouse game is their only hope. They know the FO won't lift a finger to help them and Assad certainly isn't going to point a finger at me."

"But Sarah will," Cartwright told him and knew it was an empty threat the moment Wentworth burst out laughing.

"Sarah – testify against me?" he spluttered. "You've got to be joking. Listen, I've got eight thousand in a slush fund that says your wife will make the most reluctant witness you ever heard."

It was probably true, Cartwright thought, and that was the thing that really angered him.

"It's been nice meeting you, Major, but I'm afraid it's time you were leaving." Wentworth came round the desk and began to usher him towards the PA's office. "I've got an important lunch appointment and you're keeping me from it."

"Faulkner's dead," Cartwright said, playing the only card left to him. "He was ambushed and killed near a village called Namtok."

"And Gage?"

"He died with him."

"Then I don't have a thing to worry about, do I?"

"I'm not so sure. You know the last thing Faulkner said? – 'Kimber fouled it up, they were supposed to get Matthew, not me'."

It was a barefaced lie but he could see that Wentworth believed it and was shaken. He had planted a seed of doubt in his mind; now he had to nurture the seed and make it grow.

"I don't believe Kimber fouled it up, I think it was

282

deliberate. Faulkner was becoming too much of a liability and he had to go. The same thing could happen to you."

Wentworth opened the door to the outer office. "Thanks for the tip," he said, loud enough for his PA to hear. "I hadn't realised the stock market in Hong Kong was quite so volatile. Obviously, I shall have to keep an eye on things."

He steered Cartwright through her office and out into the passageway. A moment or so ago, he had almost cracked but now it seemed to Cartwright that he had the situation back under control. The two men got out of one of the lifts at the far end of the corridor and the element of surprise worked to Wentworth's disadvantage.

"That's Detective Inspector Dalton," Cartwright said. "Looks like the Foreign Office has just pulled the rug from under your feet."

Wentworth didn't hesitate. Shoving Cartwright out of the way, he dived through a door marked Emergency Exit which led to the internal fire escape. By the time Cartwright had recovered his balance and was able to follow him, he was already halfway down the second flight of stairs.

Each flight consisted of a dozen steps; his feet scarcely touching, he took them four at a time. There was an age gap of at least a decade between them and if the years counted for anything, he should have been in far better shape, but he failed to make any impression on the lead Wentworth had established.

Cartwright heard the older man slam the exit door behind him a good five seconds before he made it to the ground floor. Emerging into a narrow alleyway, he ran towards the T-junction at the top and reached it in time to catch a fleeting glimpse of Wentworth as he disappeared into Baker Street. The traffic was stationary, held by the lights at the intersection with Marylebone Road, but they changed to green before he could get across. A taxi almost had him as he weaved a zigzag path between the moving vehicles to the accompaniment of an orchestra of strident horns.

Wentworth was obviously running blind with no pre-conceived plan in mind other than to shake off his pursuers

283

and get off the streets as quickly as possible. Baker Street Underground station was the nearest bolthole and Cartwright reckoned he would make for that. It was the interchange for the Metropolitan, Inner Circle, Jubilee and Bakerloo lines and offered him the widest choice of escap routes.

He turned into the entrance hall, raced past the booking office and ended up doing a waltz with the ticket collector the other side of the barrier who wanted to know where he thought he was going.

"For Christ's sake," Cartwright yelled, "I'm a police officer."

"That's what the other bugger said," the collector told him and reluctantly let him through.

Cartwright ran down the steps leading to the upper level and checked out the six car Uxbridge train that was drawn up alongside the island platform with its doors wide open. There was no sign of Wentworth, nor could he see him on the eastbound platform across the tracks. He hoped Dalton's non-appearance meant that the DI was taking steps to bring the whole network to a temporary standstill, but somehow he doubted it.

He went down to the next level and took the escalator to the southbound Bakerloo and Jubilee lines on the double. There were less than a dozen passengers waiting for a train to Charing Cross but the distant signal in the tunnel mouth was set to green and he knew that one hadn't gone through in the last five minutes. He trotted to the far end of the platform, cut through the connecting subway and retraced his steps on the Bakerloo platform. Long before he reached the halfway point, it was patently obvious that Wentworth had opted to take a northbound train. Raging at himself for having made the wrong choice, he raced back up the escalator, saw Dalton in the lower concourse and yelled at him to follow on, then sprinted towards the down escalator.

Presented with a choice when he stepped off at the bottom, Cartwright elected to check out the right-hand platform and worked his way to the far end before using one of the subways to cross over to the other line. The announcement which greeted him over the faulty public address system was almost unintelligible but it was clear from the number of people lined up four deep on the platform that the service to Stanmore was subject to delay. Taking his time, he began to edge his way past the crowd towards the exit. Dalton was somewhere up ahead and, with any luck, they had Wentworth sandwiched between them.

A slight breeze warned Cartwright that a train was coming long before the anonymous voice on the tannoy told everyone to stand well back. There was a ripple of movement amongst the crowd as the same announcer kept repeating that the train now approaching the station was not in service. Then suddenly he spotted Wentworth amongst the sea of faces; they were about twenty feet apart and there was no way the latter could slip past him. He sensed that Wentworth knew it too when their eyes eventually met but it didn't stop him from coming on. Side-stepping out of the crowd to give himself a clear run, he put his head down and charged.

Out of the corner of his eye, Cartwright could see the twin headlights of the motorman's cab in the tunnel and in that same instant knew Wentworth intended to push him on to the track. Moving one pace to the left, he crouched down and struck the former SAS man with his right shoulder as he came abreast. Knocked off balance, Wentworth flailed the air with his arms in a desperate attempt to stay upright, then like a rotten tree uprooted by a gale force wind, he toppled off the platform and fell across the live rail. Seconds later, the oncoming train ploughed into his body.

The evening sky was the colour of dark blue velvet and not the menacing overcast it had been a fortnight ago when he'd returned home to find the house empty. This time it was different: a light was on in the hall and the Volkswagen Golf which Sarah had borrowed from her mother was parked in the drive. Dipping into his wallet, Cartwright paid off the taxi driver who'd picked him up from Salisbury station and

285

got out of the car. The porch light came on and Sarah met him at the door as the driver made a U-turn and then went on up the lane to Codford St Mary.

Sarah was wearing a short-sleeved jersey with a simple navy blue skirt and apart from the Band-aids on both palms, she looked completely unscarred. She kissed him softly and he held her close, savouring her love and affection; then arms entwined, they walked into the living room.

"Is Helen asleep?" he asked, stifling a yawn.

"I tucked her up in bed hours ago, she could hardly keep her eyes open." Sarah wandered over to the drinks cabinet and fixed him a large whisky soda. "You look all in too, darling."

"I am a little bushed," he admitted.

"I knew I should have met you at the station."

He had called Sarah a couple of times from Brentford where he had gone with Dalton to make a statement and Sarah had wanted to ask Jennifer Tyson to babysit for them but he'd felt that her absence might alarm Helen. There had also been another reason why he hadn't wanted her to drive into Salisbury.

"You could have been waiting there all night," he said. "There were times when I thought the police were going to detain me indefinitely."

"Was it as bad as that?"

"Dalton wasn't too pleased with me; he acted as though I had deliberately shoved Wentworth off the platform."

"For God's sake, Tom, they're not going to charge you with manslaughter, are they?"

She sounded anxious and apprehensive. He guessed she was thinking about Bergitta and knew that she felt partly responsible for what had happened to her and also to Ellen Rothman, and now she was about to blame herself for his predicament.

"No, of course not," he said soothingly.

"Then it's all over?"

Cartwright drank his whisky, then choosing his words carefully, he said, "The Fraud Squad will be taking a long

286

hard look at Euro Time Sharing and I know you've received dividends from them over the years."

"That's because the SIS got Kimber to set up a special trust fund for every Intelligence officer they sent into Vietnam. It was meant to protect our pension rights should Century House have to disown us for political reasons, which is exactly what happened to me."

"Does the Inland Revenue know about this trust fund?" he asked.

"I never declared it in my tax returns, if that's what you mean." Sarah fixed herself a whisky soda, then turned about to face him. "There was no need to, the tax was paid by Euro Time Sharing when the money was received from Lichtenstein."

No one could ever accuse Sarah of being naive and deep down she must have known there was something very fishy about the arrangement. She had just preferred not to think about it.

"There are some things you have to take on trust," Cartwright told her. "But all the same, darling, I think you should have a word with Bream, Cotton and Roose."